THE PASSIONATE ONES

THE PASSIONATE ONES

A Novel Inspired by the Pop Opera Super Group Il Divo

Kellie Tayer

iUniverse, Inc.
New York Lincoln Shanghai

The Passionate Ones

A Novel Inspired by the Pop Opera Super Group Il Divo

iUniverse books may be ordered through booksellers or by contacting:

iUniverse
2021 Pine Lake Road, Suite 100
Lincoln, NE 68512
www.iuniverse.com
1-800-Authors (1-800-288-4677)

ISBN-13: 978-0-595-38237-8 (pbk)
ISBN-13: 978-0-595-82603-2 (ebk)
ISBN-10: 0-595-38237-1 (pbk)
ISBN-10: 0-595-82603-2 (ebk)

Printed in the United States of America

ACKNOWLEDGMENTS

I would like to thank the usual suspects, my best friends scattered around the globe, Dana Scott, Melissa Myers and Fiona Sassenfeld, and my local buddies Kim Hering and the Patties (White and Taylor). Also, a special thank you to my family who has had to listen to Il Divo 24/7 for the past year whether they wanted to or not. A very special thank you to Simon Cowell for finding these four amazing men and bringing them together. I don't know how you did it. And, of course, thank you to Il Divo—Carlos, David, Sebastien and Urs. Your talent, charm and gorgeous smiles have raised the standard for excellence in music (and romance!) to a new level. Thank you for your inspiration and please, keep singing and keep romancing the world! Long live Il Divo!

"Surrender to Me"

by Les Passionistes

The day we met I made a bet that you would be the one
To set me free from broken dreams and lead me to the sun.
I'd given up on love and hope and waved my flag in loss,
And now with you the win is sweet, my battle gladly lost.
So here you are, you're with me now.
You've conquered and you've won.
But I'm the victor, too, my love, now we are as one.

Chorus:
Surrender to me your body and soul,
Your heart and your mind,
Your love and your woe.
I'll be your keeper, protector and guard,
In truth you will know…
That I have surrendered to you,
That I gave my life to you.

Don't ever fear the dark of night or worry that all is lost.
I promise to protect you no matter what the cost.
And if all I ever want from you is more than you can give,
The smallest gift you give me is all I'll need to live.
From now until the end of time always know it's true,
That on the day I lost my heart, I found my life in you.

Chorus:
Surrender to me your body and soul,
Your heart and your mind,
Your love and your woe.
I'll be your keeper, protector and guard,
In truth you will know…
That I have surrendered to you,
That I gave my life to you.

Know that I have surrendered to you,
That I gave my life to you.

Know that I have surrendered to you,
That I gave my life to you.

CHAPTER 1

"Lars!" Andrew waved his hand in front of Lars' face to get his attention. He waited a moment and tried again.

"Hey, *Lars*!" Andrew said again, a little louder this time and with a slight punch to Lars' shoulder. "Earth to Lars!"

Lars blinked slowly and looked around at the group. He shrugged his shoulders, a sheepish look washing over his face.

"What? Did I miss my cue?" he asked, embarrassed.

"Yes. You have the lead, remember?" Andrew smiled patiently at Lars and signaled to the technician to start the music again.

"Sorry, guys. But do we really have to rehearse this so much? I mean, it's "Happy Birthday" for crying out loud, as you Americans like to say. I don't think we even rehearsed Puccini this much." He passed a hand through his longish black hair and sighed deeply.

"Yes, but it's "Happy Birthday" in Greek and that is a language none of us speaks, you might recall," Andrew reminded him.

"Point well taken. From the top, guys." Lars cleared his throat and the music started again. A few minutes later they declared themselves proficient in wishing a musical birthday greeting in the Greek language and they called it a wrap.

"I'll see you guys later tonight at Annabel's," said Andrew. He and Antoine headed for the door, waving good-bye over their shoulders as they stepped out of the recording studio into the late September London afternoon.

"Want a ride home?" asked Javier. They spoke to the technician in the booth and then stepped out onto the sidewalk just in time to see Andrew and Antoine getting into Antoine's sleek, black Mercedes.

"Sure, thanks." Lars followed Javier to the dark green Jaguar parked down the street. They got in and when Javier started the engine their ears were assaulted by Tom Jones's voice blaring from the CD player.

"Still into Tom Jones, huh, Javier?" laughed Lars. He settled into the cream leather seat and leaned his head back against the headrest.

"Always," chuckled Javier. He put the car in drive and remembered to look right first instead of left as he pulled into the flow of traffic. "Damn English, driving on the wrong side of the road," he muttered to himself.

Javier Garza, Antoine de Cadenet, Andrew Jones and Lars Kohler made up the newly minted and now mega-famous pop-opera group, Les Passionistes. They were an international group, ranging in age from twenty eight to thirty four, each representing a different nation: Javier from Spain, Antoine from France, Andrew from the United States and Lars from Switzerland. And they all spoke different languages, too. Though the three Europeans had learned English in school, Andrew had the advantage of having English as his first language. His knowledge of foreign languages was limited to Italian and Spanish operas and the occasional French or Gaelic song. They were brought together after a two-year search led by the world famous talent scout Samuel Bowles, whose girlfriend Melina was celebrating her thirty-third birthday tonight at Annabel's nightclub and for which Les Passionistes had learned "Happy Birthday" in Greek to serenade her in her native tongue.

"So, Lars, how are things at home in Switzerland?" asked Javier cautiously. He sensed that something had been troubling Lars and he didn't want to pry, but likewise, he wanted to give his friend a chance to unload if there was something on his mind he needed to get off.

"About the same. My mother is still leaving my father for some old boyfriend and I still have that business with Katarina to tend to when I get home this weekend. I'm not looking forward to going home. What I really want to do is disappear for a few weeks where no one knows me and I am not responsible for anyone but myself." Lars sighed and stared out of the window at the passing buildings.

"I'm sorry, man. I know it's going to be hard but you will get through it. I had a hard time with Marina but eventually she got the message and we both have now moved on." Javier turned on the air conditioner and adjusted the vents.

"Tell me again exactly how Marina handled the news that you wanted to break up?" Lars glanced over at Javier briefly and then fixed his gaze on the license plate of the blue Citroen in front of them.

"She punched me in the nose," Javier chuckled, rubbing his nose, the memory not that old and the pain still a little fresh in his mind.

"Right. I hope Katarina punches me, too. I will deserve it," Lars said in a dejected voice.

"Listen, Lars," said Javier. "You have to do what you have to do, even if it hurts. And I mean even if it hurts her *and* you. Which it will, I might add."

Lars didn't respond. He thought about the four of them and their crazy lives and wondered about the others' relationships. He knew that Andrew was still dating the same girl, Jenna. She turned up from time to time in London and other cities where they were performing and they still seemed happy to be together. And Antoine had recently ended his relationship with his girlfriend, Sophie, but that situation had been different. Sophie had cheated on Antoine with her boss at the advertising agency where she worked in Paris. Antoine had learned of this from his mother and when he confronted Sophie she had not denied it. They had ended their one-year relationship and Antoine had not spoken of Sophie in several weeks now. He had apparently moved on. Antoine was the only one in the group who was self-taught musically, and as such, he was a little more reserved than the others, feeling sometimes that perhaps he didn't measure up to the classically trained talents of the other three. But in reality, he had the purest voice of them all and often sang lead on the classic operas, especially the Italian ones. If his heart was still broken over Sophie he wasn't letting on and Lars hoped he would be as professional when the time came. At least he would have a month to himself to recover from the trauma before Les Passionistes met again in London to resume work. He blinked back to the present and decided to put Katarina out of his mind for the moment.

"So this party is at eight o'clock, yes?" he asked as Javier pulled up in front of Chelsea House where Lars lived in a rented, furnished, first floor apartment.

"Yes. Shall I pick you up? About seven-thirty?" asked Javier.

"OK. See you then." Lars stepped out of the car and waved good-bye as Javier sped off down the street.

Just as Lars let himself into the flat, he felt his cell phone vibrate in his pocket. He pulled it out and looked at it, feeling his heart sink as he saw Katarina's name on the dial. *I should answer this,* he thought, *but I just can't.* Just as he was about to bite the bullet and answer the phone anyway, it suddenly lay still and quiet in his hand. He sighed deeply, tossed it onto the sofa and headed down the hall to take a shower and try to relax. In a few days he and his band-mates would embark upon a month-long break and go their separate ways to unwind, tend to issues in their personal lives and then reunite in November to begin work on their second album. That would be followed by a concert tour, personal appearances and many weeks of promoting the album all over the world. No wonder their relationships were ending. What woman could put up with all the separations and crazed fans and lonely nights? He turned on the shower and stepped in, reveling in the hot water as it washed over his tense muscles. He pushed thoughts of Katarina out of his mind and tried not to think about his father's heartbreak, his mother's deceit and his beloved grandmother who had passed away earlier in the summer. Yes, he needed this break. He only hoped it would be enough to sustain him through the busy times ahead.

* * * *

"Your father wants to see you in his office before you go home for the night," Carly's astoundingly high-pitched voice resounded in Antonia's ear. "Don't forget."

"OK, thanks. I won't." Antonia sighed and put the phone back in its cradle. She looked at her watch and noted that it was already nearly five o'clock. Carly was one of her father's secretaries and she had already called an hour earlier to tell Antonia about meeting with her father before she headed home for the night. Antonia wondered what her father wanted. He had been in a surprisingly good mood this morning at the weekly content meeting. He had been overflowing with ideas for the special issue of *Passion* magazine they were preparing for the first of the year. Ted Taylor was the creator and editor-in-chief of *Passion* magazine and Antonia, at twenty-eight, was already one of the senior writers. She suspected that her father was grooming her to take over his position one day as editor but she was nowhere near ready for that kind of pressure and dedication. It was all she could do sometimes to meet the deadlines for her stories and her monthly pop culture column.

She tidied her desk and wrote out her nightly to-do list for tomorrow. After a glance around her desk, she put her computer to sleep for the night and headed up to her father's office. She hoped this would be over with quickly so she could get home and fix dinner. She had skipped lunch today to be sure her column was finished on time and now she was ready to dive into something yummy. Maybe she would get some Indian curry take-out on the way home from that new restaurant that had just opened near her apartment building a few blocks from the United Nations.

Her father's office was on the twentieth floor of the building that was home to several magazines including *Voice, Romance, Splash* and *Oceans*, all geared to women in various stages of life. Antonia had started her journalism career after graduation from New York University at *Oceans* while she waited for a position to open at *Passion,* her personal favorite of all of the periodicals. Eventually she joined *Passion* as a researcher and occasional photographer and then finally moved into her current position as a columnist and entertainment reviewer. She always felt she had to work harder and longer than everyone else because she was the boss's daughter and now she was finally at a place where she felt she had earned the respect and admiration of her fellow journalists. She loved her job in spite of the pressures of working in such a cutthroat industry and was thrilled to have earned her father's pride. Ted Taylor had an active hand in all of the publications of the Taylor Group and *Passion* was such a success that it had led to the creation of international versions in London, Rome, Berlin, Paris, Madrid, Moscow, Tokyo, Hong Kong, Rio de Janeiro and Sydney. A Dutch version was currently in the works as well. Life was good for everyone at *Passion.* It now surpassed *Vogue* as the most widely read fashion and lifestyle magazine in the world. Antonia's older brother, Thomas, was a photographer for the magazine's Rome edition but he occasionally flew to New York and elsewhere in the world for special assignments. Her other brother, Jordan, was a dentist practicing in lower Manhattan, and Marcie Taylor, Antonia's mother, was a retired flight attendant for International Airways whose retirement package included free flying for life for her and her immediate family. You couldn't beat that perk with a stick, especially when *Passion* stories had Antonia or her father jetting off to far-flung locales.

Antonia tapped lightly on her father's partially opened door and he beckoned her in. He finished a phone call and greeted her with a beaming smile.

"Hi, honey. Finished for the day?" he asked in a lighter-than-air voice.

"Yes, finally. And what has happened to get you in such a light-hearted mood today, Dad?" she asked as she sat down in the chair opposite his desk. She glanced out the window at the beautiful skies over Manhattan. It was late September and the trees were just starting their color-change and the air was getting that familiar nip in the early mornings and late evenings. Antonia was not a winter person and she was not looking forward to snow and cold and ice. She wished her father would relocate the entire operation to Miami.

"I'm in a good mood for a couple of reasons. The first is because I saw an old friend today who is in New York on business. His name is Juan Garza. He is a Spanish architect on whom I once did a story when I worked at *Architectural Digest* many years ago. We've stayed in touch, exchanging emails and notes over the years with updates on work and family and such, but I hadn't heard from him in about a year. Anyway, we had lunch today and it was nice to reminisce. His son has become quite a well-known opera singer in some new group called Les Passionistes. Have you heard of them?"

"I have their album, as a matter of fact. They are quite amazing." Antonia was duly impressed that her father had such a close connection to Les Passionistes. "I'll burn you a copy if you like."

"Please do. I'd love to hear it. Anyway, Juan gave me an excellent idea for a story and I think you would be the perfect person to make the story happen. That is the second reason for my good mood."

Antonia felt a knot begin to form in her stomach. She had just returned from covering a film festival in Canada for an upcoming issue and wasn't sure she was in the mood to handle anything too major, especially if it meant packing again and leaving the familiar cocoon of her apartment.

"What is it?" she asked tentatively.

"Well, Juan has a vacation home on an island off the coast of Spain. The island is called Isla Marta and it's somewhere south of Majorca, I think he said. Anyway, as you know, our special issue is all about global travel and while I originally wanted you to do the Iceland piece, I've decided you should go to Isla Marta and write about this island that Juan says is a place like no other. He has offered us the use of his home there for the month of October. He says his family vacates the place in September and heads back to Madrid. He has a small staff there and he even keeps a car there that you can use. It's a stick shift, though. You'd have to have someone show you how to drive it. But you can take as much of October as you need to get the work done and you will have to take the pictures as well unless I can spare Thomas or one of the other photographers. But you're a good photographer in your own right. And it can be the lead story for the special issue. What do you say?"

Antonia didn't realize she had been holding her breath the whole time her father was pitching his proposal to her. Now she let out a huge sigh and smiled widely.

"Oh, Dad. I can't tell you how much I didn't want to go to Iceland. I mean, it's a beautiful country and all and the one time I was there I had a great time, but I really wasn't looking forward to going again, So, yes, I would much rather go to Spain—without a doubt." Of course, it would mean a massive packing job and leaving her nest again, but for Spain, she could stand it.

"Excellent." Ted stood up and came around the desk and pulled Antonia to her feet. He embraced her warmly and then asked her the one question she knew he would ask before letting her go home for the night.

"Are you OK? I mean about Jeff. Are you getting over that…situation, for lack of a better word?"

"I'm fine, Dad. I have moved on. And you think if I'm out of the country for the whole month of October then I won't be around to crash his wedding, right?"

"Well, it had occurred to me. I just want you to be happy, sweetheart. I know how much he hurt you and I think getting away for a few weeks will be good for you—for your heart. Plus, you are the best writer at this magazine and I am not saying that just because you're my daughter. I'm saying it because it's true. You *are* the best one for the job."

Antonia smiled at her father and nodded, embarrassed at his compliment and his obvious concern regarding the matter of her broken heart.

"When do you want me to leave? I will need to do some research before I go." Antonia walked toward the door and looked back her at father.

"How about the first of the month, which, I realize, is next week already—where does the time go? I will have the travel department make the arrangements and I'll get the particulars from Juan about the house. We'll have you hooked up and ready to go in no time."

"OK, Dad. See you Monday. I'll research Isla Marta over the weekend so I can see what to expect. It sounds fun."

She waved good night and headed to the elevators. On the way home she bought some Indian curry and the latest copy of *Hello!* magazine from the newsstand near her apartment building. She would have a leisurely dinner, a long hot soak in the tub with the juicy British tabloid magazine and blow her mind playing Internet spades and listening to music all evening. Tomorrow would be soon enough to research Isla Marta. What an exciting life she did lead now that she was no longer one half of New York's golden couple: The up and coming magazine journalist and the assistant conductor of the New York Philharmonic. Jeff Cranston, her former fiancé, had left her earlier in the summer for the first chair clarinetist of the Philharmonic. Now he and Tamara Mason would be tying the knot on October thirteenth in St. Peter's Episcopalian Church, the same church where Antonia had planned to marry Jeff in June of the coming year. The months since Jeff left had been hard, but thankfully, Antonia had a supportive family and wonderful friends and a demanding job to help her through the tough times. She finally had begun feeling some peace of late and now she didn't cry every time she read something in the paper about Jeff or heard a song on the radio that they had listened to together. Life was slowly sorting itself out and she was getting back to normal. This trip would be good for her. She hurried on to her apartment and waved at her doorman as she headed to the elevator with a spring in her step.

CHAPTER 2

"Well, now that that's over with, is there any reason why we have to stick around here?" asked Lars. They had just serenaded Melina in song, indulged in cake and beer and now Lars was ready to get the hell out of the place and go home.

"I'm ready to go, too. I'll give you a lift home. I want to talk to you about something anyway. Let's go say good night to Samuel and Melina and then get out of here." Javier led the way to where they could see Samuel holding court in the rear of Annabel's.

They found Antoine and Andrew talking to Samuel, their mentor and creator in the far corner of the club where they were celebrating with Greek food and ouzo shots. Antoine was looking none the worse for wear when they arrived at the table. Andrew was practically holding him up.

"I thought you French could hold your liquor better than that," Lars teased Antoine. He pointed at the empty shot glasses on the table in front of Antoine.

"We are experts at holding our liquor. You're just jealous," Antoine smiled sleepily at Lars and Javier. "Anyway, I'm drowning my sorrows."

"What's the sad occasion?" Javier asked with interest.

"Somewhere in the world another woman is going to sleep tonight without me. That is a sad occasion for all."

Lars grinned and just shook his head at Antoine. They said their goodnights and Samuel wished them a safe and relaxing vacation.

"I will see you all back at the studio on the first of November, ready to get back to work. Protect those voices—that's my retirement, you know." He held up his glass and toasted them.

Javier and Lars shook Samuel's hand and gave affectionate hugs to their fellow band-mates. They wished Melina a happy birthday one more time and then they headed out to Javier's Jaguar.

Once in the car, Javier suggested stopping for a nightcap at Paddy's Pub down the street from Lars' apartment. He parked the car out front and they went inside the dark pub and took up spots at the long, shiny oak bar. Four beers later, after idle conversation about sports, music and women, Javier made Lars an offer he couldn't refuse.

"I know you have some tough times in the coming days, my friend, and I want to offer you sanctuary. You said you wanted to escape where no one knows you and I know the perfect place. I would go there myself but I think you need it more."

"Where is this perfect place and when do I leave?" laughed Lars, draining the last drops from his beer stein.

"My family owns a vacation home on this little island called Isla Marta off the coast of Spain. It's beautiful there and quiet and relaxing. You can stay as long as you like. My family summers there but they will be returning to Madrid this weekend so it will be available starting the first of October. There's a car there you can use and a housekeeper who happens to be a great cook. Her name is Marta, too, like the island, and she will take care of you. Go. It will be good for you."

"I don't know what to say, Javier. It sounds too good to be true. I would love to take you up on it. I have to spend a few days in Switzerland first, break a few hearts and all, and then I will more than likely need an escape. Yes, I'd love to go. Thank you."

They finished their beers and left the pub. Javier told Lars he would call him tomorrow with the particulars about the house and how to get there. He drove off to his place in Notting Hill and Lars walked to his own apartment a few blocks from the pub. Tomorrow he would prepare to leave London and consider what he would say to Katarina when he saw her this weekend. He needed to get the break-up over with as soon as possible, so the healing could begin for them both. And he would be seeing his parents for the first time since his mother's announcement that she had someone else in her life. Lars hoped his father was OK. It occurred to him that what his father was experiencing right now was exactly what Katarina would soon face on a lesser—to some degree—scale. But a broken heart was a broken heart—there was no way to avoid what he had to do. He realized months ago that Katarina was a part of his old life and he needed to let her go so he could move on in this new world that Samuel Bowles had created for him and the rest of Les Passionistes. Katarina had not adjusted well to his sudden fame and she was jealous all the time of every fan letter and every mention of his success. Every phone call had resulted in an argument leaving Katarina in tears. Lars knew it was the end, and what's more, he was sad more for her than for himself—not because he thought of himself as such a great catch, but because he could have given Katarina such a wonderful life if she only could have accepted and embraced his new success. He was anxious to let her go and move on and to open himself up to the possibility of real love, should it ever happen. But it wasn't real with Katarina and he knew it now. It was time to move on.

* * * *

"I wish I had your job, you lucky broad," said Deanna Scott to Antonia who was searching through her underwear drawer for her passport. "I'm getting tired of rubbing the backs of rich society bitches and listening to them complain about whether to celebrate their anniversaries in the Hamptons or the Caribbean or on a cruise or at an all-inclusive. And listening to them complain about the lazy help or their philandering husbands. I need a new job." She sighed deeply and threw herself back on Antonia's bed, banging her head against the headboard in the process. "Ouch! Dammit!"

"Geez, Dee—you do that all the time. You're going to get a hematoma or whatever the technical term is for smashed brains. Now where is that damned passport? I swear it was here three days ago." She continued rummaging through the drawers eventually finding the passport tucked between her new Victoria's Secret bras. She held it up in triumph, a satiny pink bra hanging off of it. "Eureka. I found it!" she exclaimed.

Deanna glanced at the clock on Antonia's nightstand and noted that it was nearly six.

"I have a client at seven so I better get a move on. I'm massaging Julia Roberts's personal assistant's personal assistant tonight. Wonder who's footing the bill for that one?" She laughed and hoisted herself off the bed.

"You enjoy your near brush with greatness. I'm going to start packing. If you think about it, ask the personal assistant's personal assistant if she has any idea what Julia was thinking when she named her twins."

"Will do. I'm off. Don't over-pack. Will I see you before you leave?" she asked in a voice tinged with wistfulness. Deanna and Antonia had been friends since their college days and had maintained the friendship throughout the years. Deanna had a successful massage therapy business and yoga studio that catered to

Manhattan's elite. Antonia had written a story about Deanna's business a few months ago for *Passion* magazine regarding Deanna's efforts to bring massage therapy and yoga to the less fortunate citizens of New York. She would often take a portable studio around the streets of Manhattan and offer free classes at homeless shelters and halfway houses primarily for women who were trying to get their lives together after having experienced abuse, illness or other misfortunes that life had thrown at them. Deanna had a big heart and it was one of the qualities Antonia loved most about her friend.

"Of course. I don't leave until late Tuesday night. Let's have dinner Monday."

"Sounds good. Oh, before I forget. Didn't you mention that the guy who owns this house where you'll be staying is the father of the hot Spanish guy in Les Passionistes?" She grabbed her handbag from where it was hanging on the doorknob and draped it over her shoulder.

"Yeah. Isn't that strange? I love that group. Wouldn't it be weird if the hot Spanish guy showed up?" Antonia smiled at the thought.

"Spanish, French, American, any of them could eat crackers in my bed. And what's the other guy? German?"

"I believe he's Swiss but maybe he speaks German. Something like that."

"Whatever he is, he is mighty delicious. Well, I've gotta go. Later, girlfriend."

Antonia walked her friend to the door then went back to her bedroom to put her underwear drawer back into some kind of order.

Later that evening, Antonia sat down at the computer and began researching Isla Marta on the Internet. There wasn't a whole lot of information to be found about the place so she figured that it must be one of Spain's well-kept secrets. She did discover that Isla Marta celebrated its birthday in mid-October in a weekend-long celebration called *Festival de los Amantes Muertos* which, upon learning through translation.com that it literally meant "Festival of the Dead Lovers," left Antonia feeling a little creeped out.

"Well, that's an odd name for a birthday celebration," she thought. She printed off the couple of pages of information she was able to gather and made a mental note to go to the bookstore tomorrow and purchase a couple of travel books on Spain. Maybe she could learn more the good old-fashioned way—from reading books. She pulled her suitcases from their storage space beneath her bed and set them in the corner by the window. Looking down on the late September evening, she noticed the dark clouds coming in from the east. If she didn't know better she would swear those were snow clouds, impossible for this time of year. She shuddered at the thought of winter and then smiled to herself upon thinking of Spanish beaches and festivals for dead lovers. "This could be one interesting trip," she said aloud.

She went into the kitchen to empty the dishwasher, stopping first in the living room to pop a CD into the stereo. She put in Les Passionistes and headed into the kitchen as the sound of the Spanish opera song "*A la Mer*" filled the apartment. As she put silverware in the drawer she listened to each distinctive voice, wondering who was who. One voice in particular stood out from the others. She wondered if the tenor voice she was drawn to was the American's voice. What was his name again? She would have to read the liner notes later and see if she could figure out who was who. In the meantime she let the music carry her away to romantic places as she put away plates and glasses. She tried not to think of Jeff and what he would have to say about Les Passionistes. Antonia figured he would love them. She pushed thoughts of Jeff from her mind and finished putting the dishes away then settled down on the sofa to listen to the music and read the CD's liner notes. Later that night she slept soundly, in a dreamless state, that left her refreshed and ready for the new day.

*   *   *   *

The house was quiet when Lars entered through the back door. He walked through the rooms looking for his parents or one of his brothers but all was silent and still. It occurred to him that his mother didn't technically live here any longer, having moved into his grandmother's house after Grandmother had passed away. He wondered where everyone was and was a little disappointed that his arrival wasn't higher on everyone's list of important events.

He found his younger brother, Urs, in the office sitting at the computer with headphones on, apparently rocking out to some heavy metal band. He walked up behind him and tapped his shoulder. Urs screeched a profane epithet and knocked the chair over as he jumped to his feet ready to do battle with the intruder.

"Jeez, Lars! What the hell are you doing here?" Urs' face paled at the fright Lars had given him.

"Sorry, Urs. Didn't mean to scare you. I'm home—a little early. Aren't you happy to see me?" He opened his arms to his brother, who at age twenty-four, four years younger than Lars, towered over him, which said a lot considering Lars was more than six feet tall himself.

"My world famous big brother Lars has returned to the nest. Good to see you in person as opposed to on television singing your brains out all over the world. How did you get home from the airport?" Urs grinned at him.

Lars ruffled his brother's dark hair and sat down on the leather loveseat across from the desk in their father's home office. He ran his hand through his own long, dark hair and sighed deeply.

"I took a cab."

"Why didn't you call someone? I would have picked you up." Urs turned off the music he had been listening to and looked at Lars. "You look tired. Everything OK?"

"Of course. Where is everyone?"

"Dad's at work. No one expected you home this early or we would have all been here to greet you with open arms."

"I decided to get the hell out of London early but I didn't tell anyone I was taking an earlier flight."

"Not even Katarina?" Urs asked, surprised.

"Not even Katarina." Lars tried to mask the pain he felt just hearing and saying her name but he didn't do a very good job.

"She would freak out if she knew you were here and you didn't tell her. I thought she would be the first person you would want to see." Urs looked quizzically at Lars, sensing that something wasn't right in paradise.

"I will see her—tomorrow. Please don't tell her I'm here. Listen, Urs. I'm telling you this straight up but don't mention it to a soul. I'm ending things with Katarina this weekend and then after I've visited with the family for a few days I'm going away to Spain for a couple of weeks to relax. You can't tell anyone."

Urs took a moment to process what his brother had just said. He didn't speak for a moment but when he did, Lars was surprised at his brother's words.

"I saw this coming months ago, the first time I watched you guys perform on that British show *Parkinson's Starburst.* I knew everything would be different for you from that moment on. Katarina was here and we all watched it together. She sensed it, too. It was a surreal moment for us but it must have been even more so for you as it was your life changing so drastically right before all of our eyes."

A pensive look came over Lars' face as he remembered Les Passionistes' first public appearance.

"Yes, Urs, my life has most definitely changed in ways I would never have expected. I've become a pampered celebrity almost overnight. Isn't that sickening?" He laughed. "Ermenegildo Zegna makes all of our clothes, I have drivers at my disposal and we stay at only the finest hotels when we travel, not to mention we eat at the finest restaurants and fly first class. Samuel Bowles has us so spoiled it's disgusting. But do you know what Lars?"

"What?"

"I am loving this life. It suits me immensely but there has been so much so soon that I feel a need to pull back for a few weeks and regroup. We have traveled and performed and recorded for more than a year non-stop and I'm already feeling burned out. I like my leisure time so this trip to Spain will be good for me. As for Katarina, she isn't interested in my lifestyle and it isn't fair of me to try to change her into becoming something she doesn't want to be. Did you know that I asked her to move to London with me last year?"

"No, I had no idea. She never mentioned it. Why wouldn't she go?" Urs replied.

"Because she won't leave her family. You know how close she is to her parents and her grandparents and her siblings and her family's restaurant. The one time we took a trip together before Les Passionistes happened was when we went to Amsterdam so I could work with that opera coach. She hated being away from Lucerne and spent the whole time we were there on her cell phone calling back here. It was very annoying. And when I asked her to go to Milan with me for the opera festival she refused. Just going across town is a major ordeal for her."

"No matter, this is going to devastate her, Lars. Are you sure this is the right thing to do? Maybe if you talk it over with her and let her know how much having her support would mean to you then she would be more supportive of your career." Urs didn't sound all that convincing and he knew it.

"I have to do it now—tomorrow. I hate myself for this but it has to be. I just don't love her that way anymore. Does this make me a bad person?"

"Not to me but I suspect it will to her family. But life goes on and she will get over it. You must have women throwing themselves at you now." Urs laughed at the mental image his words conjured up.

"Oh, little brother, you have no idea." They laughed heartily and then wandered into the kitchen to check out the contents of the refrigerator.

"Where is all the food? There is nothing to eat in here," Lars exclaimed as he rummaged around in the drawers finding nothing but cheese and jam and several bottles of beer and one jug of cream. "Let's go get Dad at his office and get some dinner. We can stop and see Mother first and see if she wants to join us."

"I wouldn't count on that, if I were you. But call her and let her know you're home. We can go see her after we eat. I hope you're paying, moneybags. You must be rolling in the francs."

"I'm not doing too badly," Lars laughed. Urs grabbed his car keys and they left through the back door out to where Urs's red Renault was parked.

"You'll have to slum it in my five-year old Renault. It's not the limousines I'm sure you've become accustomed to, but it will have to do."

"I may have grown to love the finer things in life, Urs, but I am not spoiled. I like simple things, too, and I will never forget where I came from. My family will never let that happen and I wouldn't want you to."

"Here, here," laughed Urs as they drove into Lucerne to their father's law office located in the heart of the city.

On the way into the city, Lars asked about their older brother Frederick who worked with their father at the firm. He inquired about Urs and his work. Urs had finished university in the spring after six years of figuring out what he wanted to do with his life and was now working as a chemist at an engineering firm in Lucerne. He'd had the day off and had been passing his time listening to music, searching for songs for his band to cover. He was in a group of rockers that played a mix of metal and techno in area clubs on weekends. He played one of their CD's for Lars as they drove. Lars was very impressed with the band—they called themselves Darkstar—and he encouraged Urs to consider writing some original music. Urs turned up the volume and Lars settled in for the ride.

CHAPTER 3

Deanna's boyfriend, Sean Miller, held up the bottle of Merlot and asked Antonia if she wanted a refill. They were having dinner together at Deanna's apartment—penne pasta in alfredo sauce with smoked bacon bits and aged parmesan and a green salad with fresh garlic breadsticks. Sean had cooked for them displaying yet another of his many talents, not the least of which was cooking gourmet meals and desserts from scratch.

"No, thanks," Antonia sighed, putting her hand over the top of her glass to prevent Sean from emptying the bottle into it. "I can't eat another bite or drink another drop. I'm going to burst. I'll have to ask the flight attendant for a seatbelt extender on my flight tomorrow night," she laughed.

"As if," snorted Deanna. "You're looking thinner than ever and your hair seems different, too. What did you do to it?"

"I had two inches cut off and had it colored chocolate royale, like the ice-cream, or so the girl at the salon said yesterday." She pushed her slightly longer than shoulder-length hair back out of her way.

"Well, you look lovely. Those Spanish guys aren't going to know what hit them," Deanna said approvingly. "Those amber eyes of yours and that milky complexion will be their undoing."

"Oh, please," Antonia grimaced. "My milky complexion will fry and no one will see my eyes which will be hidden behind my new sunglasses. But thanks for saying so." She gathered her dishes and took them into the kitchen.

Sean put the dishes in the dishwasher while Antonia and Deanna went into the living room to talk about the trip. Deanna had agreed to keep an eye on Antonia's apartment although the mail and the papers would be put on hold. She would check in occasionally to make sure all was well though Antonia expected no problems to arise while she was gone.

Sean came in a few minutes later with three cappuccinos and a plate of biscotti. They sipped and munched and Sean regaled them with tales from his job at Kennedy airport where he was an Immigrations officer.

Antonia noticed the time and stood up, slipping her feet back into her shoes.

"Thanks for a lovely dinner, you guys. Behave while I'm gone and don't do anything weird like run off to Vegas and get married or move to Queens. Wish me luck on my latest assignment." She headed toward the door.

"You'll do fine," said Deanna. "And you have to promise me something."

"What's that?" asked Antonia, her interest peaked.

"If the Spanish hottie from Les Passionistes shows up, and I have a funny feeling he will—don't ask me why—you have to call me immediately." She gave Antonia a sly grin and wiggled her eyebrows.

"Hey, now. I heard that," Sean called from the living room. He came over and gave Antonia a hug good-bye. "Don't be teasing my girl with thoughts of foreign lovers and sexy opera singers. My ego can't handle it, considering I'm a native Long Islander who can't sing a note.

They laughed and hugged and Antonia set out for home. She had a little more packing to do and she needed to get the apartment completely tidied before she left tomorrow.

Back at her place, she put Les Passionistes on the CD player and cleaned the bathroom and kitchen. She finished packing her suitcases and then packed her briefcase with materials on Isla Marta, the two new Spain travel books she had purchased plus some magazines and a couple of paperback novels in case she could get in some quality reading time on the beach. A hardworking journalist needed some downtime, even when on special assignment, she figured.

She glanced around the rooms and decided everything was fine as is and then tried to get some sleep. But she tossed and turned as she always did the night before a big trip, her mind unable to shut down as she mentally ran through her list of important things not to forget. She planned to go into the office tomorrow morning to say good-bye to her dad and get any last minute instructions he might have for her. She had talked to her mother earlier this evening and Marcie had wished her a safe and productive adventure. She was all set to go and she couldn't wait.

* * * *

The look on Katarina's face nearly broke Lars' heart. She was so damned happy to see him. She had literally thrown herself into his arms and wrapped herself, arms, legs and all, around his body. He hugged her hard, all the while struggling to keep his balance—both physically and emotionally. They were in Katarina's apartment—he had called and told her he was back and on his way over. She had sounded so excited on the phone and the closer Lars got to her apartment the more his stomach filled with dread. He felt like he might actually vomit if he didn't get this over with quickly. He went so far as to ask Katarina for a glass of water.

"Since when do you have to ask for anything around here?" she laughed, grabbing a glass from the cupboard and handing it to him. "You know where the water is. Help yourself."

Lars slowly and deliberately helped himself to ice-cubes from the freezer and even more slowly filled his glass to the top with water at the kitchen sink. His movements were slow and seemingly calculated in his quest to buy himself as much time as possible to preserve Katarina's world. He took a sip of the water and decided he had to somehow stop stalling. Maybe he was slightly overstating his hold over her. It was quite possible that she would not be as destroyed over the demise of the relationship as he expected her to be. He wondered if his ego could handle that. *Am I becoming an egotistical bastard*? He thought. *God, I hope not.*

He turned to Katarina and looked at her as she stood silently by the dining table. She looked sweet with her short, blonde hair, blue eyes and multiple earrings in both ears. She was tiny and looked vulnerable but Lars knew there was a steeliness underneath that she rarely showed to anyone until she felt the need to right a wrong or lash out against what she deemed an injustice of any kind. She was four years older than Lars but seemed so much younger than him in so many ways besides years. He looked away and took another sip from his water glass.

"Lars. Something's wrong, isn't it?" Katarina asked quietly. "Come sit in the living room with me and tell me what's on your mind."

Reluctantly, Lars followed her into the sitting room and perched on the edge of the dark blue sofa. Katarina sat next to him, her feet curled underneath herself. She reached for Lars' cold hand and he allowed her to hold it in her warm ones.

"Talk to me, Lars. I'm ready to hear whatever you have to say to me." Katarina spoke quietly with the slightest quiver in her soft voice.

"Katarina." Her name came out of his mouth cloaked in a sigh—a deep sigh that started at his feet and pushed its way up into his throat and out of his mouth. "Katarina. I think we have to…"

She stopped him before he could finish the statement.

"It's over, isn't Lars?" She blinked at him knowingly.

"I'm so sorry, Kat." He tried to look into her eyes but she turned away.

She pulled her hands away from his and folded her arms protectively around herself.

"What's her name?" she asked quietly.

"Whose name?" Lars asked in surprise.

"The girl you're leaving me for. What's her name?" Her voice threatened to crack.

"There is no one else, I swear to you. There has never been anyone else. I would never cheat on you." Lars had not prepared himself for this reaction though he supposed it made sense. If the tables were turned he would probably be asking for the name of the guy she was leaving him for.

"That's what they all say," she sighed. Her voice became thick with the tears that threatened at the backs of her eyes and Lars saw them begin to pool in the blue depths.

"But it's the truth, Kat. It isn't about someone else. It's about me and my life and how much it's changed over the past year. And you haven't wanted to be a part of it. I know you're proud of me, I don't doubt that, but you don't seem to be supportive. And you know what? I'm OK with that now. I understand your attachment to your family. You prefer to live here in Switzerland and that's fine. But my life is in London now, for the time being anyway. And I need to know that I'm free to live my life the way I want to and not have to worry about hurting you."

"It's too late for that, Lars. You've just broken my heart into a million pieces. I can't believe you're throwing away what we have together. And for what? A career as an opera singer? Well, you know what? I don't even like fucking opera. But I love you."

Lars forced a laugh at her profanity, such a rarity from her usually pure lips. He reached for her hand but she turned away, getting up from the couch and walking over to the window. He saw her shoulders shaking in silent sobs and he felt helpless as to what he should do next.

After a moment she composed herself and turned to him.

"Is your mind made up, Lars? Is there anything I can do to change it?" she asked quietly.

"I'm sorry," he said again. He truly had no idea what else to say to her in that moment. Her next words surprised him.

She suddenly closed the distance between them, wrapping her arms around his neck and burying her face into his chest. She breathed in his scent, so sexy and musky. She couldn't bear the thought of his leaving her this way and not sharing their lives together. It seemed impossible.

"Stay with me tonight, Lars. I want to make love to you the way we used to before you left for London. Remember? It's been so long." She reached up to kiss his mouth but he turned his cheek to her instead.

"No, Kat. It wouldn't change anything and it would just make it harder in the end. I should go. I hope someday you can forgive me and see that this was the right thing to do." He gently pried her arms away from him and slowly put them back down to her sides. "I'm sorry," he said again.

"Stop apologizing. I don't want to hear it. Just go, Lars. Go live your exotic, high society life. My mother told me you would do this to me and she was absolutely right. I'm not good enough for you anymore, am I? That's what this is about, isn't it, Lars? I just don't measure up now that you're rich and famous." She sobbed and reached for a tissue from the box on the end table, wiping her tears and her nose.

"That could *not* be further from the truth, Kat. You can't possibly believe that!" Lars had not expected this reaction and her words felt like knives stabbing into his heart. He walked toward the door and stopped, his hand on the knob.

"There will always be a place in my heart for you. I want you to know that. I have to go now. Please take care. I'm so sorry." He opened the door and walked out before she could say another word. As he started Urs's car, which he had borrowed for the day, he caught a glimpse of Katarina in the living room window watching him leave. She was crying and holding herself. Lars backed out of the parking spot and drove quickly away. He felt tightness in his throat and tears were burning behind his eyes. He had never deliberately hurt another human being in his life like that before and it hurt like hell.

* * * *

The sleek, silver BMW convertible threaded its way through the streets of Madrid like a lightning bolt, weaving in and out of the busy mid-afternoon traffic. Jaime took the traffic circle by storm, laughing and singing at the top of his tenor voice as he sped around the circle, too fast for the sharp curve and barely keeping the car on all four wheels as he dashed down the *Avenida Maestra* toward the outskirts of the city.

"¡*Jésus Cristo*! Jaime! Slow this damned car down now or I will never let you drive again!" Javier yelled at the top of his voice as he held onto the dashboard for dear life. "What has gotten into you?"

"Sorry, Uncle Javier. But I love to drive fast. Isn't it an amazing feeling?" Jaime slowed the car to a more respectable, not to mention legal, speed and after a couple of minutes Javier felt himself finally beginning to relax. They still had a ten-minute drive ahead of them and he decided that his young nephew needed a lecture on the subject of responsibility and safety.

"Jaime, listen to me. You have a promising future ahead of you. Why would you want to destroy your life by getting yourself hurt or worse in a car accident? And if something were to happen to you it would kill my sister and your grandparents and all of us. No more of this irresponsible behavior. You must think of others first, before your own selfish desires. Do you understand me, boy?"

"Yes, Uncle Javier. I understand you and I'm sorry. My mom would freak if she knew I was driving too fast. Promise not to tell about this?" Jaime actually sounded contrite and Javier wanted to believe that his eighteen-year old nephew had gotten the message.

"I will not tell my sister if you promise to obey the speed limit. Now swear on the souls of the most holy saints of Spain and then tell me about your audition at the Royal Music Academy. I want to hear what opera you chose."

Jaime promised on the souls of the saints to be a more conscientious driver and proceeded to tell Javier about his performance of the Italian piece "Amor Ti Vieta."

"I rocked out on that song, Uncle Javier—totally." Jaime steered the car down a cobbled lane that led to the Garza estate just north of Madrid. He drove the car through groves of lemon and orange trees lining the lane on each side and brought the car to a stop in front of the large white house Juan Garza, Javier's father and Jaime's grandfather, had designed and built himself twenty years ago for his growing family.

"And you lost your humility, I see." Javier playfully punched Jaime in the stomach as they grabbed Javier's suitcases from the trunk of the car. "Well, you will have to perform it for me after dinner. I want to see if you can sing as amazingly as your Uncle Javier."

"Now who has lost his humility?" Jaime laughed. They carried the suitcases into the rambling front hall and set them down at the bottom of the wide spiral staircase.

"Mama! We're home. Uncle Javier is here!" Jaime yelled loudly. His voice echoed off the walls. Javier suppressed a smile and felt pride wash over him for his beloved nephew whose vocal talents even extended to musical yelling. There was no end to what the boy could accomplish if he buckled down and studied his music seriously.

Javier's sister, Analeza, appeared in the foyer, one arm outstretched toward Javier, the other firmly planted behind her back.

"Javier, the world famous opera singer has returned to the fold." She beamed at him, embracing him with her extended arm.

"Mama, what are you hiding behind your back?" asked Jaime? "Did the letter come?" He tried to see what she was hiding.

Analeza brought her hand out and put an already opened white envelope into Jaime's hand. Her face gave nothing away regarding what the contents held.

"I'm so sorry, Jaime, but I couldn't wait to open it. I know it was wrong of me but I had to know," she said softly.

Jaime didn't say anything. He pulled the folded paper from the envelope and slowly opened it, holding his breath with anticipation.

Javier and Analeza stood silently while they watched his face as he read the words that would change his life.

"I got in! I got in!" Jaime screamed the words like a little girl and they all laughed and hugged and cheered.

"Congratulations, Jaime. You got into the Royal Music Academy on your very first try. *Muy excelente*! It took me two tries before I got in." Javier was bursting with pride and affection for his nephew. The entire family knew that Jaime had a gift that exceeded any they had ever witnessed, and Javier was no slouch opera singer himself. He was genuinely thrilled for Jaime.

"We have already planned a celebratory dinner for tonight," said Analeza. "And we have two guests of honor: Jaime, my beautiful opera singer-to-be and Javier, my now famous the world over brother who has somehow managed to pass his talent onto my son and for that I am forever grateful." She hugged them both and steered them toward the kitchen located at the rear of the house.

Javier greeted the cook, Alma, who was busy chopping vegetables for a salad and waiting for bread to rise that she would later bake in the old-fashioned stone hearth at one end of the kitchen.

"Where are Mother and Father?" asked Javier. He poured himself a glass of lemonade and sat down at the round oak kitchen table. Jaime had run off to put away his letter and more than likely to phone his best friend with his news.

"They're at the club golfing but should be here soon," said Analeza. "Father just returned from New York a couple of days ago. I guess he had a really good trip—even got to see an old friend he hadn't seen in years."

"It wasn't a woman, was it?" Javier asked, suddenly thinking of Lars' mother who had recently left his father for someone she had known many years before. The thought sent a shiver down his spine.

"Why on earth would you ask a question like that?" Analeza frowned at him. She joined him at the table with a glass of lemonade for herself and brought a package of macaroons. She took a cookie from the bag and pushed them toward Javier.

"Just kidding," he forced a smile. "Seriously though. Was it a woman?"

"*Dios mio,* Javier—Mr. Suspicious all of a sudden. No. It was a man—an old friend who once interviewed him. Remember a long time ago when Father was featured in *Architectural Digest*? The article is framed and hanging in Dad's study. It's the guy who wrote the article." She popped another cookie into her mouth and chewed slowly.

"Oh. That's nice. Get these things away from me. I can't stop eating them and I don't even like coconut." He laughed, pushing the bag away.

Analeza proceeded to catch him up on local and family news and he answered her many questions about Les Passionistes and what it was like to be suddenly famous and wanted by women all over the world. That had made him laugh heartily which caused him to snort lemonade out of his nose.

"If all those women could have just seen that slick move, brother, they might think twice about lusting after this famous opera singer," Analeza teased.

At that moment Juan and Maria Garza walked into the kitchen and Maria went straight to her son and hugged him fiercely.

"Welcome home, son," she said. "The only time we ever see you anymore is on television or in the papers. How are you?"

"Great. It's good to be home. I'm ready to relax and play for awhile."

The four of them sat together at the table, talking and soon Jaime joined them and told his great news to his grandparents.

Juan immediately got up and went to the bar and selected a bottle of *Dom Perignon* and the five of them toasted both Jaime's and Javier's successes.

Later that evening after they had dined on a sumptuous feast of steaks, fried potatoes, egg tortillas, salad and homemade bread, Javier and his father sat together on the front porch and sipped cognacs and talked about life in general. It was a nice change of pace for Javier after the constant activity of the past year. It felt good to relax and breathe in the nighttime air. He could smell the late summer blooms in the gardens below the porch. He hadn't felt such peace in a long time.

"Javier, you weren't planning to go to Isla Marta while you're on your break, were you?" Juan asked.

"I had considered it, but, no. Speaking of Isla Marta..." He started to mention his loan of the place to Lars.

But Juan was already speaking.

"That's good because I've loaned the house out to the daughter of an old friend of mine that I saw recently in New York. My old friend Ted Taylor is a magazine editor and I suggested he do a travel story about the place. So he's sending his daughter there for a few weeks to write it."

Javier swallowed a lump in his throat. This could be a big problem considering the circumstances. He should probably tell his father that he had already loaned the house out to Lars but since, technically, it wasn't his house to loan out in the first place he decided to keep quiet. He was quite certain his father wouldn't normally mind his letting Lars stay there and he had not felt the need to check first, it never having occurred to him that the place would not be available. He would just have to call Lars and change the plans. He hoped Lars wouldn't mind.

They finished their drinks and headed inside for a friendly game of cards before retiring for the night. Javier resolved that he would call Lars first thing tomorrow morning about Isla Marta.

CHAPTER 4

It had been a long twenty or so hours and Antonia was feeling every minute of every one of those hours in her bones. She was dog-tired and so ready to crash into a soft, warm bed and sleep away the jetlag that threatened to do her in. And finally she was nearing the end of her journey. She had left Kennedy airport on time last night and flown all night to Barcelona. She had whiled away the long flight reading through the new books on Spain and the latest issues of *Passion's* competitors, *Vogue* and *Harper's Bazaar,* figuring it was always good to know what the competition was up to. She'd even had time to start a new chick lit novel that Deanna had loaned her. She had never been one to sleep on an airplane though she envied those who could. And the in-flight movie had been one she had seen before so she had passed the hours reading, taking the odd moment here and there to rest her tired eyes.

She had had a bit of a problem getting to the right part of the huge airport to catch her charter flight to Isla Marta and had made it there at the last possible moment, dragging her heavy luggage behind her. She had been warned in advance by the travel office at *Passion* that her luggage had to be collected at the baggage claim for the customs inspection and that she would have to transport it herself to the part of the airport where charter flights departed. And just her luck that it was on the far side of the airport. By the time she had settled into her seat on the impossibly tiny aircraft she was utterly exhausted and could feel the mother of all headaches threatening. And if she even took one moment to consider the size of this plane, she would probably faint in fear so she just sat still in her seat and tried to stay calm, keeping negative thoughts at bay as best she could.

The flight to Isla Marta was not terribly long and soon Antonia was on the ground and collecting her bags at the small baggage claim area. After she had all of her bags together she took a moment to check out her surroundings. She immediately felt the change in the air temperature—a good change. She could feel the tropical heat and noted that it wasn't oppressive but rather welcoming and soothing. The place wasn't at all crowded and she had a momentary feeling of helplessness. Someone was supposed to be here to meet her and drive her to the Garza house but there didn't appear to be anyone waiting for her.

I won't panic, she thought as she made her way slowly to the small terminal's front doors. *Someone will be here soon.* The automatic doors opened and she stepped out into the heat of the afternoon, dragging all of her gear behind her.

"¿Señorita Taylor?"

Antonia looked to her left where an older, white-haired man was just alighting from a light blue vintage Volvo.

"Yes, that's me," Antonia smiled at the man. "*Buenos tardes.*" She didn't know much Spanish but she did know how to say 'good afternoon.'

"I am sorry to be late in arriving. So many sheep and goats on the roadways and I had to wait for them all to pass. Please forgive me," said the man. He offered her his hand. "I am Manolo. I am to take you to the house. Please forgive if my English is not so good." He smiled at Antonia warmly.

"Your English is fine but my Spanish is non-existent. And you aren't late. I've only just arrived myself." She shook his outstretched hand firmly and together they loaded her luggage into the boot of the Volvo. She climbed in beside him and fastened her seatbelt. Manolo started the car and the sound of Les Passionistes immediately filled the car and spilled out of the open windows.

Antonia laughed and glanced at Manolo who looked sheepish.

"I am sorry for the music is too loud for your ears." He reached to turn it down but Antonia stopped him.

"It's OK," she smiled. "I know this group. I have this CD, too. It's beautiful."

"Do you know that one of these singers is the son of Juan Garza? You are going to Juan's house now," he said a little haltingly.

"Yes, I heard that. That's really cool," She realized too late that using the word 'cool' probably made her sound like a star-struck teen, assuming Manolo even knew what she meant by that.

They left the airport grounds and pulled out onto a two-lane road that led away from the area where the airport was located and into a wooded area that went on for a couple of miles. Manolo eventually turned onto another road that took them between beautiful grassy fields to the left and a rocky cliff to the right.

The road became twistier with each passing minute and Antonia noticed that they were ascending a rather tall hill that could almost be classified as a mountain. When they reached the summit, Antonia glanced down to her right and gasped audibly at the sight before her. Her reaction made Manolo laugh heartily.

"Everybody makes that sound the first time they see it," he said, turning the music down a little bit. "It is fantastical, no?"

"Oh, my god," Antonia whispered. "This is breathtakingly exquisite."

Unfolding before her eyes was the Mediterranean Sea in all its amazing turquoise splendor. White sandy beaches curved for miles around the edge of the sea and wild sea-grasses danced gently in the breeze along the cliff's side. Late summer wildflowers in brilliant shades of pink, purple and yellow still bloomed along the rocky road as they crossed the summit of the mountain and began the descent toward the sea. Soon little white structures—islanders' home, shops and cafes—began to appear on both sides of the road, which had finally widened out a bit. They passed through two small white villages both dominated by old stone churches before they arrived at the Garza compound. Tall palm trees dominated the grounds and Antonia caught a glimpse of the Mediterranean Sea at the end of a footpath that led off from where the driveway ended at the side of the house. The house itself was stucco-style with a red-tiled roof, very traditional for this part of the world. The out buildings, including a garage and what appeared to be a bathhouse were made of white stone. The grounds were thick with exotic foliage and Antonia could see hibiscus bushes growing in front of the veranda and purple and pink bougainvillea trailing over the roof and dangling over the veranda awning. Late summer roses in shades of tangerine, white and red grew alongside the house along with what appeared to be wild herbs. She had landed in paradise and though she was exhausted she could hardly contain her excitement. Discovering the joys of Isla Marta would not be a difficult task at all.

* * * *

"You can't go to Spain, darling. You only just got here," Mona Kohler said to Lars, a note of sadness in her voice. They were in the living room of Lars' grandmother's house, now his mother's home.

"I'll make a deal with you, Mother. I won't leave until this weekend. That will give us more time to catch up and see all the cousins. But you and I need to talk about what's going on with you and Dad. And don't tell me it isn't my business."

Mona smiled half-heartedly at Lars but didn't say anything. Not about her marital situation anyway.

"I like your hair long like that, darling. It suits you." She ran her fingers through the long, thick hair at the back of his neck.

"It sets me apart from the others," Lars laughed.

"Tell me about your life in London. I want to hear everything. And when you are finished filling me in, I will tell you about me. And, darling...thanks for agreeing to stay a few days longer. I need quality time with my son. The world sees more of you than I do."

Lars answered his mother's many questions about his life as an opera star and after awhile she did the talking. When she had finished telling him about meeting up again with a long lost love he decided he must tell her about Katarina. He had resisted mentioning it at first because he knew how much his mother loved Katarina and she would probably not take the news well. But she surprised him.

"One thing I have learned Lars, and I have learned this lesson the hard way, is that you must follow your heart. Your head will talk you into and out of situations all the time, but your heart knows best. Even if the outcome is unknown, you must obey your heart's requests. If you don't, the pain you feel will overwhelm you—maybe not right away, but one day it will come back to haunt you. I know it sounds corny and trite, but it is the truth. Always remember that."

"I will, Mother. Now what have you got to eat around here? I'm starved."

They laughed and went to the kitchen where they sat at the table, talking and eating homemade beef noodle soup and crusty bread.

Later that evening it occurred to Lars that perhaps he should contact Javier and let him know that he wouldn't be arriving at the house on Isla Marta until the weekend, but then again, what did it really matter to Javier? He wouldn't care one way or another. It wasn't like he was going to be there himself. Lars decided it didn't matter that much since he wasn't inconveniencing anyone with his late arrival and decided not to worry about it. He changed his flight plans and then gave his family his undivided attention for the rest of the week, indulging his mother and father's wishes to talk, eat, shop and just generally be together as a family. Of course, he had to divide his time between his two parents but somehow it all worked out and he managed to please everybody, including the local paper, which wanted photos and an interview. Lars was so ready for this break from his job that it didn't even occur to him to check his cell phone to see if Samuel or one of the producers or his band-mates had been trying to reach him. As a matter of fact, he couldn't even remember where he had left his cell phone. *Oh, well, if someone needs to reach me, they'll find a way,* he thought. As it happened, the next time Lars would see his cell phone would be on Isla Marta but he didn't know that now.

* * * *

I give up, thought Javier. *Lars must have lost his phone. I'm just going to have to go down there and head him off at the pass.*

He had been trying to contact Lars all day and had had no luck. He cursed himself for not getting Lars', Antoine's and Andrew's home phone numbers just in case he needed or wanted to talk to them during their break.

He told his parents that he had decided to get away after all to Isla Marta and he wanted to leave the next morning. He was afraid they would be hurt that he was rushing off so soon after just getting home, but he only intended to stay a couple of days, talk to Lars about going to his aunt's home on Majorca, or maybe this Antonia Taylor would be OK with sharing the house with Lars. They didn't have to entertain each other and goodness knew the house was big enough for the both of them. It would all work out one way or another, of that Javier was sure.

"So all of a sudden you need to get away from it all, is that it?" asked his father in a teasing voice as they sat outside on the front porch once again, this time with tumblers of whisky. Juan smoked a Cuban cigar and looked at Javier with a twinkle in his eye.

Javier could tell that something unsaid was implied by his father's tone of voice but he truly had no clue what it could be. He would soon find out.

"Maybe for a couple of days. Is that so unusual?" Javier wondered what his father was getting at.

"Or perhaps the knowledge that there is a pretty girl staying in the house is the real reason you suddenly need to go to Isla Marta. Could that be it?" he joked.

Shit, Javier thought. He felt his cheeks grow hot with embarrassment. Why had it not occurred to him that his father might get the wrong idea about his sudden desire to go to Isla Marta?

"How do you know she's pretty?" asked Javier. *Good comeback*, he thought.

"Because Ted showed me her picture and I must say, she is a beauty—just you're kind of girl, I would say. So you want to check her out? Well, that's fine by me. But I must warn you, Ted mentioned that Antonia recently had her heart broken so you must not go down there and try anything funny. I would not want my old friend's daughter to be hurt again."

This conversation is getting way out of hand, thought Javier, *but I guess I had better play along.*

"I promise I will not hurt a soul. I'll stay a couple of days and then come back here and challenge you to a round of golf. How does that sound?" Javier was pleased with that response. Distracting his father with golf talk worked every time.

"Sounds perfect." Juan ground out his cigar, finished his whisky and wished Javier a good night.

Javier sat on the porch a few minutes more, listening to the night-sounds. And he couldn't help it. He had to admit to himself that while he had not previously given even one thought to the mystery girl staying at the house on Isla Marta, now this Antonia had him wondering. He was intrigued and couldn't wait to get to the island and see her for himself.

* * * *

Antonia tried several times to wake up and join the world, especially the glorious world that literally waited at her feet, but the effects of jetlag and a lingering headache had gotten the best of her and she had slept for nearly fifteen hours straight. When she finally forced herself to sit up in the bed in the darkened room, she felt a moment of disorientation. She looked around the room, trying to remember where she was when suddenly the metaphorical light dawned—Spain. She got up from the bed and walked over to the white wicker dresser where she had laid her watch last night. She picked it up and turned it over and was shocked at the time. Nine-thirty! How could it only be nine-thirty? She had the feeling that she had been out as long as Rip Van Winkle yet it was only nine-thirty? She padded in her bare feet across the cool stone floor over to the window and pulled the shade back expecting to see darkness.

"Yeow!" she screeched, covering her eyes quickly from the blinding light. "Damn!" She must have set her watch wrong. It was broad daylight outside. She looked quickly around the room and noticed a clock hanging on the wall next to the entrance to the bathroom. It did indeed say nine-thirty. It was nine-thirty *the next day*. "I guess I was more tired than I thought," she said aloud.

She hurried through a shower, washing her hair and dressing quickly. She was afraid that Marta and Manolo would think she had died in here or worse, that she was some lazy American who was going to sleep her life away and as such she was anxious to make an appearance.

Last night she had met Marta, Manolo's wife, who had shown her the house and her room and the kitchen and using hand motions and barebones English had told her to make herself at home—at least that's what Antonia had taken away from the conversation. Marta had fed her a light supper and then she had hit the sack—hard.

Antonia walked through the tastefully decorated living and dining rooms into the bright yellow kitchen where she found Marta squeezing oranges presumably for juice. Marta smiled in greeting, said something she didn't understand and indicated the kitchen table. Antonia sat down and watched as Marta prepared and served her a feast of fresh juice, scrambled eggs, serrano ham, a flaky, golden croissant with strawberry preserves and several slices of pineapple. Antonia ate like she had never eaten before and enjoyed every bite. She thanked Marta profusely who seemed happy that Antonia had cleaned her plate.

"Now you walk," Marta said. "Now you walk."

"Now I walk?" Antonia was confused but impressed that Marta had spoken words she had understood even if she didn't know why Marta had said those particular words.

"Now you walk." Marta gently pushed Antonia toward the back door where Marta pointed in the direction of the sea.

Antonia decided it was better not to argue and nodded to Marta who smiled widely at her.

"*Vaya a la playa, chica,*" said Marta.

And then Antonia understood completely what she meant: 'Go to the beach, girl.'

"OK. *A la playa.*" Antonia laughed. She waved to Marta over her shoulder and headed down the path to the sea. She couldn't wait to test the waters.

* * * *

Manolo had been surprised to hear from Javier who had called him from the airport on his cell phone and so he had dropped his gardening tools in the dirt, hopped in the Volvo and dashed to the airport without even telling Marta he was leaving.

Now they were turning into the driveway and they could see Marta standing on the steps wringing her hands in apparent worry.

"I think I'm in trouble, son," laughed Manolo as he parked the Volvo under a stately palm tree.

Marta gave Manolo a half-angry look, hugged Javier warmly, surprised and delighted to see him, and then ordered them to go find the girl. She had gone to the beach ages ago and had not returned. Marta was too afraid to go herself fearing she would find Antonia dead in the water.

"Go!" she ordered Manolo.

"I'm sure she's fine," said Javier. "I'll go, Manolo. You stay here and make nice with your wife. I'll find the girl—Antonia."

He started down the half rocky, half-grassy path to the beach. A minute or so later he was out of sight of the house and standing in the sand. He looked up and down the beach but saw no sign of Antonia. He felt a sinking sensation in his stomach and immediately remembered his father's admonition not to hurt this girl. He hadn't said anything about the possibility of the girl hurting herself. He started down the beach and walked quite a distance, coming to a small cove where he had spent many summers of his childhood playing in the water with his cousins and sisters. And there sitting on a rock was the woman he presumed to be Antonia. Her back was to him and not wanting to sneak up on her and scare her to death, he called out to her.

"Hello...Antonia?"

She turned and looked at him over her shoulder, then got up from the rock and stood a few feet away from him.

"Yes?" She looked warily at him, keeping a respectable distance between them.

"Hi. I'm Javier Garza. I'm Juan's son." He walked toward her, extending his hand.

Antonia took his hand and shook it firmly. She instantly recognized him and made a concerted effort to remain composed. It seemed that Deanna's prophecy or wish or portent, whatever it was, had come true.

"Hello. It's nice to meet you and thank you for letting me stay here while I work on my story about Isla Marta. I haven't seen much of the place yet but what I've seen so far is unbelievably gorgeous." The words tumbled out of her mouth like a nervous waterfall.

Nothing could be more gorgeous than you, thought Javier. *I must be dreaming.* Aloud he said something completely different.

"Welcome. Glad you could come. I only hope that your article isn't so great that Isla Marta loses her innocence and becomes overrun with tourists," Javier smiled.

"Well, that is a possibility, but on the bright side, the tourists bring lots of money and that would give a boost to the economy—if it needs one." Antonia smoothed her white, cotton T-shirt down over her khaki shorts and wished fervently that she was better dressed and wearing some make-up, at least lip gloss and mascara.

"That is true," Javier wanted to study her features but staring seemed rude so he looked down at her feet—which seemed like the safest body part to look at. She was wearing pink flip-flops and he noted with amusement that her toenails were painted pink as well. He wondered if she had any idea at all who he was. He and his band-mates had had their faces plastered all over the globe for the better part of the past year so it was entirely possible that she had heard of Les Passionistes. But Javier found himself hoping that she didn't have a clue.

"I didn't realize that anyone else would be here," Antonia said. She removed her flip-flops and began to walk along in the sand with him in the direction of the house.

"I decided to take a break now that summer is over and all of those tourists who have already discovered Isla Marta are no longer here," said Javier, telling a little white lie, as he fell into step beside her.

"You're so lucky to have a place like this paradise to escape to. I live in New York City and most days I'm happy just to escape into my own apartment." She laughed and Javier felt as if his insides were turning into jelly.

"I love New York. We had such a wonderful time there and the people were so generous to us. I mean to me…when I was there." Javier wanted to kick himself. If he didn't want her to figure out who he was then he had better choose his words a lot more carefully than that.

Antonia wondered why he had suddenly corrected himself and it dawned on her that he might not want her to know about his profession. She couldn't imagine why that would bother him but she decided to err on the side of caution and not mention that she already knew who he was until he brought the subject up himself.

They walked back to the house and on the way Javier asked Antonia about the story she would be writing about Isla Marta. She explained that she planned to interview shopkeepers and other local residents, including Manolo and Marta if they were willing, about life on the island. She wanted to write about the topography, the weather, the commerce and also the cultural aspects of Isla Marta including its music, food and traditions. She wanted to learn everything there was to know about this enchanted locale.

Javier told her about the upcoming birthday celebration that paid homage to dead lovers, advising her to enjoy the celebration even as she would be studying its rituals and customs so she could write about it for the article. She assured him she intended to enjoy it as this trip would be as much about relaxing and having a good time as it was about getting the work done.

Back at the house, Marta clapped her hands at the sight of Antonia alive and well. She brought them soft drinks and banana cake still warm from the oven, giving a sly little wink to Javier as she handed him his plate. He looked at Antonia to see if she had seen the wink but she was looking out toward the sea, which was visible between the trees. They sat on the veranda eating and talking, the conversation flowing easily back and forth between them. Suddenly, a familiar sound floated from the house, through the open windows, enveloping them. Javier nearly choked on a piece of the cake when he heard the sound of his own voice singing "Nella Fantasia" in Italian, along with Antoine, Lars and Andrew. He felt his face redden and shook his head slowly. Apparently Manolo or Marta, more than likely, wanted to impress Antonia on his behalf. He feared his cover was now officially blown. He was correct.

"Les Passionistes," said Antonia. "I have that CD. I brought it with me. Would it be rude of me to ask you to autograph it sometime?" She smiled at him and took a sip of her drink. *Why did I say that?* she asked herself, suddenly feeling self-conscious.

"So you know. I wasn't sure and I didn't want to bring it up. I was afraid you might think me pretentious or something," Javier said a little sheepishly. Why did it matter that she knew who he was? It had never bothered him before when he met new people. Why did it now? These questions floated across his mind as he looked into Antonia's amber eyes.

"I knew but I didn't want you to think I was some sort of freaky, groupie stalker type or something who managed to get here under false pretenses. Of course, if you want to participate in my article in any capacity you are more than welcome," she laughed.

"I would be happy to contribute any way I can," he replied.

They spent the next couple of hours talking and getting to know one another with Antonia assuring Javier that their conversation was strictly off the record and they were simply two people enjoying one another's company.

After lunch Javier took Antonia into the village and showed her around. She snapped a few photos with her personal camera as they walked around the plaza and he treated her to an ice-cream cone at a quaint little shop. While they sat outside on a bench eating their cones, a young woman came toward them clutching a CD in her hand.

"Javier. It's so nice to see you. I can't believe you're here on Isla Marta." She held out the CD. "Everyone here has heard about your success. Will you please sign my CD?" She handed him the CD's liner notes and a pen and he signed his name and thanked her. She walked happily away, staring at the CD as she walked back to her clothing boutique.

"Do you know her?" asked Antonia.

"No clue," said Javier. They both laughed and finished their cones, then went back to the Volvo and drove to the house.

Antonia went to her room to make a phone call so she could check in with the office and let her father know she had arrived safely. Javier sat on the veranda to wait for her, his thoughts drifting. He felt himself getting carried away by Antonia's beauty and intelligence and her sense of fun. He knew already that he was falling for her and he wasn't quite sure what to do about it. When Marta came out to offer him a drink, she made mention of how lovely Antonia was and had he noticed? Javier nodded and smiled but remained silent so as to discourage conversation on the subject. He declined the drink offer and just sat staring into space.

Back in her room, Antonia felt a giddiness that she had been suppressing from the moment she had first laid eyes on Javier. He was so sexy and sweet. She felt a full-blown crush developing and the thought scared her. She had not felt anything for any man since Jeff and a world famous opera star was the last person she should be having feelings for. She bet Jeff would be impressed with her crush—maybe even jealous, though for musical reasons only. She made her phone call and then rejoined Javier on the veranda where they talked all evening long. Antonia couldn't remember when she had felt so relaxed and comfortable with someone while Javier wondered how he would get through the night without touching her honey-brown hair or kissing her full pink lips. It was going to be nearly impossible. He even forgot that Lars was probably on his way. He wondered what his band-mates would think of Antonia. If he only knew.

CHAPTER 5

For the next couple of days Antonia and Javier were inseparable. They spent entirely too much time on the beach, walking, swimming in the cerulean water, collecting shells and sometimes napping on blankets, letting the October sun wash over them. Even though he tried to keep his thoughts clean and aboveboard, by the end of the second day of beach-combing and visiting the local villages so Antonia could take notes and pictures for her story, Javier knew that the time had come for him to make his move. He sat by a fountain in the plaza in the little, whitewashed village of Dos Passos watching her interview the village's *alcalde,* or mayor, about the festival which was scheduled to begin with a parade in a couple of weeks. All of the villages held their own special events pertaining to the festival and she wanted to know how Dos Passos would be celebrating it. Javier had acted as her translator for several interviews but this *alcalde* spoke English quite well so she hadn't needed his help. He sat on the bench holding two cold bottles of Coke while she finished her interview.

He watched as she concluded her conversation with the *alcalde*, who, if Javier was not mistaken, was flirting with her rather shamelessly. Antonia laughed at something the *alcalde* said and then came over to join him.

"He gave me great information. By the time I get finished here I'll have enough material for a whole series of articles," she said animatedly, sitting down quite close to him on the stone bench. "This festival for dead lovers sounds like a fun fiesta, in spite of its downer name."

"It's great," agreed Javier. "The whole island gets caught up in it." He handed her a Coke and watched as she drank thirstily from the bottle. Her lips and creamy neck were disturbing him to the point that he had to clear his throat and look away. He could feel his heart beating rapidly in his chest and even though they were in a very public locale, and there were many people walking about the plaza, he felt had to kiss her now.

Noting his silence, Antonia glanced at Javier, completely unaware of his inner turmoil. She noticed that his eyes had taken on an almost wild-eyed, heavy-lidded look and it began to dawn on her that something was about to happen—right here in the town square. In seeming slow motion, Javier placed his arm along the bench behind her shoulders and weaved his hand sensuously into the back of her thick, brown hair.

"Antonia…" he whispered her name. It sounded like honey dripping from his lips. "You are very beautiful."

She blushed and looked down at her lap. "I bet you say that to all the girls." She felt flustered and wondered if anyone was paying any attention to them. As attracted as she was to Javier, she also felt a strange sense of confusion—something she couldn't define, but felt quite sure was related to the fact that he was a sexy Spaniard who might or might not be one of those famed Don Juan types—the ultimate Latin lover—who would love you one moment and break your heart the next.

"Only when it's true," he smiled, leaning close enough to her that he could smell the freesia scent of her shampoo. "I've been wanting to kiss you all day and if I don't do it soon the sun will set and I will miss my chance."

"You don't kiss after sunset?" she asked teasingly. She could smell his skin, he was so close to her now. Her flesh prickled with anticipation.

"Oh, believe me, I kiss after sunset, among other things. May I?"

In answer, Antonia turned her face to his and their lips touched tentatively. Javier groaned from deep within his throat and willed himself to remember they were in public so as not to ravish here on this stone bench. She put her hand up to his face and the kiss deepened. His tongue pushed slowly between her lips and even, white teeth and tangled with hers. He pulled her closer to his chest and breathed her in.

"Maybe we should go home," he whispered into her hair. He was about to stand up when he realized that standing up right now was impossible without showing his desire so blatantly to the villagers who went about their evening shopping and strolling all around them. "But give me a moment."

Antonia grinned and covered her mouth with her hand.

"Technical difficulties?" she asked teasingly.

"You could say that." Javier removed his arm from around her shoulders and leaned forward a moment, resting his elbows on his knees.

Antonia looked around the plaza and saw that several women were looking their way and appeared to be preparing to approach them.

"Javier…we're about to get company. Some fans I'm guessing," She indicated with a nod of her head in the women's direction.

"OK. We can go now." He stood up, taking her hand and led her to where they had parked the car in front of the little tourist office. He opened the door for her and they got in, driving westward into the setting sun.

Antonia was quiet on the ride back to the house. She had a sense that they were about to cross into dangerous territory and she resolved not to lose her head and do something crazy, like let this sexy Spaniard seduce her. He seemed so genuine and kind but he was a famous, opera singer after all and she couldn't be entirely sure of his motives. She couldn't be sure if he intended to make love to her because he wanted *her* specifically, or because she happened to be available and present. She prayed she would have the resolve to resist his charms.

She watched him shift gears and averted her gaze. She preferred to look out the window, anywhere but at his beautiful hands, which she imagined could do some amazing things to her body. She felt the attraction, the powerful lust, growing between them and feared she wouldn't be able to resist if and when the time came.

The house was quiet. Manolo and Marta had apparently retired to their cottage for dinner. In the kitchen, Javier pointed to the paella on the stove that Marta had left for them.

"Are you hungry?" he asked.

"I could eat," she said. "I need to wash up first." She went to the bathroom to wash her hands and comb her hair. She studied her face in the mirror, noting how the sun and wind had put a pinkish glow in her skin. She felt her stomach rumble with a combination of hunger pangs and nerves about what the night held.

Javier got plates from the cupboard and chose a bottle of wine from the wine rack. He put a CD of bolero music on the little boom box that Marta kept in the kitchen and lit a candle, setting it in the middle of the dining table.

When Antonia returned from the bathroom she noticed the music and the candle but didn't comment on it. It all seemed like so much—almost too much—for her mind to take in. A few days ago she had been in New York living her boring but safe life, writing articles about movies and fashion and now here she was in Spain about to have dinner with a hot, sex and very famous Spaniard. How had this happened? She tried to stop analyzing the situation and just let it be.

They fixed their plates and Javier poured the wine. At the table, he pulled out her chair and she sat down, commenting on his chivalry.

"Such a gentleman," she smiled.

"I try." He sat down across from her and immediately lifted his wineglass in a toast.

"To Antonia, the beautiful journalist from America who has suddenly appeared in my life like magic. I pray this is not a dream."

"Thank you. That was sweet." Antonia blushed, embarrassed.

They touched glasses and drank slowly. Antonia felt the wine go immediately to her head and took that as a sign that she had better eat something fast. She stabbed a fat, pink shrimp and bit into it as Javier watched.

"Tell me more about your life in New York, Antonia. I want to hear everything." He picked up his fork and speared a piece of chorizo.

"There isn't all that much to tell really," she demurred.

"Tell me what there is then," He gave her a disarming smile.

And so they spent the next hour eating and talking, eventually taking their wine into the living room where they sat side by side on the sofa in the darkened living room.

When their glasses were empty and they had finished the entire bottle of wine, Javier set their glasses down and turned to Antonia. He took her hands in his and kissed them both softly.

"While I admit that we have not known each other very long, can I just say to you that I have an intense desire to make love to you? Does that shock you?" Javier looked into her eyes and waited for her answer.

Antonia felt dizzy—from the wine and from Javier's words. Her senses were heightened and on alert. She wanted Javier to make love to her but way down deep in the recesses of her mind, her instincts were begging her to be strong and resist anything beyond passionate kisses and tender touches until she knew him better and could trust him with her heart.

She wasn't sure why she felt this strange resistance but guessed protecting her barely healed heart had to be the reason. She wasn't the type to engage in casual sex with someone she barely knew and she sure as hell didn't want to be another land conquered by Don Juan if Javier turned out to be that type. She was torn.

"No, it doesn't shock me," she said quietly. "But, I'm not sure..."

"Shhh..." Javier touched her lips gently with his fingers, preventing her from finishing her thought. "Don't say anything. Just sit here with me and let me hold you and breathe you in." He enveloped her in his arms and held her closely for a few moments. Then he cupped her chin in his hand and turned her to face him, kissing her gently. His tongue ran over her lips feather-lightly causing her to shudder visibly. The kiss deepened and Antonia felt herself floating away. It was as if she had sprouted wings and was hovering above herself watching two strangers surrender to passion. She felt Javier's hand slide up her blouse and stop just beneath her breast, waiting to see if she would stop him. When she didn't, he slid his fingertips beneath her lacy bra, up over her breast but again stopping short of touching her hardened nipple. She didn't move and so he ran his thumb over her nipple and she involuntarily arched her back and gasped. Javier cupped her breast and buried his face into her neck, trailing kisses across her throat.

Antonia was going mad with longing but still she heard the voice of reason whispering to her to stop this now. Stop this before something happened that could never be undone.

"Javier," she whispered, taking his hand and slowly pulling it away from her breast. "We have to stop before we can't stop."

"Why would you want to stop something so beautiful from happening between us? I want you, Antonia, and I'm fairly sure you want me, too. Or am I wrong?" He touched her cheek, rubbing his thumb along the line of her jaw.

"No, you're not wrong. It's just that I hardly know you and you barely know me. Besides what would you think of me if I fell so easily into bed with you?" She pushed away a lock of hair from his forehead where it kept falling just above his right eye.

"I would think you are a passionate woman who knows what she wants and isn't afraid to go for it," he said, kissing her eyebrows.

Antonia sighed and laid her head back against the sofa, closing her eyes. She tried to gather her thoughts and interpret his words in such a way as to make them sweet and innocent and not a ticket to buy his way into bed with her.

Javier sensed that he had gone too far and now needed to do some serious damage control. As much as he wanted her he would never try to sweet talk his way into her bed. She had to want it as much as he did or it wouldn't be nearly as beautiful as he intended it to be.

"It's OK, Antonia. You're probably right. I'm a patient man. I can wait. You are worth it." He kissed her again and pulled her to her feet. Those words had been difficult to say but Javier hoped it would appease her. He walked her to her room and kissed her good night in the hallway. She closed the door and leaned against it, sighing deeply. She hoped she had done the right thing.

Javier slept badly that night, thoughts of Antonia making him crazy. He made a vow to himself that no matter what, he would be on his best behavior and let her make the next move. The proverbial ball was in her court. He would just have to wait it out.

The next day, after breakfast on the veranda, Javier took Antonia to the gypsy market in a neighboring village and acted as translator for her as she gathered information for her article. She moved from stall to stall purchasing little trinkets of handmade jewelry, shawls, almonds and hair clips for gifts for family members and friends—as well as to be used in photos for her story. In the afternoon when they returned to the house she went to her room to do some writing and Javier used the time to help Manolo make an outdoor fire pit for roasting a pig during the upcoming festival. It was a tradition to eat pork on Isla Marta's birthday and Manolo built a new pit every year for the occasion.

Antonia developed a headache, probably from drinking too much wine at the dinner of fresh seafood and salad prepared by Marta that they'd shared together on the veranda, and had to excuse herself to go to bed early. Javier looked in on her a couple of times during the night, nearly desperate to lie down beside her but always resisting. She looked so lovely in sleep and he hoped her headache would be gone in the morning.

* * * *

As much as Lars loved his family, he was more than ready to go to Isla Marta for that much needed break. After several days of singing for aunts and uncles and eating pastries and meat pies he was anxious to be alone. Urs dropped him off at the airport on his way to work and wished Lars a peaceful break. After settling into his seat on the plane bound for Barcelona, Lars opened the new book he had just bought in the airport's gift shop—*The Da Vinci Code*, in German. He had almost purchased the English version but decided he didn't want to have work that hard on something that was supposed to be pure fun escapism. He was hooked on the first page and nearly halfway through it when the plane landed in Barcelona. He made his way to baggage claim and after a long walk to the other side of the airport, he was on another plane to the island. There he would take a taxi to the house. He thought about what he would do first when he got there and decided a dip in the Mediterranean Sea would be in order. He continued reading, losing himself in the plot.

At the airport on Isla Marta, Lars claimed his suitcase and walked through the automatic doors to the taxi stand where a yellow cab sat idling. He got the driver's attention and then began to dig around in his flight bag trying to find the paper on which he had written the address of Javier's family's house. He felt a slight tear in the bottom of the bag and shoved his hand inside, finding both the paper and his missing cell phone.

"Ah, there you are," he muttered, opening his cell phone and turning it on. He thought he had lost the damned thing forever. He handed the paper to the taxi driver who had been waiting patiently for him to find the address.

As they rode along, Lars checked out the scenery as he sifted through his many messages. He listened to Javier's message about there being a slight problem with the house, his father having promised it to the daughter of an old friend. *Too late now*, he thought. *I hope this girl doesn't mind sharing.* He finished listening and flipped the phone closed. He could see the Mediterranean Sea and it sent a warm feeling into the pit of his stomach. *This is going to be great*, he thought.

A few minutes later, the taxi drove up the driveway and came to a stop near the veranda. Lars handed the driver a wad of Euros and hopped out of the car, pulling his flight bag and black suitcase behind him. He walked up the steps to the front door and was just about to knock when Javier appeared in the doorway.

Javier had nearly forgotten that Lars was even coming, thinking that perhaps he'd changed his mind. And as much as he hated to think about it, he wished Lars had. But he was happy to see his friend and welcomed him with open arms just the same.

"Lars! It's about damned time," Javier exclaimed. "Where the hell have you been?"

"I've been in Switzerland with my family. My mother didn't want me to leave right away so I stayed a few extra days for some 'quality family time.'" He used his fingers to make air quotes around the words. "What are you doing here?" Lars dropped his bag onto the wooden porch floor and sat down in one of the white wicker chairs grouped in front of the large picture window.

"I've been trying to reach you for days. Did you ever get my messages?" Javier glanced in the window then sat down in the chair next to Lars.

"Would you believe I only just found my cell phone a few minutes ago stuck in the torn lining of my bag? Sorry, mate, that I didn't get the message sooner. Now, what are you doing here?"

"I came here to see you to let you know there was a mix-up about the house. I've been here a couple of days. I was about to call Samuel back in London and have him track you down. I thought maybe you'd changed your mind about coming."

"No. I couldn't wait to get here. Did that American girl show up?"

"Yes, she's here. She's in the house looking at pictures or something. Speaking of girls, how did it go with Katarina? Did you do it?"

Lars' face fell and he looked off in the direction of the sea.

"Yes, I did it. But I don't want to talk about it if you don't mind. It's still way too fresh."

"Sure. Sorry, man," Javier patted Lars' knee, offering silent support. "You want a beer?" He stood and moved to the door.

"I would love one." Lars smiled widely, leaning back in the chair and stretching his long legs out in front of him.

Javier went inside through the living room and into the kitchen. He grabbed two Coronas from the fridge and rejoined Lars on the porch.

They popped off the tops and clinked their bottles together in a silent toast.

"Is there a problem with my being here?" Lars asked. "Did you tell that girl I was coming? Maybe she won't mind sharing the place. I certainly won't bother her."

Oh, yes, you will, thought Javier, *when you see her*. He felt something akin to jealousy threatening to invade his psyche. All of a sudden having Lars here on the island seemed like the worst possible idea ever. But it was probably too late now.

"I have another suggestion," said Javier. "You can go to Majorca to my aunt's place. She isn't there right now and she said it's fine if you want to use it. Her house is magnificent—much nicer than this place." Javier waved his hand around indicating the house and grounds.

"Looks like paradise to me," Lars responded. "I will be perfectly happy here."

At that moment, the screen door opened and Antonia walked out onto the porch. Javier and Lars immediately jumped to their feet. She stopped in front of the doorway and smiled at them both, unable to hide the recognition on her face upon seeing Lars.

"Hello," she said to Lars. She looked questioningly at Javier and waited for an introduction.

"Antonia. This is Lars Kohler. Lars, Antonia Taylor." He watched as the two of them shook hands longer than he thought necessary. They waited for her to be seated before sitting down themselves. Javier saw her glance at the beers in their hands and immediately offered to get her one.

"That would be great, thanks," she replied. She crossed her tanned legs, tucking them under the chair and smoothed her white linen skirt over her knees. Javier watched Lars, gauging his reaction to her. Lars had a poker face but Javier could swear he saw some kind of glint in his eyes.

He hurried to the kitchen, not wanting to leave them alone for too long. If there was one thing he had learned during the past year of working and touring and doing interviews with Lars and the other members of Les Passionistes, Lars was the one who attracted the most ladies. Women of every age and ethnic group flocked to him like moths to the proverbial flame. While the others certainly had their share of female attention, Lars was the one the girls wanted most. To their credit, they had never had any jealous fits or ego wars but suddenly Javier felt the green-eyed dragon breathing down his neck and he didn't like it.

Lars studied Antonia for a moment. She was quite arguably one of the most beautiful women he had ever laid eyes on. She made his pulse race and that surprised him. He fidgeted slightly in his seat and crossed his legs

"I'm sorry about the mix up," he said to her. "Do you have a problem sharing the house with me? I promise not to leave the toilet seat up. Isn't that the one thing that drives women crazy more than any other?" Lars smiled.

"I'm sorry?" Antonia asked, frowning. "What do you mean?"

"Don't tell me Javier didn't mention I was coming?" Lars couldn't believe it. How could Javier forget to tell her? He suddenly remembered the offer of the aunt's house in Majorca and it started to make sense.

"He didn't mention it," she said. "But there is more than one bathroom so the toilet seat issue should not be a problem." She smiled sweetly at him.

Javier returned with Antonia's beer just in time to hear her laughing. *Jesus, he doesn't waste any time, does he*? Javier felt a slight annoyance but was determined to shrug it off.

"Javier, you never mentioned that Lars was coming to stay at the house." Antonia looked quizzically at him, reaching for her beer.

"Must have slipped my mind," he said with the slightest edge to his voice. He had to get a grip and stop acting so territorial. What was coming over him?

The hell it slipped your mind, thought Lars. Aloud he said, "I don't want to intrude on you guys or anything…"

Antonia stopped him. "Stay please. The more the merrier," she smiled at them both apparently not noticing the crackling in the air all around them.

Antonia's words irritated Javier to no end. *What the hell is wrong with me*? he wondered. *I'm being ridiculous*. He took a long pull on his beer and tried to relax.

"Forgive me if I sound rude, but aren't you the Swiss member of the group?" Antonia asked Lars.

"Yes, I am. So you know Les Passionistes?" he asked with interest.

"I do. I have your album and I think it's beautiful. The world needs more of the kind of music you make." She smiled at them both as she spoke.

"What is your favorite song on the album?" asked Lars, testing her.

She didn't hesitate.

"The fifth one, 'Surrender to Me,' without a doubt. Which one of you is singing lead on that one?"

"I sing the first verse and Andrew sings the second. We all sing the chorus and the big ending together," answered Lars.

"Well, it's breathtakingly beautiful," she sighed, a look of something akin to rapture on her face.

"Thank you," Javier and Lars said at the same time. Lars laughed. Javier just looked uncomfortable.

At that moment Marta walked up the path carrying a bag of groceries. Javier jumped to his feet and ran down the steps to take the bag from her. He introduced her to Lars and they all went into the house. Lars brought his suitcase and carry-on bag inside and Javier showed him to his room while Antonia visited with Marta in the kitchen.

When they were alone in Lars' room, Lars turned to Javier.

"Have I walked into the middle of something, man?" he asked.

"What do you mean?" said Javier, feigning ignorance.

"You know exactly what I mean. Is something going on with you two?"

"Maybe. She is beautiful, isn't she?"

"Nothing like stating the obvious," said Lars, grinning.

"So you *did* notice?" said Javier with an edge to his voice.

"Hard to miss. Should I leave?"

"Nah, of course not. But don't try anything. I saw her first," Javier said it jokingly but Lars suspected that he wasn't kidding around.

"No worries," said Lars. "Now can we get some food around here? I'm starving." He squeezed Javier's shoulder and followed him to the kitchen.

Javier and Marta exchanged words in Spanish—something about chicken and vegetables. Neither Antonia nor Lars understood them.

"Marta has an appointment in town tonight so we are cooking our own dinner. How about chicken on the grill?" Javier asked them.

"Sounds great," said Lars. "Let's get started, shall we?"

They gathered around the kitchen's marble-topped island, each settling into a different task. Lars peeled potatoes, Antonia chopped vegetables for salad and Javier tenderized and seasoned the chicken breasts, readying them for the grill. They listened to rock music on the radio as they worked and shared a bottle of wine.

As she chopped spinach, Antonia's mind was working in high gear. She stole glances at Lars and Javier from time to time, all the while trying to calm her quaking her nerves. As crazy and improbable as it seemed, she felt as if she were in the company of greatness. The keepers of two of the four most exquisite voices in the world were standing mere inches away from her, performing mundane tasks involving potatoes and chicken. It was surreal. She wished she had a witness. Deanna should be here experiencing this with her. She thought about the slight change in Javier that she had detected upon Lars' arrival. What was that about? Jealousy? It couldn't be, she tried to convince herself. She studied Lars, intent over his potatoes. He was gorgeous. Antonia looked at his hair, which was long and curled around his neck. He had almond-shaped, light brown eyes and glorious cheekbones. And those lips...She heard a loud whacking sound and glanced in the direction of the noise. Javier was beating the hell out of a pound of chicken breasts and he was looking at her as he did it. She saw something almost dangerous in his eyes and a shiver ran down her spine. Lars looked over at Javier and laughed.

"Hey, man. They're already dead, you know," he said teasingly.

"Sorry, I got carried away." Javier gave the chicken one more hard thwack and then carried them out back to the grill. Antonia avoided making eye contact with Lars and carried the salad out to the back patio. They finished cooking dinner and sat together outside and ate and drank another bottle of wine. Antonia was careful not to overindulge-she didn't need another headache. Javier seemed to relax and she enjoyed listening to them talk shop. Lars' arrival had certainly caused a sea change. Antonia wondered how the rest of her time here would play out. It was certainly going to be interesting.

* * * *

Later that night, while Lars was taking a shower, Javier asked Antonia if she would like to take a walk on the beach.

"There is a full moon tonight," he said. She had been going over some notes she had taken earlier about the festival but had been having a hell of a time concentrating. She'd wandered into the kitchen where Javier was having an espresso. She declined his offer to make her one, fearing it would keep her awake all night.

"A walk sounds nice. Let me just change my shoes," she said excitedly and dashed off to her room.

Javier put his cup in the sink and went down the hall past Antonia's room to the bathroom at the far end of the hall. He heard Lars turn off the water and open the shower curtain. He tapped on the door and a moment later Lars opened it, wrapped in a towel.

"Yes?" He looked surprised to see Javier standing there, as if he had been expecting to see someone else, or so Javier thought.

"Antonia and I are going for a walk along the beach. You won't mind, will you…if we leave you alone for an hour or so?"

"No, of course not. Have fun." Lars smiled and stepped back into the bathroom and shut the door.

Javier stood outside the bathroom for a moment listening to the silence on the other side of the door and then met Antonia as she came out of her room.

Lars heard Antonia ask if he would be coming with them but they had already gone outside before he could hear Javier's response. He went into his room and finished drying off, then changed into jeans and a T-shirt. He took his book out to the front porch where an electric light hung from the porch's overhang. He sat down on the wicker loveseat and tried to concentrate on the words but his mind kept wandering. He caught a glimpse of the spectacular moon through the fronds of the palm trees and noticed that it was huge tonight. He sighed and tried again to concentrate on his book.

Antonia and Javier walked slowly in the direction of the cove where Javier had first seen her, neither of them talking. Antonia was worried that Lars might be offended at being left behind but she didn't dare say anything about that to Javier for fear of opening Pandora's box. And Javier was thinking only about kissing her. He reached for her hand and held it tightly as they walked along the water's edge. The air was cool but not too much so and the sound of the water lapping against the shore had a musical quality to it.

"It's beautiful here," breathed Antonia. "So quiet and peaceful, like being at the end of the earth."

"It is," agreed Javier. He stopped walking and pulled her into his arms. The moonlight shone on her face and he traced the outline of her jaw with his finger. "Antonia…I love your name."

"Thank you," she smiled at his unexpected compliment. She looked into his brown eyes and noticed that the same lock of hair had fallen on his forehead again. She resisted the urge to push it back. He was only about two inches taller than she was and she could smell the espresso on his breath as he leaned into her and let his lips graze hers gently. His tongue tangled with hers and he moaned against her mouth. After a long moment, he pulled back and looked into her eyes.

Antonia wondered what he was thinking. She felt his arousal against her thigh and it made her feel strangely uncomfortable. She was attracted to him, she was certain of that, but something seemed off. She had no idea what, or if it was to do with her or Javier. She just knew that something wasn't right that needed to be for her to give herself to him physically the way he so clearly wanted. She was glad now that she had resisted making love with him even though she was sure it would be amazing in every way. He certainly knew how to kiss. She sensed that Javier would be an attentive and unselfish lover and though she wanted him, why was she so afraid to find out?

"What are you thinking about?" Javier asked. He slid his hand into her hair and pushed it back behind her ear.

"I was thinking about you," she said. Her answer surprised him and gave him hope.

"What about me?" he pressed, nuzzling into her neck.

"I was thinking that you want me," she said quietly. She looked beyond him out to sea.

"Yes, I do. But why did you say it like that?" he asked, a faint hint of alarm in his voice.

"What way?" she asked.

"Like maybe you wish I didn't want you."

"I'm not sure. Maybe I'm afraid."

"You have nothing to fear from me, Antonia. Is it because I'm famous and you think I must do this with women all over the world—love them and leave them, as they say in America?"

"Yes, that must be it," she sighed and laid her head on his shoulder. They stood there in the sand, holding one another, not speaking for several moments. Javier wanted to kiss her again but he sensed it would be better to hold back.

"Well, just so you know, Antonia, I don't."

"I believe you," she raised her head and they resumed walking, back the way they had come. Javier gathered that their walk was coming to an end and he was right. Antonia led them back to the house where they found Lars reading on the veranda.

The phone rang inside the house and Javier went to answer it.

Antonia leaned against the porch railing a few inches away from where Lars sat.

"How was your walk?" he asked her.

"Nice," she said quietly. "What are you reading?"

He held up his book for her to see.

"Ah, *The Da Vinci Code*. Excellent book. Are you reading it in English?"

"No. German. I wanted to enjoy it," he laughed.

"Your English is excellent though. So is Javier's. Does Antoine speak English, too?" she asked with interest.

"Yes, but not as well as Javier and I. Andrew has mastered the language though."

"Very funny," Antonia laughed.

Javier returned to the veranda, a stricken look on his face. Antonia jumped up and went to him immediately.

"What is it, Javier?" she asked.

"That was my sister. My father has had a heart attack and I must return to Madrid right away."

Lars jumped to his feet instantly. "I'm so sorry. What is his condition?"

"He's stable but they don't know how much damage has been done to his heart yet. I have to get Madrid as soon as possible. I'm sorry to run out on you."

"It's OK," Antonia said, concern in her voice. "You go. We'll think good thoughts and keep your father in our prayers."

Javier tried not to dwell on the fact that she had said 'we' and 'our.' This was not the time to sink into a jealous funk. He had to think of his father.

"Thank you," he said. "I'd better go pack. I can get the first flight out tomorrow. Also I need to speak with Marta and Manolo. I will be sure to say good-bye in the morning before I leave." He turned and left them and went back inside to get ready.

"How horrible for him and his family," Antonia said, wrapping her arms around herself to ward off a sudden chill that was washing over her.

"Yes, it is very sad. I hope he will be OK. I met Javier's father once. He is a nice man. Javier talks about him all the time. I think they are very proud of one another," said Lars.

"They must be." Antonia walked to the door. "I'm going to call my father, just to check in. It's afternoon in New York. I just need to hear his voice."

"Good idea. I will do the same."

They went in search of their cell phones both needing to make sure their loved ones were safe and sound.

CHAPTER 6

The next morning, Antonia awoke early, anxious that she might miss saying good-bye to Javier. She took a quick shower, dressed in jeans and a pale yellow blouse and put on minimal make-up, leaving her hair to air-dry. She found Lars and Javier in the kitchen, sitting at the table talking quietly. Marta was cooking eggs at the stove and Manolo was standing just outside the back door smoking a cigarette.

"Good morning," Antonia said, joining them at the table. "Any news about your father?"

"Yes. I called my sister first thing this morning. She said Father made it through the night peacefully but he is to have surgery later this morning—a by-pass operation. I'm very anxious to get there. I'm booked on a flight that leaves in one hour so I'd better get to the airport." He pushed back from the table, leaving his breakfast uneaten. Marta chastised him about not eating properly—at least that's what Antonia guessed she was saying—and hugged him affectionately. They all walked outside and Manolo brought the car around and loaded Javier's luggage into the trunk.

Lars took Javier's hand in his to shake it, then pulled him close in a tight hug. "Be safe, my friend. Think positive thoughts. Call if you need anything at all," he said, his voice sounding deep with concern.

Antonia walked over to Javier and put her arms around him, pulling him close. He tilted his head and kissed her tenderly on the lips, a lingering kiss that was meant to send a message to Lars as well as to remind Antonia of the way he felt about her. It was so hard to let her go, especially when he wasn't sure how she felt about him. He would just have to trust that she would miss him as much he knew he was going to miss her.

"Good-bye. I'll call as soon as I get there and have any news. Take care, you two. Marta and Manolo will take good care of you." He got into the front seat with Manolo and they drove away.

Lars and Antonia walked back into the house where Marta had just set their breakfast on the table—eggs, bacon and lemon muffins. She gave them both a mysterious look before saying, in pretty good English, that she would see them later and then headed home to her cottage.

They ate in silence for a few minutes. Antonia felt a strange nervousness slowly creeping into her bones, making its way to her stomach, threatening to shut down her appetite. She tried to ignore it and took a bite of muffin, wiping the crumbs from her lips with a napkin.

Lars was feeling an awkwardness of his own that had gone undetected as long as Javier had been on the scene. He finished his breakfast quickly and asked Antonia if she would like coffee.

"Yes, please. Do you want me to make it?" she asked, getting up from the table.

"That's OK. I've got it." He found a canister of coffee and began to heat the water. When the coffee was ready they took their cups to the front porch and sat together in the quiet of the morning.

Lars studied her profile as she gazed in the direction of the sea. She held her cup close to her face, both hands holding it tightly. He noticed her nose, a perfect nose, and her lips, so plump and pink. Her skin shone in the early morning sunlight. He wondered what she was thinking. He could understand Javier's falling for her. It would be easy to do. He forced himself to think about Katarina for a moment, so tiny and blonde and innocent. When he thought of her now, she seemed more like a sister to him and he felt a stab of guilt at her distant memory, already receding to the back of his mind.

Antonia was aware that Lars was staring at her. She kept her gaze on the sea and tried to think of Javier. But for some inexplicable reason, thoughts of Lars kept crowding out thoughts of Javier. She suddenly remembered the first time she had seen Les Passionistes on TV. They had performed on *Live with Regis and Kelly,* which Antonia was not normally home to see at that time of the morning, but on that particular day she was going in to work late because she had a dentist appointment. She had recently read an article about the group in *USA TODAY* and now she was thrilled to be home to see them perform live on TV. She had studied each of them intently as they sang their first hit, "Something About the

Way You Look Tonight." It was the Elton John song, translated into Italian and sung as an opera and it was out of this world beautiful. She had noted the way the Spanish guy had seemed to make love to the microphone and seduce the audience with his voice, and the Frenchman who had seemed shy somehow though it didn't show in his voice, only his body language. She had watched as the American hit some amazingly high notes, which gave her chills, they were so beautiful. And then the Swiss one, who stood slightly apart from the others with his longer hair and exquisite cheekbones. When he had sung those romantic words with his tenor voice she'd held her breath as long as he held the last note, the sight and sound of him causing her heart to skip a beat. She'd nearly convinced herself that these four men had been created in a lab by Samuel Bowles. They couldn't possibly be real. On her way to her dental appointment, she had stopped at the music store and purchased the CD, anxious to get home later that night so she could listen to every song and try to pick out the voices on each track. And now here she was, half a world a way from home on a tiny island in the Mediterranean Sea with Lars Kohler sitting next to her. It didn't seem possible.

"A franc for your thoughts," said Lars quietly, interrupting her memory.

Antonia laughed. "Don't you have the Euro in Switzerland?" she asked.

"No. We have yet to join the EU. We're neutral, remember?" he said teasingly.

"Yes, you are. I remember now," she nodded. "I was just thinking about this article I'm working on for *Passion*, the magazine where I work," she lied. Lars didn't need to know what was really going on in her head.

"Ah, yes. Javier mentioned you were here on assignment. Are you getting much done?" he asked.

Antonia wondered if that was some sort of a slam—an implication that she'd gotten more done with Javier than on her article.

"Quite a bit, actually." She decided to let the comment go, hoping he meant nothing by it. "As a matter of fact, I have to go all the way over to the other side of the island today to check out some little villages there and take more pictures. But I have a slight problem." She felt embarrassment wash over her face at the admission she was about to make.

"What's that?" asked Lars with great interest, noting the high color coming into her cheeks.

"I need to drive over there in the Volvo but I don't know how to drive a stick shift. I mean I sort of know but I'm not very good at it."

Lars laughed hysterically. For some reason her words cracked him up.

"It isn't that funny," said Antonia, annoyed at his unexpected reaction. "I bet lots of people don't know how to drive stick shifts."

"I'm sorry," Lars smiled, shaking his head in amusement. "You're right. It isn't that funny. I don't why I laughed. Would you like me to teach you?"

"I don't want to bother you or anything. If you could just tell me what to do I can probably figure it out on my own." Antonia tried to hide her annoyance.

"I would have to be crazy to let you loose on this island with a car you can't drive. Anyway, you can't *tell* someone how to drive a stick, you have to show them."

"If isn't too much trouble then I…"

He cut her off.

"It's my pleasure. Let me know when you're ready and we shall begin lessons in Lars' Driving School. Tuition is free—for you." He winked at her, sending an electric jolt down her spine.

They got up and went inside where Antonia tidied the kitchen and Lars went to change his shoes. When he returned he noted that she was wearing flip-flops and advised her to go change her shoes as well.

"When you become proficient at driving, you can wear whatever kind of shoes you like but until then you should wear tennis shoes or something that won't slip off."

"OK. Makes sense," she responded and went to her room to change into her white Adidas sneakers. On impulse, she ran a brush through her hair, put on lipstick and some translucent powder on her cheeks and forehead. She felt excitement tingling in her veins as she grabbed her notebook, purse and camera. With one more glance in the mirror, she took a deep breath and joined Lars in the driveway where he was talking to Manolo about the car.

"Ready?" asked Lars.

"As ready as I'll ever be," she laughed.

She went to get in on the driver's side but Lars cleared his throat loudly stopping her from getting in.

"What?" she asked innocently.

"Lesson number one: I drive. You observe." He took the keys from Manolo who shook his head and crossed himself, then walked toward the house muttering under his breath.

"Fine," Antonia said a little huffily getting into the passenger side and fastening her seatbelt. Lars climbed in and did the same. He started the car, adjusted the seat and the mirrors and turned off the radio.

As soon as he placed his right hand on the gearshift, Antonia felt a rush of oxygen to her brain. Or maybe it was a mass exodus of the oxygen, but whatever it was it left her feeling dizzy and weak. Lars' hand caressing the gearshift threatened to be her undoing, just as Javier's hand manipulating the gearshift had gotten under her skin. What was it with her and gearshifts anyway? She swallowed a non-existent lump in her throat and averted her gaze, looking at a purple flowering bush bordering the driveway. She knew instantly that this driving lesson was going to be a disaster and she wasn't even in the driver's seat.

"Ready?" asked Lars. He looked at her profile, noting that she suddenly looked pale. He mistook her demeanor for nerves related to personal safety and reassured her in kind. "You don't have to worry. I'm a very good driver."

"I'm sure you are." She barely managed to get the words out. She cleared her throat and spoke a little more loudly. "So what do you do first?"

Lars proceeded to show her how to shift into reverse, explaining how and when to use the clutch and how to get the car back into drive. He turned the car around in the driveway and pulled out onto the road and they slowly began to drive away. He glanced at her out of the corner of his eye and noted that she was looking out her window and didn't seem to be paying attention to his driving.

"Antonia…?"

"Yes," she responded in a whisper, still not looking at him.

"You're going to have watch me drive if you want to learn how to do this." He reached over and gently grasped her chin in his warm fingertips, turning her face toward him. His hand felt like a brand burning into her skin and for one awful moment she feared she might lose consciousness.

Oh, my god, she thought. *What is wrong with me? I don't think I can do this.* She tried very hard to compose herself and act as if his presence were not having an effect on her. Why had she thought this would be a good idea? And why did she think that she would be just fine if it were Javier in the driver's seat?

"I'm sorry. I'm paying attention now," she said. "So what happens at that stop sign up there?" She pointed to the sign at the end of the road where they would make a left turn along the coast road that led to the northern side of the island.

Lars showed her how to shift and brake, coming to a stop. He signaled a left turn and then pulled the car onto the coast road, picking up speed as they drove. The sea sparkled in the sunlight below them, stretching out in all its glory to the horizon.

"You have to be careful of that view when you're driving, Antonia. It could get you killed." He smiled mischievously. She watched as he shifted back and forth from gear to gear explaining about the clutch and the gas and the importance of getting your feet in sync. She tried to concentrate on his words and not on his hands and let the information sink into her brain. He was more than likely going to pass over the controls to her soon and she didn't want to make a fool of herself the first time she drove.

They drove several miles, eventually arriving in the little town of La Forza. Antonia asked Lars to park near the old church so she could get some photos and make notes about the little shops and boutiques in the town square. They spent the next hour wandering around the village, chatting with both tourists and locals, then decided they needed a snack and cold drink. They sat at an outdoor table at a little café and shared a plate of churros with chocolate sauce and orange sodas.

It suddenly occurred to Antonia that she might be boring Lars out of his mind and decided she had better offer an apology. He was here on vacation after all and she shouldn't be dragging him all over Isla Marta just because she had a job to do.

"Lars, I'm so sorry. You must be bored senseless following me all over the place while I interview people and take endless pictures. I'm almost finished here. I'm really sorry I dragged you out here." She impulsively touched his arm as she apologized.

"I couldn't let you come alone, you know. Anyway, I'm enjoying this. This island is quite lovely and I might not have seen much of it if I weren't with you now. So, thank you for the tour." He looked down at the spot on his arm where her hand had touched him a second ago. He put his hand over the spot and pressed down, then finished off his orange soda in one long pull.

Antonia saw his gesture and wondered about it but said nothing. "Still, if there is anything I can do for you, please let me return the favor."

"Actually, there is something you could do if you wanted..." he said mysteriously.

"What's that?" She looked at him quizzically.

"When we get back to the house I really want to go for a swim in the Mediterranean Sea. Will you come with me?"

"I would love to," she answered quickly, wishing she hadn't eaten so many churros now. Would her bathing suit look bulgy? Oh, well, too late now. She would just have to suck it in.

When they finished their food, Lars paid the tab against Antonia's wishes and they walked back to the car. He held the keys out to her.

"You feel ready to drive now?" he asked.

Antonia felt fear rush over her. "Are you sure?" she asked breathlessly. "What if I get us killed?" she laughed nervously.

"I won't let that happen," said Lars confidently. "Go ahead. Give it a try. You'll be fine."

Antonia climbed reluctantly behind the wheel, adjusted the mirrors and the seat and fastened herself in. Lars secured his belt and then very dramatically, made the sign of the cross against his chest.

"Hey, now. It won't be that bad," she grinned nervously.

"Just kidding," he teased, giving her a wink.

He watched as she started the car, eased into gear and drove down the street. Everything seemed to be going well until time to proceed up a hill after stopping at a stop sign. Antonia popped the clutch and killed the engine. They jerked to a stop and the car began to roll backward.

"Oh, my god," Antonia exclaimed. She put her foot on the brake but the car continued to move. "What happened?"

"It's OK. Start the car and then just keep your foot on the brake, let up on the clutch and give it some gas," Lars said patiently.

She did exactly as he said and they jerked forward violently, the engine dying again.

"Oh, no!" she screeched, feeling panic set in. "This is way harder than I thought it would be." She felt defeat washing over her and she'd only just begun.

"It's OK," Lars said soothingly. "Just try it again."

She tried it again and the same thing happened with the car continuing to roll backward.

"It's my damned feet. I'm not coordinated enough!" She sounded panicked.

Lars looked over his shoulder and saw that a car was fast approaching them. He reached down between them and pulled the emergency brake, bringing them to a sudden stop. He felt a thin bead of sweat on his forehead and noticed that Antonia had gone pale.

"You can do it, Antonia. Let's just wait for this car to pass and then try it again."

"No. I can't. I'm too stressed out now. Will you drive, please?" she begged.

"Sure, if you want," he said, feeling a sense of relief. This was scarier than he had expected it to be and his stomach was churning.

They got out and switched seats and both breathed a sigh of relief at the same time.

They laughed nervously and then sudden tears fell down onto Antonia's cheeks.

"Hey, now. It's OK," he said, reaching over and wiping her tears with his thumb. "You'll get the hang of it eventually."

"I'm not so sure about that. You must think I'm a total loser," she said dejectedly.

"No way," he said, smiling reassuringly at her. "We'll try again later at the house away from traffic until you get comfortable behind the wheel. It will be fine."

"Thank you for being so patient with me. I probably scared you to death." She smiled sheepishly and clutched her hands together tightly in her lap. She resisted the urge to touch her face where his hand had just brushed away her tears. She could still feel the pressure of his fingertips there.

He reached over and took her cold hands in his and held them there in her lap. She looked down at his hand on hers and felt a wave of emotion run over her. Her senses were on high alert and her stomach roiled. She held her breath unknowingly until Lars removed his hand to shift gears. She looked everywhere but at him for the remainder of the ride.

Lars kept his hand on the gearshift as they drove back to the house in silence. He parked the car and turned off the engine then turned to her.

"OK, now?" he asked softly. "Feel like that swim?"

"Absolutely. I'll just get changed and meet you out front," she said, still feeling embarrassed about her bad driving and the silly tears.

Lars went to his room to change into his swimming trunks. He sat on the bed for a minute thinking about Antonia. He had enjoyed being with her this morning, watching her try to grasp the seeming complexities of driving a standard. He had admired the way she had interacted with the people she had interviewed and hell, he had even enjoyed the way she had eaten her churros, chocolate dripping onto her chin and the way she had licked the sugar off of her fingertips. He imagined what it would be like to kiss her, realizing in that moment that Javier already knew what it was like. That's when he realized that he could never know. No matter how attracted he was to Antonia, she was off limits to him. He had to remember that, no matter what.

But when they got to the beach a few minutes later and Antonia dropped her swimsuit cover-up to the sand, Lars nearly forgot. She was wearing a pale blue bikini and he saw that she had a tiny diamond stud in her navel. She looked so beautiful that he had an instant physical reaction that caused him to drop to the blanket she had spread out for them and pretend to fiddle with his tennis shoes.

My god, this is not good, he thought. *Not good at all. This cannot be happening. I came here to get away from it all and now look.*

Antonia was experiencing some anxiety of her own. She felt naked in front of him and yet at the same time she felt a sudden urge to make him want her the way Javier had wanted her. More than anything, Antonia had the sense that if she did not kiss Lars she would go mad with want. *Where is this coming from?* she wondered as she walked toward the water, stopping to look back, checking to see if he was going to follow her.

He got up from the blanket, removed his T-shirt and walked toward her. She drank in his tall, naturally tanned skin and long legs and felt her stomach clench. She hurriedly turned away and walked into the cool water. He followed her and they slowly waded out to waist-level, then stopped, standing close to one another. Antonia shivered from the sudden chill and saw Lars look down at her breasts where her nipples were straining against the thin material of her bathing suit top. She self-consciously crossed her arms over her breasts and looked away from his piercing gaze.

Lars felt foolish, like the proverbial child getting caught with his hand in the cookie jar. He was torn between sinking under the water head and all or taking her into his arms and holding her until the goose bumps on her body disappeared. Suddenly this swim didn't seem like such a great idea but they were here now so he would just have to get his mind off of her body and what he wanted to do to it.

"See that rock out there?" Antonia said, pointing quite a way out from the shore.

"Yes," said Lars, fearing the reason for her question.

"Race you to it," she smiled.

"Oh, no. It's way too far." Alarmed, Lars grabbed her arm just as she was about to dive under the water. "Antonia, it's too far. There could be a dangerous undertow. Don't be crazy."

She looked down to where his hand was holding tightly to her forearm.

"Are you afraid, Lars?" she asked him, an almost seductive tone to her voice.

"No...yes...maybe," he stammered. "You are quite a contradiction, Ms. Taylor. Less than hour ago you were afraid to drive a stick shift and now you want us both to drown just so you can show me what a great swimmer you are?" Lars had not meant to come across as so chastising but was aware that he sounded that way.

"I'm sorry," she said contritely. "When you put it that way, I get your point. But I could make it if I wanted to."

"I have no doubt about that."

They both noticed at the same time that he was still holding onto her arm. She looked down at his hand, and, in a move that shocked even herself, she gave her arm a sudden twist and was now holding onto his arm instead. They stood there looking at one another, each waiting for the other to move. Antonia wanted to pull him to her and kiss him. She had never been sexually aggressive in her life and she knew deep down that she didn't have the nerve to start now no matter how powerful the urge. And Lars wanted to taste her lips, run his hands through her hair and smell her skin but he didn't dare betray Javier that way. He slowly pulled his arm out of Antonia's grasp and dropped down below the water up to his neck.

"I'm going for a swim. I'll be back," said Lars, suddenly feeling the need to get some distance between them. "Don't you go near that rock," he indicated the rock with his head. He disappeared beneath the water and began to swim parallel to the beach. She watched him for a few minutes, his long, lean strokes cutting through the water, then went up onshore and wrapped herself in her cover-up and sat on the blanket trying to sort through her emotions.

Antonia wanted Lars more than she had ever wanted any man in her life. More than Jeff, more than Javier, more than anyone. She sensed he was attracted to her as well but he also seemed damned resistant. Maybe he was more of a danger to her heart than Javier was. She shuddered from a sudden internal chill and pulled her wrap closer around herself. She sat with her knees drawn up to her chest, her chin resting on them watching Lars. She watched as he swam back and walked out of the water toward her, his long hair dark and dripping, his body shiny with wetness. As he got closer to the blanket, she had to avert her gaze at the sight of his clinging trunks hugging his body like a second skin. He sat down beside her and rubbed his hair with a towel and then draped it around his shoulders.

While he had been swimming back and forth, Lars had been in a race with his thoughts. He tried to figure out what was happening between him and Antonia. He had never met a woman quite like her—so full of contradictions and sweetness. So sexy and beautiful. More than anything he had wanted to kiss her when they were standing there in the water, her hand on his arm. He wondered if she and Javier had made love and he decided that he had to find out. He wasn't sure that it would make a difference but he had to know.

They were sitting so closely that their thighs touched when one or the other of them moved even the slightest bit. Lars gathered his courage and waded into dangerous waters.

"Antonia…?" he turned to her and looked into her eyes.

"Yes?" she asked quietly, turning her gaze away toward the horizon.

"I know it's none of my business but I'm curious about something," he said slowly.

"Yes?" she asked again, still looking straight ahead.

"What happened between you and Javier…before I got here?" He looked at her profile. She turned toward him, then fixed her gaze on the sand at their feet.

"What do you mean?" she asked quietly.

"You know what I mean. Is there something going on between you two?"

"Why do you ask?"

Lars wanted to tell her the truth—that he needed to know if had a chance with her without destroying his friendship, not to mention working relationship with someone he considered a close friend. But instead he took the safer route.

"Because it sure seemed like it, the way you two looked at each other. I'm just curious. Sorry for prying." He poked his fingers into the sand beside the blanket and found a little seashell with a chip on its edge. He picked it up and fiddled with it as he waited to see if she would answer his question.

Finally she spoke and her words sent him into a state of confusion.

"There was something going on, sort of, *until* you got here."

Something about the way she had said the word 'until' put his mind in a tailspin.

"Can you explain that?" he asked, tossing the seashell back into the sand.

"There was an attraction, I think, forming. Javier has a very magnetic personality, almost overwhelming and I think for a moment there I was getting caught up in him."

"But what about now?"

"I don't know. Javier is a great guy. He's a sexy guy. But I sort of held myself back a bit. I guess you could say I had reservations. I *have* reservations."

Lars thought about this for a moment. He still did not know the answer to the question he needed an answer for most and he didn't know how to ask it without sounding lewd and invasive of her privacy. But he had to know so he took a mental breath and asked—sort of.

"Um, did you and Javier…you know…ever…" he stopped, unable to say the words which would sound like such a betrayal to his friend.

"Make love?" she asked, not mincing words.

"You don't have to answer that. It isn't my business. I'm sorry. I shouldn't have pried."

"I'll answer your question if you tell me why you want to know." She turned her body toward him and looked into his eyes, wanting so much to touch his cheekbones and feel the five o'clock shadow she saw forming along his jaw and chin.

"I don't need to know. I shouldn't know. I'm sorry, Antonia. You must think I'm a rude Swiss prick," he replied, forcing a smile.

"No, I don't think that at all. I'll tell you anyway. No, we didn't. Javier wanted to, but I couldn't. I'm not sure why." She sighed deeply and laid back on the blanket, her legs bent at the knees, her eyes closed.

Powerful emotions flowed through Lars' body. He thought about what she had just said and decided that it didn't make a difference. As long as Javier had feelings for Antonia she had to remain off limits to him. But God help him, he had to know what her lips felt like, tasted like, just once. He promised himself he would kiss her one time and then never again. But it would prove to be an impossible promise to keep as he would soon find out.

Without giving her any advance warning, he turned and leaned over her, lowering himself down until he was only an inch away from her face. She felt his presence and opened her eyes in surprise. He touched his lips slowly and gently to hers and felt her arms come up around his torso, pulling him closer to her. She opened her mouth, welcoming his tongue inside. It touched hers gently and then more urgently as their passion grew. He kissed the corners of her mouth and trailed his tongue along her jaw. She arched her back and he glanced down at her breasts pushing up into the bikini top, trying to break free. He wanted to touch her breasts and take them in his mouth. There was so much he wanted to do to her that it nearly made him crazy. He wanted to bury himself inside of her until they both couldn't take it any more.

Antonia was nearly overcome with the passion she felt for Lars. She returned his kisses ardently and rubbed her hand down his back, stopping at the top of his swim trunks. The devil on her shoulder whispered to her to touch him, to take him in her hands, to give herself to him right here on the beach. The angel on the other shoulder told her to wait—be sure it's real, not lust or just a vacation fling to be tossed aside in a couple of weeks and forgotten about. *Hold back, Antonia, don't give it way*, it whispered. *Don't do something you might regret.* She had been able to resist Javier but this was different. This was Lars and she wanted him badly.

Just as their kiss threatened to overwhelm them, Lars caught himself and pulled away and looked down at her. He kept seeing Javier's face and he felt guilty. He couldn't, *shouldn't*, be doing this. He had to be the strong one and make it stop.

He kissed her tenderly on the lips one more time and pulled her arms away and sat up.

"We better go," he said quietly. He got up and wrapped his towel around his waist and offered his hand to help her up. She took it and he pulled her to her feet. Neither said another word as they gathered their belongings and walked back to the house.

CHAPTER 7

Javier and his sisters left the hospital together to go home for dinner and a change of clothes. Juan had made it through surgery without complications and they all felt a sense of relief. Their mother and Jaime remained at the hospital but had promised Javier that later that night they would come home to eat and change. Javier was worried about his mother who looked exhausted and had refused to eat all day.

"The doctors have said that everything will be fine with Father, yes?" Anabela needed reassurance again. She was Javier's younger sister by two years who lived in Salamanca and taught world history at the university there.

"Yes, the prognosis is good. But Father will have to cut back on the cigars and the cognac, I think. And he may have to give up his beloved fried foods." Javier laughed at the thought of their father giving up his favorite vices. "We will have to watch him carefully."

At the house, they fixed themselves sandwiches of serrano ham with huge chunks of manchego cheese, all the while wondering if they should be eating such rich foods in light of their father's condition. They laughed guiltily at the irony of their lunch choices but still ate the food anyway.

Javier excused himself to go to his father's study to make some phone calls. He had promised Samuel that he would call him at his office in London with an update on his father's condition as soon as he was out of surgery. He also needed to call the house on Isla Marta to see what was going on there. He had been unable to shake the feeling that something might develop between Lars and Antonia if they were left alone too long. He didn't think she was the type of girl to fall all over a hot superstar, even one as irresistible as Lars but then again he had yet to meet a woman who didn't flock toward Lars like a magnet to steel. He realized what he had just thought about Antonia falling for a hot superstar and hoped that that didn't apply to him. Then he had a laugh at the thought of himself that way.

He called the house on Isla Marta first and Marta answered the phone. They had a short conversation in Spanish that left Javier feeling slightly unsettled. She had inquired about his father's health and asked how the family was coping. Then she mentioned that Lars and Antonia had returned earlier from swimming and had been avoiding each other ever since. Marta told him that Antonia was now asleep and Lars had taken the Volvo into town. He heard Manolo in the background asking for the phone. He asked after Juan's health before they hung up with Javier promising to call again soon.

Javier replaced the phone in its cradle and stared out the window in the direction of his mother's prized orange and lemon groves. What had Marta meant about them avoiding each other? Was that a good sign or a bad one? He felt a sense of unease as he reached for the phone again. He needed to give Samuel a call with an update.

* * * *

Samuel Bowles was arguably the most famous and most prolific talent scout in the world. He was responsible for the United Kingdom's hottest television show, "Search for a Star," which had spawned copycat shows in twelve nations, all of which paid him handsome royalties and back-end fees. He had discovered the Outback Babes on a jaunt across Australia and the all-girl pop group was now the hottest quartet of young teen singers in their country as well as Europe. He had discovered Emma O'Dwyer, a young folk singer from Ireland and had signed her to his agency immediately. She was now a huge star in the United Kingdom and would be soon in Europe and the rest of the world. But out of all his new talent, Samuel was most proud of Les Passionistes. It had taken the better part of two years to find the magical combination of four voices who could do for him the one thing that no other singer in the world had ever been able to do. They had made him like opera. More than that, they had made him fall in love with opera in a way he never would have thought possible. He had auditioned various combinations of voices, searching for a group that would make him understand the genre and actually want to listen to it. And one day, Antoine, Andrew, Lars and Javier were the four men standing before him, having been randomly selected from a group of hundreds of male singers of a certain age and a certain look that his scouts around the globe had sent to audition for him. They sang the song that all the candidates were required to sing, as well as songs of their own choosing, and they had blown him away. For the first time in his life Samuel Bowles was speechless and intimidated. He had signed them on the spot and called a halt to all other scheduled auditions. Now he was introducing opera in a whole new way to the rest of the world and evidently, judging by the millions of albums sold to date, the world was loving opera, too. Or loving Les Passionistes. Sometimes Samuel thought they could sing the phonebook and people would love them, especially the ladies.

And so it was with great annoyance that he read the paper handed to him by his assistant Colin Parker. He was not happy but also not *completely* surprised by the turn of events of this day. Colin had reminded him, not that he needed reminding, that the four men who comprised Les Passionistes were young and handsome and had talents bigger than any the world had ever seen. They were sexy, hot-blooded, straight males and the world was taking notice fast. In the course of this very long day, disturbing information had been passed to him via emails from associates in Paris and New York and from insiders at the hungry-for-a-story London tabloids. He bet Les Passionistes didn't even know they were making news all over the world and not the good kind either. Many had said that any publicity is good publicity but Samuel did not buy into that nonsense. His newest find had only been on vacation for a week, and already they were getting themselves into trouble on two continents. He would be glad when they were all back in London at the end of the month where he could keep an eye on them.

He opened the advance issue of the *London Inquisition,* the one that would be on newsstands tomorrow, and read the article, assessing as he read how to do damage control. He looked at Colin who sat across from him in the plush suite of offices on Essex Street, then began to reread the article. Colin waited quietly, his nerves on edge.

"What are you thinking, Antoine?" Samuel muttered to himself. He continued reading, making disgruntled noises under his breath. "And you, Andrew. Why now would you make such a foolish mistake, when your career is so new? At least Javier has a legitimate reason to be in the news, albeit a sad one. Thank God for Lars, At least he is flying under the radar and not getting into trouble on his vacation wherever he is."

"I've taken the liberty of calling the lawyers regarding the Andrew situation, as that seems to be the most dire," said Colin. "I think the Antoine situation is mostly out of our hands for the moment."

"Yes," said Samuel. "I may need to go to America and see Andrew. He has made one fine mess and I hope he understands the consequences of his actions and what an impact it could have on Les Passionistes. These men have to learn that they are a team and not just musically, but in all aspects of life. When one does something foolish, it hurts them all."

"I couldn't agree more. Shall I book you a flight to America then?" Colin stood and moved toward the door.

"Yes, and get Antoine on the phone for me. He and I need to have a fireside chat."

"Will do," Colin exited the office, leaving Samuel to ponder the situation. What he didn't say to Colin but he was sure Colin knew anyway, was that their foolishness hurt *everyone*, not just the four of them. And by everyone, he meant himself and his wallet.

* * * *

After their trip to the beach that afternoon Lars and Antonia had gone to their separate rooms to shower and change. Lars had finished first and taken the Volvo into town where he had sat at a bar and nursed a beer or two. Kissing Antonia had been a mistake and now there would be awkwardness between them. Maybe he should cut his losses and go back to Switzerland, or go to America and check in on Andrew. He was missing his band-mates a lot more than he thought he would and realized that he—*they*—were safer somehow, though from what he wasn't entirely sure, in their protected work environment. He tried to assess his feelings for Antonia. There was no way he could be in love with her after having known her for barely two days. Hell, it had taken months for him to fall in love with Katarina. Or had he ever been in love with Katarina? Now he wasn't so sure. But Antonia stirred something in him that Katarina hadn't—a deep passion akin to lust—and it shook him to his core. The thought of going back to the house and being in such close confines with her rattled him. He didn't remember ever having been rattled by Katarina, except for maybe at the end, last week when he'd crushed her. He finished his beer, left several Euros on the table and headed back to the house. He would have to return sooner or later anyway, may as well get it over with.

*   *   *   *

Antonia sat on her bed, trying to formulate words about Isla Marta on her laptop but the screen remained largely blank. She couldn't concentrate on her article and she had made herself feel even worse by putting on her Sony Walkman and listening to Les Passionistes. She played "Something About the Way You Look Tonight" over and over again until she thought she would go out of her mind. She and Lars had kissed and it had been pure bliss. She didn't remember ever feeling this way about anyone—not even Jeff—and she had been engaged to marry him. When she had finished showering and changing, she'd gone out to the kitchen for a drink. The house had been eerily quiet. She'd walked quietly from room to room but Lars was not in the house—or on the grounds. And then she'd noticed that the car was gone and figured he had gone out somewhere. The longer he stayed away the worse she felt. So now she sat on her bed, staring at the blank screen feeling miserable and fighting tears. When the song started to play again, she ripped the headset from her ears and shut off the Walkman. She went out to the veranda where she would wait for Lars. They needed to talk so that they could share this house peacefully.

It was getting dark when Antonia saw the Volvo's headlights coming up the driveway. Her stomach automatically began its churning and chills ran over her, causing her teeth to chatter. She wrapped her sweater tighter around herself and sat still on the loveseat waiting for Lars.

He cut off the engine and sat for a moment in the stillness of the dark car. He could see Antonia sitting on the porch and he felt his breath catch in his throat. She looked beautiful sitting there, a shaft of moonlight shining across the lower half of her face, illuminating her full lips and delicate chin. Lars groaned inwardly as he opened the door, slamming it shut a little too hard. He climbed the steps and stopped near where she sat looking expectantly at him.

"Hello," Lars said quietly. He stood between her and the moonlight, her face now in shadows.

"Hi," she replied. "Lars…," she said his name then hesitated, not sure how to open a dialogue between them.

"Antonia, listen," Lars began. "About this afternoon at the beach. I shouldn't have kissed you. I was wrong to do that and I apologize if I've made you feel uncomfortable now. I don't know what's going on with you and Javier but one thing I'm fairly sure of is that he has feelings for you. And he's my friend. I cannot betray his friendship. I'm a guest in his home and I have no right to anything or anyone he has a prior claim on. I don't even know if I'm making any sense with my English," he finished his speech in German with words that Antonia suspected might be profane.

"First of all," Antonia replied fiercely, "Javier has no claim on me. Yes, we kissed a couple of times but that's all. I am not in love with him and I would bet you a hundred damned Swiss franks that he isn't in love with me either. Second of all, I am a guest in his house, too, and I would never abuse my status here. And third of all, you don't have to apologize for kissing me. I know you didn't mean anything by it. Let's just forget about it." She stood up and walked past him down the steps and stopped at the bottom on the brick walkway. She had hated making that last statement but felt she had to give Lars an out—a way to dismiss the kiss as a little nothing that had no lingering effects on her. Hell, he was a man, he would forget easily anyway.

But in actuality the kiss was all Lars could think of. That and her skin and the smell of her sunscreen and her hair and the way her hand had felt on his arm and on his back. He looked down at her, wanting to pull her into his arms and bury his face in her hair and taste her lips but he couldn't do it. It wouldn't be right. But he couldn't stay here in this house with her, knowing she was sleeping just down the hall and would be sharing meals with him. This wasn't how he had planned to spend his vacation—wanting something he couldn't have. He was a world famous opera star—he should be able to have whatever he wanted—shouldn't he?

"Maybe it would be better if I left Isla Marta," he said, his voice deep with regret. "After all, you were here first."

"You don't have to leave, Lars. I want you to stay." Antonia responded quickly, without hesitation. If Lars left she would be crushed. She couldn't imagine being here without him now. "I mean," she amended, "this place is big enough for the both of us. Please don't go." She hoped she didn't sound desperate but that was how she felt.

At that moment Manolo walked up the path from his cottage and joined them.

"Hello. I have a message for you both from Javier. He called earlier to say that his father had surgery and it was a success. He will call tomorrow morning to speak to you both."

"Thanks," Lars said. "I'm glad Javier's father made it through OK."

Manolo wished them both a goodnight and went back to his home.

"Are you about to go somewhere?" Lars asked her.

"I was going for a walk on the beach," she responded.

"Well, be careful," he said. He smiled at her and went into the house leaving her there in the moonlight. She sighed deeply and walked down the path to the sea feeling suddenly bereft. She wished Lars had offered to accompany her. She felt confusion about what was happening or *not happening* between them. How did everything get so complicated? She turned her thoughts to Javier, suddenly seeing his handsome face in her mind and hearing his sexy voice whispering in Spanish to her. She had a feeling that if Lars had not shown up on Isla Marta that she would be deeply in love with Javier right now. Lars' presence had certainly complicated things and she wasn't sure how to deal with the complication. She walked for about a half an hour and then returned to the house. When she walked past Lars' room she could hear him talking in German to someone on his phone. She wondered whom he had called and what they were talking about. She went to bed and spent a restless night filled with worry about what the next day would hold.

* * * *

Deanna and Sean were enjoying a leisurely day off together at Sean's apartment starting with a breakfast of sausage, bagels, juice and the *New York Post*. Sean was poring over the crossword puzzle while Deanna searched through the entertainment section looking for the movie times. She turned to page six and noticed a headline near the bottom of the page in the gossip section that caused her to nearly choke on her sun-dried tomato bagel.

"Oh, my god!" she croaked, grabbing her napkin to stifle the coughing jag that followed. "Sean, listen to this!"

Sean dropped his pen and turned his attention to her immediately. She was obviously agitated by something earthshaking in the fashion world, like a shoe sale at Barney's and he knew better than not to give her his undivided attention.

"What is it, darling?" he asked sweetly, preparing himself for the inevitable onslaught of shoe talk not to mention bags and belts and thongs.

"Listen to this headline. Oh, my god. I have to call Antonia. This is unbelievable!"

"What is it?" Sean wondered how a shoe sale at Barney's would benefit Antonia who was presently on another continent but maybe Deanna was her shoe-shopping proxy and had authorization to make important purchases in absentia.

Deanna read the headline out loud:

"*Scandal and tragedy rock Pop-opera group Les Passionistes.*"

"Can you believe this?" she asked, incredulous.

"Read it to me," said Sean, definitely interested now.

"Scandal has rocked the hot new group, Les Passionistes, discovered by Samuel Bowles, creator of the world famous TV show Search for a Star. *American tenor and heartthrob Andrew Jones was arrested yesterday on charges of disturbing the peace at the Dockside Restaurant in lower Manhattan. The dashing Jones reportedly had a major row with his girlfriend, Jenna Ashcourt, at the restaurant, which resulted in his throwing chairs and breaking bottles of beer on the tables. Anonymous sources at the restaurant say that Ashcourt, 30, had just broken off their relationship of five years and that apparently Jones, also 30, had not taken the news well. He allegedly became enraged, began to break things and had to be subdued by wait-staff until local police arrived on the scene to take him into custody. He is scheduled to appear in court on October 18. His representatives could not be reached for comment."*

"In related news, a late breaking story out of Paris indicates that singer Antoine de Cadenet, 32, the suave former pop singer turned Les Passionistes member, is purportedly having an affair with American starlet and former Playboy Bunny Cassie Kendall, 25, wife of Hollywood's hottest star Tom Booth. The couple was reportedly seen leaving the rear exit of the Ritz Carlton just before dawn yesterday morning, looking 'none the worse for wear' according to a hotel staff member who spoke on condition of anonymity. De Cadenet's publicity department could not be reached for comment."

"And sad news regarding Les Passionistes member Javier Garza, 34, of Spain. His father, noted architect Juan Garza of El Grupo Garza, Madrid's largest and most prestigious architectural corporation, has reportedly suffered a heart attack and is in a Madrid hospital. His condition was not known at press time. The younger Garza was called away from his exotic island vacation and has been at his father's bedside since the attack. Garza's handlers could not be reached for comment.

The other member of the famous group, Lars Kohler, 28, of Switzerland, is vacationing at an unknown destination in Europe and so far has stayed beneath the news radar."

Deanna finished reading the article and looked at Sean in amazement.

"Can you believe this? I have to call Antonia. I wonder if she knows about any of this?" She jumped up from the table and ran for her phone, calling Antonia's cell, thankful that Antonia had the sense to get an international number so she could be reached anywhere, anytime.

"Dammit! She's not picking up!" Deanna came back into the kitchen where Sean was rereading the article. "This is weird. Do you think Antonia knows anything about any of this?"

"I don't know," said Sean. "Have you heard from her since she's been gone?"

"Oh, I forgot to tell you what with your working such long hours lately, that I had an email from her the other day and she told me that the Spanish guy showed up at the house. She said he was hot and they had made a 'connection.' I haven't heard anything since and I've been going nuts. I've left messages but she hasn't called back. If I don't hear from her soon then I'm calling her father to see if he's heard from her. In the meantime I'm going to check the Internet and see if I can learn anything else about these guys. Isn't this amazing?" With that, she dashed off to the computer in Sean's spare bedroom.

"Quite," said Sean to her retreating back. "Does this mean we aren't going to a movie today?" he asked the air.

* * * *

Antonia finally gave up on sleep a few minutes before dawn. She could see from her bedroom window that the sky was just beginning to turn a pinkish, orangey tinge at the horizon and so she decided she would walk down to the beach and watch the sun rise in all its glory. She had intended to do it at least once on this trip anyway and since she was already awake, sleep having been impossible, she may as well not miss her chance to see nature in one of its most divine moments.

In the bathroom she washed her face and brushed her brown hair, which had taken on auburn highlights from several days in the sun, into a ponytail. She changed from her worn out university nightshirt into a pair of navy shorts, a white cotton tank top and her tennis shoes and slipped quietly from her room into the darkened hall. She lingered for a moment outside Lars' bedroom door, wondering if he had slept well last night. He probably had slept longer than she had, she figured. She looked for a moment at the door-knob, wishing she had the courage to open it and slip inside, if only just to watch him sleep. But instead, she went to the kitchen and grabbed an apple from the fruit bowl on the kitchen table and stepped outside the house into the still of the morning. She was surprised to notice that there was the slightest hint of a chill in the air. The silence was interrupted from time to time by chirping birds and the sound of the tide as it washed ashore, then slid back out to sea. She started down the path walking slowly, stopping to smell the purple flowering bush that bordered one side of the driveway. Several bees were already awake, buzzing from flower to flower. She watched them a moment and then continued down the path. A minute later she was standing on the water's edge staring at the sight of the sun breaking free over the horizon. The fiery orange ball rose slowly in the sky and in a matter of only a few minutes Antonia was awash in warmth, the morning's chill turning to a comforting heat.

Lars had heard Antonia moving about the house. He had not slept either though not for a lack of trying. He lay in his bed staring at the ceiling thinking about what he should do. And then it occurred to him. He didn't have to do a damned thing except what he had originally planned to do. And that was relax, swim in the Mediterranean Sea, eat himself silly and every so often, sing pieces of Les Passionistes' repertoire so he would not forget the words to all the complicated songs in Italian, Spanish and English. He made a mental note to suggest to the guys that they tackle a German opera just once, then thought better of it—figuring Antoine would whine for a French one. He got up, showered and then went out to the kitchen for coffee and sweet rolls. Taking his breakfast outside he walked slowly about the grounds thinking about Antonia. They could co-exist peacefully for a couple of weeks. Shouldn't be a problem. He stopped to examine the same purple bush Antonia had breathed deeply of earlier. He wondered what it was. It looked like his mother's lilac bush but it didn't smell the same. He broke off a stem and studied the petals, lightly covered with dew. He turned his face up to the sky and breathed deeply. Why did everything smell like her? He dropped the flower to the ground and walked back toward the house, pouring out the rest of his now cold coffee in the grass. It might be early in the day but for Lars it was time to sing.

* * * *

The closer Antonia got to the house, the louder the sound got. It was one quarter of the same sound she had been listening to for days in her headset. And it was amazing. She recognized the song from the CD—"*Miserere*"—it was one of her favorites. Lars was somewhere at the back of the house singing in his gorgeous tenor voice. She had to see him sing. She walked through the house, following the sound of his voice, and saw that he was in the back garden standing like a statue, his arms outstretched and his face skyward as if in supplication. She watched from the window of the library that looked out over the garden as he sang, hitting the notes, sometimes stopping himself to sing a measure over again. When he seemed satisfied, he stopped and hummed under his breath and then began to sing "Surrender to Me." Antonia held her breath as his voice rose, its silkiness pouring over her, giving her goose bumps and making the hair on the back of her neck prickle. This was her favorite song on the album and she just had to get closer. She walked out of the library and over to the door that opened onto the garden patio. She quietly opened the door and stepped outside, easing the door shut behind her. Lars' eyes were closed as he sang and he didn't see her enter the garden. She stopped under a tree and watched, listening in silence.

As Lars sang he began to sense that he was not alone but he did not stop singing "Surrender to Me." He opened his eyes and looked at Antonia and sang the last line to her, *"...Surrender to me your body and soul, your heart and your mind, your love and your woe. I'll be your keeper, protector and guard, in truth you will know...that I have surrendered to you, that I gave my life to you."*

Antonia felt light-headed. Hearing the words to that song as it played on a machine was one thing, but to hear Lars Kohler sing them in the flesh was out of this world. She knew he had just sealed her fate and he probably didn't have a clue.

"That was beautiful," she whispered. "My favorite."

"Thank you. I hope I didn't disturb you but I have to practice from time to time so I don't get, how do you say in English—rusty—and also so I don't forget the words. Singing in a foreign language is difficult, especially in English." Lars had remembered that Antonia had said "Surrender to Me" was her favorite song and it was not by accident that he had chosen to sing it, hoping she would hear him. If he couldn't have her then he would make damned sure she didn't forget him.

"Well, you certainly aren't rusty." She longed to walk up to him and take him in her arms. She wanted him to sing to her for the rest of her life. She also had to be realistic. It wasn't going to happen. As long he believed he was betraying Javier in some way then nothing would ever happen between them.

"Have you had breakfast?" Lars asked as he walked toward her, holding the door open and following her inside.

"Only an apple. Have you?"

"Yes, but I'm still hungry. Shall we make something?"

"Sure." Antonia went to the fridge and set out eggs and bacon. She stole a look at Lars as he searched in the pantry for more breakfast options. It seemed that he was going to play it cool and casual. So then would she.

The phone rang and Antonia picked it up.

"Javier!" she exclaimed, looking over at Lars. Lars stopped mixing the pancake batter to listen.

"Antonia, how are you? And Lars? I called the other day but you were sleeping and Lars was out. Is everything OK there?"

"Everything is fine here but how about with you? How is your father?"

"He's doing well. His heart attack was—how do you say in English—a wake-up call, but he will make a full recovery if he behaves himself."

"That's excellent news, Javier. I'm thrilled for him—and you."

"I miss you, Antonia," Javier said, his voice deepening.

Antonia hesitated, her eyes on Lars. She had only a second to respond before Javier would feel slighted. The truth was she did miss him, but saying so in front of Lars seemed wrong somehow.

"You, too," was all she could muster. "Would you like to speak with Lars?"

"Yes, please." She thought she heard a touch of sadness in those two words and she felt a pang of guilt. She handed the phone to Lars and took over the pancake making duty.

Lars and Javier spoke a few minutes and then Lars said *adios* and hung up the phone. He was quiet, not mentioning the conversation he's just had with Javier. Antonia wondered about that.

"So what did Javier have to say?" she asked innocently.

"Not much. Same thing he said to you." Lars didn't sound convincing. "He said to send his best to Marta and Manolo."

He began to set the table, putting out glasses and plates. He felt out of sorts now, after talking to Javier, and in need of a diversion.

"Would you like another driving lesson after breakfast?" he asked, grinning at the sight of her face as it paled at the question.

"I suppose I will never learn if I don't try," she said reluctantly. "But I think I might be a hopeless case."

"Never that, Antonia. Today is the day. Think positive thoughts."

They ate together sharing casual conservation about the progress of Antonia's article with Lars recounting stories from his time so far with the his band-mates. Antoine sounded like a wild one and Andrew seemed like the serious type, according to Lars' descriptions of their characters. Antonia wondered if she would ever get to meet them. When they finished eating they cleared away the dishes, then left for the driving lesson. Antonia was filled with determination to master the Volvo come hell or high water and couldn't wait to try it again.

CHAPTER 8

"You need to go back to Isla Marta, Javier. Soon it will be festival time and you haven't been to the *Festival de Los Amantes Muertos* in a very long time. You can accompany the young lady and help her with her article about the island," Juan said, his voice sounding stronger by the hour.

"I won't leave you and Mama, Father. Not until you are home and settled into your new routine and the doctor has cleared you to return to work," Javier was adamant about remaining in Madrid to tend to his father.

"I'm not returning to work," said Juan. He saw the look of shock on Javier's face and held up his hand. "Not right away anyway. Your mother has pointed out to me that it has been much too long since we have taken a vacation. I was thinking that we would go to Australia for a month. It would mean the world to your mother to see her old school friends who now live in Sydney. And Anabela needs to get back to Salamanca to her students. And, of course, we have Analeza here, and Jaime. Jaime is such a blessing. I want to take him to Australia with us before he starts his musical studies in January."

"But I won't feel right leaving you like this," Javier felt guilt already about being away from his father and he hadn't even left the room.

"You won't be leaving me like this. I only had a double by-pass son. I got off easy. And besides I'm going home tomorrow. They're letting me out early for good behavior." Juan laughed and adjusted the white hospital blanket over his legs.

"When we get you home I will see how I feel about leaving you. But you can't get rid of me that easily." Javier smiled warmly at his father.

"Tell me about the girl—Ted's daughter," said Juan, not realizing he was treading on shaky ground.

Javier told his father as little as he could without giving his feelings away. But his father was an astute man and he heard what Javier didn't say.

"You like this girl don't you, son?" Juan grinned at Javier, ruffling his hair.

"Papa! Why would you think that?" Javier laughed.

"You wear your heart on your sleeve. Now I *know* you should get back to Isla Marta. You shouldn't leave such a lovely girl there alone. A bandito may come along and sweep her off her feet."

Javier laughed at his father's joke, but inside he felt a knot of fear forming. His father didn't know Antonia was alone with someone far more dangerous than a bandito. She was with Lars, his close friend and colleague—Lars, the one man no one woman could resist.

* * * *

The second driving lesson went much better than the first. Antonia had driven them around the compound for a while and then Lars had given her the OK to go into the village nearest the house. She had done a fine job of shifting the gears, going uphill after coming to a stop and parking. They had stopped for *café con leche* in town and Antonia bought a *Hello!* magazine at the little newsstand near the café. It was in Spanish but she figured she could figure out what the stories were about using rusty high school Spanish and looking at the pictures. She drove them back to the house without incident and Lars declared her nearly ready for a solo outing.

"But not yet. And I'd feel better if I borrowed Manolo's old Fiat and followed you."

"It's OK. I think I've got the hang of it now," Antonia declared.

"Still, let's not be too—what is the word in English I mean to say?" Lars asked, stumped.

"Hasty?"

"Yes, hasty."

Antonia got out of the car and yawned and stretched, her lack of sleep the night before catching up to her.

"I think I'm going to lie down for about an hour and then get back to work on my article. I have to send my father some copy so he can see how it's going. And Lars, I have a question…?" She looked demurely at her feet.

"Yes?"

"I need to visit some nightclubs on the island. Would you want to come with me? I haven't learned much about the nightlife on Isla Marta."

"Now that sounds like a good time. Should we start tonight?" Lars was excited at the thought of finding a club and listening to some harder edged music than his usual pop and opera.

"Tonight it is," she smiled at him and headed to her room. She brushed her teeth and stretched out on the bed with the new magazine. She had intended to look at the pictures and try to decipher some of the juicy gossip inside but she felt too tired. Had she opened the magazine she would have seen some interesting pictures of Lars' band-mates up to their eyeballs in trouble.

* * * *

The sound of her cell phone ringing shrilly woke Antonia from a deep sleep. She grabbed it and said a breathless hello.

"It's about damned time. Where the hell have you been?" Deanna exclaimed into her ear.

"Hi Deanna," Antonia laughed. "I'm sorry. Every time I've thought about calling you it's been some god-awful time in New York. What's up?"

"*What's up*? You're asking *me* what's up? All hell is breaking loose with Les Passionistes and you're asking *me* what's up?"

Alarmed, Antonia sat up in her bed, brushing the hair out of her face. The she immediately relaxed, thinking news of Juan Garza's heart attack must have made the papers back home. Her father had mentioned he was a globally known architect.

"Oh, you must mean Javier's father having had a heart attack. Yes, Javier had to go back to Madrid to be with him. He called this morning and said his father is doing amazingly well."

"That's great—really good news—but what about Antoine de Cadenet and Andrew Jones? Have you heard about them?"

Antonia jumped to her feet, her heart racing.

"What are you talking about? I haven't heard anything about them. Tell me!"

"I read in this morning's paper that Andrew got arrested for tearing a restaurant apart in a fit of anger over his girlfriend dumping him and Antoine is having an affair with that actress who's married to Tom Booth—Cassie Kendall."

"No way!" Antonia was shocked. This couldn't be true. She glanced at her new copy of *Hello!* She opened the cover and saw a picture of Les Passionistes on the first page, as they appeared on the cover of their album. She saw a lengthy article about them with smaller photos inset of Antoine leaving a Paris hotel with Cassie Kendall and a picture of Andrew in handcuffs being led out of a New York restaurant by police.

"Oh, my god, Deanna. I'm going to have to call you back. I have the newest copy of *Hello!* magazine right here in front of me but I hadn't even opened it yet. And the stories are in here. I can't believe I didn't see this sooner! I have to show this to Lars. I'll call you back." She said good-bye and hung up, then went in search of Lars. She took the magazine with her and ran down the hall stopping outside his closed door. She tapped gently but he didn't answer. She tapped a little louder but still he didn't answer. She pushed the door open slowly and peeked in. Lars was stretched out on his bed, sleeping soundly. Antonia's breath caught in her throat at the sight of him lying there. She resisted the urge to lie down beside him and curl up in the crook of his arm. He looked sexier than she thought was humanly possible. She could easily have stood there forever staring at his magnificence but she had to tell him about his friends. She walked over to the bed and shook him gently, whispering his name.

"Lars...wake up," she whispered.

"Hmm...what...?" His eyes flew open and he sat halfway up, balancing on his elbows. "What is it? Are you OK?" he sounded dazed from having been awakened so abruptly.

"Lars, I just had a phone call from my friend Deanna in New York. She told me something I think you should know. Plus it's in also in here. I only just noticed." She handed him the magazine opened to the story about his band-mates.

He looked at the story for a moment and then cursed in German.

"I can't read this. What does it say? This is Andrew in handcuffs and is that that actress with Antoine?" He sounded agitated, his breaths coming out fast.

"Deanna said something about Andrew getting arrested for busting up a restaurant when his girlfriend broke up with him and Antoine is apparently having an affair with Cassie Kendall. She's married to Tom Booth."

Lars jumped up from the bed and went to find his cell phone. He turned it on and was astounded to see that he had more than a dozen messages.

"Damn! All these messages and I had my damned phone turned off. Give me a minute to listen to these."

Antonia sat quietly on the edge of his bed as he went through his messages. His parents had called and also his brother, Samuel and Colin and even some reporters. How had they gotten his cell number? The last call was from Katarina: "Lars, I just wanted to call and say that I miss you. I hope you're having fun and getting some much-needed rest. Your mother said that you will be coming back to Lucerne before you return to London. Please call me when you get in. I love you. Good-bye." He closed his phone and turned to Antonia.

"I cannot believe this. I have to make some phone calls, Antonia. Will you give me a few minutes to sort this out?" he asked, feeling frustrated and cut off from the world.

"Sure. I'll be in my room if you need to talk. Let me know how everything is going as soon as you know anything, please." She smiled encouragingly at him and he nodded then turned back to his phone. His first call would be to Samuel. Samuel would know what was happening.

* * * *

The nights were the worst. She would fall into a troubled sleep, only to awaken a few hours later, her heart nearly pounding out of her chest, her breathing shallow and her stomach quaking. In seconds the memory would wash over her, threatening to drown her. She would be unable to go back to sleep, her mind unable to shut down, unwilling to give in to her exhaustion. The pillow would become soggy with her tears and her head would pound in pain. She couldn't go on like this. She had tried talking to her mother, but her mother was hurt, too. Lars had betrayed them all. He had been such a big part of their lives for so long and the whole family felt the pain of the break up. Life didn't seem worth living. How could she get up and face another day? Face the customers at her family's restaurant, many of them regulars asking after Lars. Asking if they'd made any wedding plans and how she felt about his new success and sudden fame—how proud and thrilled she must be for him. She couldn't take anymore of it. She had called Lars and left a message on his phone—that damned phone that he could never remember to leave turned on. There had to be something she could do—some way to get him back. Some way to make him see that he still loved her. There had to be a way. And there was the secret she had been keeping from him. The secret she had kept because she didn't want to cause problems for him during the recording and promotion of the album. The secret that had first thrilled and then nearly destroyed her. She had planned to tell him that night but he had broken her heart before she'd had the chance. Maybe it would be better to let it lie—after all, there was nothing to be done now. It wouldn't change anything. But still, he had a right to know, didn't he? Katarina got up and moved about her room, willing herself to make it through another day.

*   *   *   *

Lars hung up the phone and sat on his bed contemplating what he should do. He had just spoken to Colin who had informed him that Samuel had flown to New York to see about Andrew. But news was improving on that front—Samuel had called Andrew before catching his flight and had heard his side of the story about what had happened at the restaurant. As Samuel had suspected, and knowing Andrew as well as he did, there was more to the story than had been printed in the paper and he had been right. He'd had some doubts as to the validity of the story in the London papers anyway and Andrew had assured him that appearances were not as they had seemed and he was anxious to get everything cleared up. As for Antoine, that story had been blown out of proportion as well by the French tabloids. Lars took a closer look at the photo in *Hello!* that showed Antoine exiting the hotel with Cassie Kendall. He saw the black-clad elbow in the lower corner where the picture had been cropped to cut out the third person in the shot. Antoine told Samuel that the elbow belonged to Tom Booth who had been at the party at the Ritz Carlton along with his wife Cassie Kendall. They had all left at the same time and shared a cab back to their own hotels elsewhere in Paris. He explained that there was no affair but he had been honored at the thought that the tabloids assumed he could get someone that hot.

Lars laughed to himself thinking of Antoine and his reputation with women. He certainly had one. As for Andrew, it seemed that Samuel had everything under control or he would have when he got to New York and talked to him in person. Colin had advised Lars to stay put on the island and stay under the radar until these situations had been dealt with and put to rest permanently. So he dropped the magazine into the trash and went to find Antonia.

She was in her room, sitting Indian-style in the middle of the bed staring at her computer screen. He stuck his head in the doorway and she beckoned him inside.

"Have you learned anything about Antoine and Andrew? Are the stories true?" she asked anxiously.

He told her what he had just learned from Colin.

"So it seems that everything is going to work out. At least I hope so. The only story the tabloids appear to have gotten right is the one about Javier's father." Lars came up behind her and looked over her shoulder at the laptop screen. It was blank.

"Getting a lot accomplished, I see," he laughed.

"Very funny. I couldn't concentrate if you must know. I was worried about your friends and I don't even know them!" She closed her laptop and turned around to face him. He towered over her where she sat in the middle of her bed. The sudden silence and their proximity to one another caused a sudden electrical disturbance in the room.

Lars' gaze roamed over her hair which was held back in a loose knot at the back of her head. He had an urge to set it free and run his fingers through it. She looked up at him expectantly. Their eyes met and held one another's gaze. Antonia wanted to pull him down with her onto the bed. Lars wanted to cover her like a blanket with his body. They both began to speak at the same time.

"You go first," said Antonia sheepishly.

"I was going to ask if you wanted to go for a swim," said Lars, almost wishing he could take back the words. Seeing in her in a bathing suit was certainly not going to help matters.

"Sure," she said. "I just need to send a quick email to my father first. Give me ten minutes."

Lars nodded and backed out of the room. Antonia opened her laptop and sent her father an email apologizing for not having the copy ready for his perusal and promising to have something by tomorrow morning New York time. Then she put on a bathing suit—this time a black one-piece that she had had for years—and went to find Lars. She vowed to make every effort not to pay attention to his lean, tanned body or his gorgeous long, dark hair. She would swim for exercise sake today. Maybe later at the club they would both loosen up and Lars would feel more relaxed and less worried about what Javier would think. Maybe she would have the courage to find a way to let Lars know how attracted she was to him as if he couldn't tell already. But she would have to convince him that Javier was not in the picture and that might be hard to do without Javier here to speak for himself.

* * * *

Javier helped Alma and his sisters clear the table and went to check in on his father. His mother was sitting with him in their bedroom where Juan was now ensconced in bed with his newspapers and the television's remote control. Juan had insisted he be released from the hospital immediately even though everyone would have preferred he stay a few more days. The doctor had finally relented on the condition that a visiting nurse accompany him home and stay for a couple of days to make sure Juan experienced no complications. Juan had agreed and was now happy to be home in his own bed in his own house. Javier was thrilled at how good his father looked so soon after surgery. The nurse sat at a nearby desk by the window writing up her report. Maria sat in a wingback chair placed beside the bed with her needlepoint spread out on her lap.

"Hello Father, Mother. How are you feeling?" asked Javier.

"Like a million Euros, my son," smiled Juan. "Have you made your flight arrangements yet?"

"That's what I wanted to talk to you about," said Javier, sensing his father was going to give him trouble about leaving again. "I have October off. I can stay with you and Mama and help around here and I can make sure you obey doctor's orders. Someone needs to keep you in line." He laughed and winked at his mother who shook her head of dark curls at him.

"I have been keeping your father in line since long before you came into this world, Javier. I think I can manage a few more years."

"A *few* more years?" bellowed Juan. "Only a *few*?"

"Calm down, Señor Garza," chastised the nurse." "Remember your blood pressure."

"You know what I mean," said Maria. "Dozens and dozens of more years."

"That's more like it. For a minute there I thought you had it in for me." Juan smiled lovingly at his wife.

"Nonsense!" Maria took his hand and kissed it gently, then rubbed her fingers gently over the bruises where the IV had been.

Javier felt a catch in his throat at the sight of his parents still in love after all these years. If he ended up with half the romantic love in his life that his parents had then he figured he would be well and truly loved. He thought of Antonia and decided that maybe it *was* time to get back to Isla Marta.

"Alright then," Javier acquiesced. "I will make arrangements to fly out tomorrow. But you have to promise me you will call me at the first sign of a problem no matter how minor it may seem. Deal?"

"Deal," said Juan. "Now come over here and give your young father a hug."

Javier laughed and took his father gently into his arms being careful not to hurt him. They talked a few minutes more and then Javier left his parents and went out to find Jaime. He wanted to sing with him before leaving. He also wanted to find out if there was any new information regarding Andrew and Antoine's situations. Colin had filled him in when he'd called with an update on his father. He thought about calling the house to tell Lars and Antonia he was coming tomorrow but he decided the element of surprise would be more to his benefit. At least he hoped so.

*　*　*　*

Lars said that Antonia could drive to Dos Passos where they were going to visit *Club Vista Hermosa*, a little nightspot on the beach that Antonia had learned from locals was *the* hot place for great music, delicious tapas and colorful people on Isla Marta. It was to be her first time to drive at night and she was a little nervous.

Lars looked at her stilettos and shook his head in doubt.

"I don't know, Antonia. Those are some dangerous shoes you're wearing there," he looked down at her feet clad in three-inch silver high heels with straps that snaked sexily up her ankles. Of course, Lars was referring more to the way her legs in those shoes made him feel than for any driving dangers they posed. He took her in her short, black, clingy dress with its halter neckline and dangly seashell earrings and had to turn away. She looked gorgeous with her hair up again in a wind-tossed knot on top of her head. He wanted to skip the club and spend the night in his room having his way with her. He tried to banish the thought from his mind as she exclaimed over her shoes.

"Should I change them?" she asked. "I have shoes with shorter heels."

"No. I…you should be fine," Lars stuttered, opening the car door for her and handing her the keys.

Antonia knew she looked good tonight. She had made a point of looking extra sexy to get Lars' attention. Before this night was over she intended to, at the very least, kiss him senseless, even if it killed her.

Lars also looked incredible. He was wearing black pants that showed off his gorgeous backside and a black dress shirt that fit him snugly across his chest with just a suggestion of the taut muscles underneath. With his long, black hair and dark skin he looked like a dashing knight. Sexiness oozed from his pores. Antonia wondered if he was aware of his effect on her. She hoped not. She intended to play it cool and coy.

She drove them without incident into Dos Passos and parked the car in the beach lot. They could hear the music playing—a mix of rock and bolero—a sound Antonia had never heard before. It sounded amazing and she couldn't wait to kick up her heels.

As they walked toward the club Antonia asked Lars if he liked to dance.

"I love to dance. I hope you do, too." He placed his hand at the small of her back as they entered the club. It was dark and loud and smoky inside. They walked over to the bar and ordered drinks—a beer for Lars and a Toreador for

Antonia. She had read about this drink, a blend of tequila, crème de cacao and cocoa powder online and had been anxious to try it. She was a little alarmed at the amount of tequila the bartender put in it but figured one of these babies, nursed slowly over the course of the night should not be a problem.

They moved through the crowd to get closer to the dance floor where people were dancing and laughing and having a good time.

Lars pointed to a table that had just been vacated and they grabbed it before someone else could get it first. He pulled out her chair and she sat, taking her first sip of the Toreador. It hit her stomach like a lead balloon.

"Whoa!" she laughed. "That's a lot of tequila."

"I noticed you were getting more tequila than anything else. Be careful or you will not be allowed to drive home." He smiled, tilting his glass toward hers and taking a long drink of his beer.

They sat without talking for a while choosing to take in the music, watch the people dance and munch tapas from bowls a waitress had placed on their table. Antonia dipped a piece of bread into olive oil and took a bite. It was delicious—the bread soft, the olive oil smooth. Lars ate several green olives and some almonds. People swirled all around them, the women wearing tiny skirts and tight tops, the men dressed mostly in black. Antonia finished her drink a little too quickly, forgetting that she had planned to make it last the night, and felt her head spinning in a fast rotation.

"Wow," she laughed. "That was good. I might need another." She raised her hand, getting the waitress's attention. She ordered another Toreador for herself and a beer for Lars and the waitress went to fill the order.

Lars watched Antonia. Her eyes sparkled in the little bit of light in the club. She looked beautiful and vulnerable. He watched her take another bite of bread and olive oil. A drop of oil lingered on her lips and Lars wanted to kiss it off of her. Instead he reached over with a napkin and wiped it off.

She laughed and thanked him. Antonia couldn't remember when she had felt so free. She really liked the atmosphere in this club. It would get a nice mention in her article. The waitress returned with the drinks and Lars paid for them. He sipped his beer and watched horrified as Antonia drank her Toreador in one gulp.

"Oh, god," Lars said, taking her hand. "You should not drink so fast. You will be sorry. Come dance with me." He pulled her to feet and she wobbled a bit on her high heels. He led her to the dance floor where a techno rock song by the European group Bach and Roll was just starting.

Antonia threw her head back and danced with abandon, her hips gyrating and her feet moving in time to the music. She was a very good dancer in spite of the fact that she was a little tipsy and her shoes were like twin skyscrapers. Lars matched her move for move, at one point pulling her close and holding her against him during a key change in the music. He could smell her hair, her breath, her skin. He groaned against her as she brushed her lips against his jaw. His body tingled with desire for her. She whispered into his neck

"Kiss me, Lars," she breathed. She nuzzled into him and his lips found hers.

I need to stop this, he thought. *I can't be doing this.*

But, of course, he couldn't stop. Her tongue slipped into his mouth and ran across the edge of his teeth. He moaned as he wrapped his arms around her, his tongue meeting hers as they kissed deeply. The music suddenly changed to a hard rock song and Lars pulled back and looked into Antonia's face. Her eyes were dark with desire and slightly out of focus. He led her back to their table but someone had already taken it.

"Take me home, Lars," Antonia said. "I think I have enough information to give this place a good write-up in my article."

He led her from the club and back out to the car. They had only been there a little more than an hour. Antonia went to get in on the driver's side but Lars stopped her.

"I realize you only had two drinks but you drank them too fast. I will drive us home."

He helped her into the car. He got in beside her and saw her fumbling with the seatbelt.

"Here let me help you with that." He reached over her and felt her breath on his cheek. As he reached for her seatbelt she took his arm and held it, then pulled his face to hers and kissed him. The kiss deepened and soon their tongues were entangled once again. She kissed his jaw and his neck and smiled as he groaned with pleasure.

"Antonia, we shouldn't be doing this," he whispered. "It's going to be too hard to stop."

"I don't want to stop, Lars," she whispered. "I want you." Antonia shocked herself with her words. It must be the tequila talking, she figured.

"But…" Lars started to speak but she stopped him with a kiss. Her fingers slipped in between the buttons of his shirt, softly caressing his chest. He groaned, whispering in German. His eyes were closed as he kissed her jaw, then put his hand over hers tucked inside his shirt.

"Let's go home," she whispered, slipping off her shoes and leaning her head back on the headrest.

Lars started the car and drove back to the house. Antonia's gazed drifted to his hand on the gearshift. She knew she shouldn't look there but she couldn't help herself. He noticed her watching his hand, a look of deep desire on her face. Or maybe it was the tequila. He couldn't be sure. She was certainly bold tonight. He pulled into the driveway and parked the car near the house.

They got out and Antonia stumbled as her bare feet made contact with the graveled surface of the driveway.

"Ouch," she cried, trying to walk on tiptoes across the gravel. Lars took her hand and they walked slowly up the stairs and into the house.

As Lars closed the front door behind them, he caught sight of Manolo leaning against a tree lighting a cigarette, watching them, his face showing disapproval in the moonlight.

Once inside the house Antonia turned to Lars and slid her arms around his neck. She was feeling tipsy and bold and sensual and she wanted Lars in the worst way. She trailed kisses over his jaw, feeling the roughness of the hair there. She kissed his lips and he felt his resolve weakening. He kissed her tenderly at first then harder until they were panting, clinging together there in the darkened hallway. He let her hair free from its clip and buried his face in it, breathing her in. She could feel his hardness press into her hip and using her hand she pushed his backside into her hip, putting pressure on his hardness. He groaned, whispered German words in her hair, then English.

"Antonia, we have to stop," he tried to say but she stopped him with her lips. He could feel himself falling into the abyss and was helpless to do anything about it. He took her hand and led her down the hall to his room where he sat down on the bed, kicked off his shoes and pulled her down on top of him. He ran his hand underneath her dress and felt the tiny pair of underwear she was wearing. His hand caressed her bottom, the skin so soft and smooth. He felt her shiver as he touched her. She began to unfasten his buttons and soon his shirt was off. She kissed his chest, taking his hard nipples into her mouth. He moaned and pulled her dress over her head in one swift move. Her breasts were perfect, the pink nipples erect. He took each one in turn in his mouth suckling them, making her cry out with pleasure. Her hand slid down to the waistband of his pants and tugged at the belt, trying to unfasten it. He reached down and helped her, unzipping his fly and releasing the button. He pulled off his pants and boxers, then removed her panties and they lay there on top of his bed naked together. His tongue trailed over her stomach and down toward her belly-button where the little diamond sparkled in the dim light of the room.

"I can't wait, Lars," she breathed raggedly, reaching downward and grasping him in her hand, his hardness throbbing against her palm, wanting release. "Please, I'm going crazy."

Realization hit Lars hard. This could not happen. He was this close to betraying his best friend and there was the matter of protection. He was not prepared to make love to her. He had to find a way to stop or just take this in another direction and then make damned sure it didn't happen again.

"I don't have protection," he whispered into her hair.

"Damn it," she cursed softly. "I don't either." Then she laughed at the absurdity that she would carry condoms around in her purse. Deanna had warned her about moments like this. Why hadn't she listened?

"It's OK, there are other ways, not as perfect, but just as good." He slid down the length of her body and spread her legs apart, touching his tongue to her wetness. Antonia arched her back, moaning. Lars moved his mouth over her letting his tongue work its magic and in seconds Antonia cried out and shuddered hard. She grabbed his hair, tangling her hands in it. He climbed up to her and put her hand on him and she leaned down and took him in her mouth, sucking and manipulating him until he came as hard as she had just done.

They lay together for a long time, his arm around her, her head resting on his shoulder listening to crickets chirping outside the window. Antonia looked at Lars and kissed him tenderly on the lips.

"You're beautiful," he whispered, brushing her hair away from her face.

"So are you," she smiled.

"Antonia…" Lars felt like he needed to say something about what had just happened between them.

"Shh…don't speak," she said against his jaw. "Let's just let it be."

"Alright," said Lars reluctantly. He thought of Javier and felt a stab of guilt. He couldn't let Antonia sleep with him tonight in his bed. He knew himself too well. He would turn to her in the middle of the night, groggy with sleep and make love to her and that would be a complication he couldn't imagine. "As much as I would love to sleep all night with you, Antonia, I don't think it would be wise. I don't trust myself. We would get careless."

"I understand," she kissed him, then reached down for her dress where it lay on the floor by the bed, pulling it over her head.

He sat up and slipped back into his pants. They stood up and Antonia swayed into his arms.

"Hey, there," he grinned, catching her. "Let me help you to your room."

They walked to her room and kissed good night, a long passionate kiss that threatened to start another fire that might be impossible to put out. Lars pulled away and reluctantly went back to his room. After he had gone, Antonia floated to the bathroom, brushed her teeth and crawled into bed. She hugged the extra pillow to her chest tightly wishing it were Lars.

In his room, Lars quietly paced. He had loved holding her, kissing her, tasting her sweetness. It would be impossible to act as if nothing had happened between them tomorrow. He stretched out on the bed, his mind unable to switch off to let him sleep. He finally decided that tomorrow would just have to take care of itself.

CHAPTER 9

Once again, Antonia had a hard time sleeping. Visions of Lars kissing her lips, his body so close to hers, his silky, black hair tangled in her fingers, all swirled around in her head rendering her immune to sleep. She finally dozed off an hour before dawn into a deep slumber and when the call of nature eventually roused her into wakefulness she was shocked to see that it was after ten o'clock. She sat up, pushing the hair off of her face and rubbed the sleep from her eyes. She padded into the bathroom and took a quick shower then dressed in a pair of jeans and a light green, sleeveless sweater and stepped out into the hallway. The house was silent and still. She saw that Lars' door was ajar but he was not in the room. She walked quietly into the living room but no one was there. She went into the kitchen, noticing that it was tidy and sparkling clean, with no breakfast dishes in the sink or pans on the stove—no sign that anyone had been there this morning except for Marta who must have been here cleaning.

Wondering where everyone was, Antonia went out the front door and looked around the grounds. She noticed the Volvo parked in its usual spot under the huge palm tree. She walked around the house to the back and all was still and quiet there, too. She decided she would go back inside and make herself some breakfast and then work on her article. As she rounded the corner of the house, she saw Lars walking toward her, fresh from a swim in the sea. His wet hair was slicked back and he had a towel wrapped loosely around his waist. He looked like a god with his chest hair matted in dark swirls and the sight of his half-naked body caused her breath to catch in her throat. He looked up and saw her watching him and waved hello.

"Good morning," she said, smiling. "You should have woke me up. I would have gone swimming with you. Didn't your mother ever teach you that it's not safe to swim alone?"

"Morning. Yes, I know better but you were sleeping so soundly that I couldn't bring myself to wake you." He pulled the towel from around his waist and used it to rub excess water from his hair. When he finished his black hair was a beautiful mess around his head.

Antonia felt an internal shiver at the thought of Lars watching her sleep. She fought the urge to walk up to him and run her fingers through his hair. Lars threw the towel over his shoulder and walked past her toward the house.

"What are your plans for the day?" he asked as they went inside to the kitchen.

"I'm going to scan my pictures into my laptop and send them to the magazine and do some work on my story." She brought out two cups from the cupboard and held them up to Lars, checking to see if he wanted coffee. He nodded yes and she set about heating the water. "How about you?"

"I'm going to do absolutely nothing. Maybe go for a swim again later and a run. I talked to Manolo this morning and he said it's supposed to rain tonight. Oh, and he wondered if there was anything special we needed from the market." He sat down at the table and watched her make coffee and toast.

"Can't think of anything," she said. She set his coffee on the table and observed his elaborate way of preparing it—two sugars, a little cream, a stir and a taste, then one more sugar and more cream, another stir and then he drank it, nearly in one go round. She found the whole routine endearing and felt herself wishing she could share the ritual with him daily forever.

They finished their coffee and Lars left her to go shower. She washed their cups and plates and headed to her room to work. Concentration would be hard to come by but she would have to try.

Lars let the warm shower spray run over his body while his mind drifted to Antonia. He thought back to earlier this morning when he had walked into her room to ask her if she wanted to join him for a swim and how she had looked, curled up on her side, her face toward him, relaxed and beautiful in sleep. He had wanted to kiss her awake but knew that he would probably end up in bed with her. He made up his mind that the next time Javier called he would have a talk with him about Antonia.

* * * *

Javier had felt keyed up all day waiting to catch his flight. He had spent all morning with his father who had reassured him repeatedly not to worry about anything and to go to Isla Marta and have a good time. So now he could finally relax as the plane left the Madrid airport. He had to fly to Barcelona to catch the small plane to the island and he would be there this evening. He didn't call ahead to tell anyone he was coming and as such he wondered what he would find once he got there. His instincts were telling him that something was up, but he tried to push the thought from his mind as he settled into the flight. They landed in Barcelona just as a rainstorm was starting which resulted in a delay for his flight to the island. He waited impatiently in one of the many airport cafés drinking *café con leche* and watching people walk hurriedly about. Finally, nearly three hours after his flight was scheduled to depart he was on the plane heading to Isla Marta. It was now quite late and dark outside and Javier hoped taxis would still be available when he got there so he wouldn't have to disturb Manolo. The flight was bumpy and he sighed in relief when they finally landed in one piece at the small airport. He grabbed his bags and found one lone taxi waiting out front. He hopped in, gave the address to the driver and leaned back in his seat, his nerves strangely on edge. *Must be because of the scary flight I just survived*, he thought. That and wanting to see Antonia again.

* * * *

Lars and Antonia had passed a very strange day trying to keep low profiles but not to such an extent that they had been actively avoiding each other. She'd spent a lot of time in her room forcing herself to work on her article. She did some reading about the upcoming festival and scanned in her photos. She was delighted to see that several pictures of Lars had turned out so well and saved those for herself. She had taken a short nap and had a late lunch alone in the kitchen.

As for Lars, he'd finished his book, taken a long run followed by another swim, then a shower and a nap. He'd awakened feeling refreshed and hungry. He was surprised at how late it was when he had gone to look for Antonia. Passing through the living room he'd glanced out of the window and noticed that it was dark—not just from the lateness of the hour but from storm clouds passing overhead.

He found Antonia on the front veranda curled up on the loveseat with a book, reading under the dim porch light. He sat down next to her and she looked up from her book at him.

"Good evening, sleepyhead," she said smiling. She marked her place and made room for him on the loveseat.

"Hey, not fair. I caught you sleeping today, too, you know," he laughed.

They talked a few minutes about their day. They sat close and once again Lars could smell her perfume or her hair or whatever it was about her that overwhelmed his olfactory organs. He closed his eyes for a second and breathed in, then sighed deeply.

"You always smell so damned good," he said, his voice barely above a whisper. He had not planned to touch her or kiss her or have any physical contact with her at all but it was impossible when she looked so beautiful and smelled so good. He laid his arm on the back of the loveseat behind her shoulders and allowed his fingers to roam into her hair, which lay loosely down her back. It was so soft and silky…what was he doing? Why was he torturing himself this way?

Antonia needed no more invitation than his proximity and his fingers in her hair to turn into his arm and bury her face in his neck. Talk about smelling good. Who knew the sense of smell could have the most powerful pull of all. She smelled his Lacoste cologne, his hair, his skin and she could not stifle a groan of a pleasure. She turned her face to his and they kissed, softly at first, then more ardently, as if their lives depended on this kiss. He held her close in his arms and she wrapped her arms around his neck and they kissed like this for a long time until they were interrupted by the sound of a throat being cleared rather harshly.

"Excuse me. I don't mean to interrupt," said Manolo, a rather gruff tone to his voice. He looked at them with keen disapproval in his eyes. "I just wanted to tell you to be prepared for the electricity to go out. That happens often out here in a storm. I've brought you some candles and a lighter and two flashlights with extra batteries. Just in case." He reached out his hand and gave Lars a bag with the supplies in it.

"Thank you," said Lars. He glanced at the dark skies and noticed the scent of rain in the air.

"Be sure all the windows are closed, please," Manolo nodded good night to them and walked away as quickly as he had come.

"Wow," said Antonia. "He was not happy about something."

"I noticed. I'm sure I can guess why." Lars got up and walked down the steps into the yard and turned his face skyward. Antonia watched as he stood there silently for a minute. Then he came back up and told her could feel the rain beginning. A few seconds later they could hear it and soon it was pouring down in the darkness. Inside they dashed from room to room checking and closing windows. In the kitchen, Antonia set out the candles readying them for use should they be needed. She tried out the flashlights making sure they worked. She walked down the hall to see what Lars was doing. He had just shut the window in his bathroom and turned to see her standing in his room.

He knew he should steer her back out to the living room or to the kitchen or even outside in the downpour, anywhere but near his bed. Where was his resolve not to betray a friend? Why could he not resist her? She sensed his misgivings and closed the distance between them. They stood at the end of his bed, kissing with intense passion, a passion that threatened to be their undoing. He had his hand under her shirt, caressing her breast, his thumb manipulating her nipple. Her hand was pressed against his hardness, teasing and torturing him as their tongues waged a battle they would both have lost if it not been for the sound they both heard at the front door.

They jumped apart guiltily. Lars adjusted himself and ran a hand nervously through his hair. Antonia quickly straightened her sweater and they walked over to the door. She peered down the hall but saw no one and looked at Lars questioningly.

"It's probably Manolo coming to beat me up. I'll go check," whispered Lars forcing a grin. He walked down the dark hall into the equally dark living room and saw a shadow in the doorway.

"Why is it so dark in here?" Javier asked, flipping on the overhead light. He took in Lars' somewhat disheveled appearance and looked beyond him down the hall.

Playing it as cool as possible and without missing a beat, Lars went to him immediately and embraced him tightly.

"What are you doing here?" he asked surprised.

"My father is doing well enough to kick me out of the house and send me back on vacation," Javier said with a laugh.

"That's wonderful news," Lars exclaimed. He glanced down the hall then back at Javier. "You should have told us you were coming. We would have prepared you a meal or something."

"In my own home? I can fend for myself. Where's Antonia?" Javier started down the hall and Lars followed, fearing his reaction at finding Antonia in his room. But she wasn't there. Lars was relieved and hoped the relief didn't show on his face.

Antonia heard them talking from the other side of her bedroom door, where she'd quietly retreated upon hearing Javier's voice. She smoothed her clothing, took a deep breath and opened her door. The look on Javier's face when he saw her did something to her heart—something strange. How could she have forgotten how handsome and sexy he was? He stood there in the hallway in a matador's stance, his hands in his pockets, one foot slightly forward of the other, his back ramrod straight, looking at her with an intensity that made her shiver.

"Javier!" She exclaimed, reaching out to embrace him. He pulled his hands from his pockets and took her in his arms, holding her tightly to him. Once again her senses were assaulted by his amazing scent. What was it with these foreign men or was it just opera singers? Was there some rule that said they had to smell good enough to eat? Antonia caught Lars' eye over Javier's shoulder and he averted his gaze, staring down at the floor.

"Antonia, I have missed you. How have you been? How is your article coming along?" Javier asked, leaning back to look at her. He brushed a lock of her hair off of her cheek and took her hands in his. Then he leaned forward and kissed her softly on her lips.

Antonia felt a strange mix of emotions. She felt uncomfortable with Lars standing so close, witnessing Javier's show of affection but at the same time she felt an unexpected sense of safety with him here now. It didn't make sense nor did she know what kind of safety Javier provided. She tried to keep her voice from shaking as she answered him.

"I'm fine, thank you. And the article is coming along slowly but surely. I'm looking forward to the festival next week." She smiled feeling a rush of shyness wash over her.

"*Muy excelente*," Javier smiled. "I would love a glass of wine. I had a very nasty flight in the storm on the way here. Several times I thought we were going to crash. I need a drink. Will you both join me?"

Lars responded quickly. "I would love some wine. Red or white?"

"In the pantry there are some special bottles hidden away. I'll get a red. It's from a vineyard on Majorca." He smiled a disarming smile at Antonia.

"I'll join you in a moment. I just need to put away my computer," said Antonia glancing at Lars as she turned back into her room. He caught her eye and turned away, following Javier to the kitchen. She stepped back inside the safety zone of her room and leaned against the wall behind the door and tried to relax.

There was a strange feeling in the air. Another sea change was passing over the house. She went into the bathroom, brushed her hair and put on some pink lip-gloss. She stayed just long enough to miss the conversation between Lars and Javier.

Javier found the bottle of *Gitano Rojo* and a corkscrew in the pantry and brought them to the table.

"So, Lars, what were you doing before I arrived?" Javier asked in an almost disinterested fashion. He put the corkscrew into the cork and began to slowly turn it, burying it deep into the cork.

"Nothing much," Lars replied. For a split second he had considered telling Javier the truth but he stopped himself. "That's wonderful news about your father."

"Thank you. Have you and Antonia been getting along OK?" Again, he asked the question with an air of ambivalence as if he didn't particularly care to know the answer.

"Just fine. I've been teaching her how to drive a stick shift. She was a little shaky at first but she seems to be getting the hang of it now." Lars leaned up against the counter, crossed his legs and his arms and watched Javier work the corkscrew.

"That's nice," said Javier. "You've kept your hands off of her, I hope." It was more of a statement than a question.

Lars looked into Javier's eyes and lied through his teeth.

"Of course. You have to ask?" he said forcing a smile.

At that moment the cork on the wine bottle popped loudly. Javier set the bottle on the counter and removed the corkscrew from the cork. He poured the wine into three glasses and handed one to Lars.

"A man can never be too sure of these things," Javier smiled. At that moment Antonia joined them and Javier handed her a glass. Javier raised his glass to theirs and they toasted.

"To great friends, new and old." He observed them over the top of his wineglass as they drank.

"Is there any news about Antoine and Andrew?" asked Lars. "Colin filled me in on what's happening with them. It doesn't sound good."

"I spoke with Samuel before I came here and he says things are not as bad as they seem. He will call here in a day or two and give us an update. It sounds like everything will work out satisfactorily though."

"Thank God," sighed Lars. "All Les Passionistes needs is a scandal to kill something that's still so new."

"Samuel mentioned that we might have to return to London earlier than originally planned to take care of business," Javier said, draining his glass and refilling it.

"That makes sense," said Lars. "I'm getting rusty anyway. I forgot the words to "*Mi Fantasia*" yesterday. It kind of freaked me out."

Javier laughed. He walked closer to Antonia and topped off her drink.

"You are so quiet, Antonia," he said, putting his arm around her.

"I'm just listening to you two, trying to imagine what your professionals lives must be like. There is a romantic and mysterious air surrounding what you do. It fascinates me."

"To the outside world opera *is* mysterious and romantic, that is true," said Javier. "But learning the music is hard and sometimes we want to scream like little girls."

"Sometimes we *do* scream like little girls," Lars laughed.

They all laughed and Antonia felt a sense of calm slowly descend upon them where before there had been a strange, almost imperceptible, tenseness floating about the kitchen. They took their drinks to the living room and sat and talked. Javier sat next to Antonia on the sofa, his arm resting on the cushion behind her shoulders, and Lars sat across from them in a wingback chair. They told Antonia funny stories about fan encounters, most of them involving Antoine who they said had this sense that he had to 'connect' with every female they encountered, as if he owed them something. And they told her about Andrew who wanted to play basketball everywhere they went and carried a bag full of balls and gym gear everywhere they traveled.

At midnight, Lars told them he was going to bed. He sensed that Javier was waiting him out so he could be alone with Antonia and Lars wasn't going to make him wait any longer. He looked directly at Antonia as he said good night trying to gauge her feelings at his leaving her with Javier. She seemed serene and content but maybe that was the wine having its usual effect on her. She was not a seasoned drinker and it showed every time she imbibed. He went down the hall and shut his door wishing he could be a fly on the wall in the living room right now. He hated not knowing what was happening out there.

When Lars had gone, Javier got up and turned out the lights leaving them in darkness.

Antonia's nerve endings tingled with anticipation. She knew Javier was going to kiss her and she felt as if she were about to cheat on Lars. She felt guilty about this until Javier sank into the seat beside her and took her into his arms and touched his lips firmly to hers, kissing her so passionately that it nearly knocked her senseless. She felt the guilt ebbing away and found herself returning his kiss with a passion of her own that she didn't realize she was feeling. Javier was a master kisser, there was no doubt about that and he seemed to drink her in. She felt light-headed and overwhelmed and every part of her body suddenly sprang to life. Had Javier's absence made her heart grow fonder without her knowledge or permission? His tongue seemed to blend into hers and they kissed with an urgency that puzzled and excited her. Again she asked herself, *what is happening to me*? They slowly pulled apart and Javier whispered sweet endearments in her ear in Spanish, which sent shivers down her spine and caused her skin to tingle all over.

"Does this mean you really have missed me, Antonia?" he asked softly against her jaw, his lips tracing a line down to her chin. She moaned softly, feeling a fire in her loins that threatened to engulf her.

"Yes, more than I realized, I think" she smiled, turning her face into his and kissing him again. She thought of Lars and felt a stab of pain in her heart but, God help her, should could not pull herself away from Javier's embrace or his tender lips. It was as if a bolt of lightning from the storm outside had split her brain and her heart in two. Nothing made sense any more.

"Good. I know it's late and I will let you sleep now. I'm happy to be here with you," he smiled, pulling her to her feet. They walked down the hall to her room and he kissed her once again and said good night. She heard his footsteps recede as he walked to his room across from Lars'. She collapsed on her bed and hugged her pillow tightly to her chest and rocked slowly back and forth. She wanted to laugh and cry at the same time. This unexpected turn of events made her feel as if she were losing her mind. It didn't seem possible that she could be attracted to them both so strongly. She tried to think of Lars but now it was Javier who kept coming into her head. She screamed silently into the pillow and lay there, with swirling, confusing thoughts that kept her company for most of the night.

Chapter 10

"Have you been to the village of Maladita on the western side of Isla Marta?" Javier asked Antonia over breakfast the next morning.

She and Javier were eating sweet rolls on the veranda, which Marta had made fresh that morning. Marta had been keeping a low profile of late but she'd magically resurfaced with Javier's return. She had been rather cool to Antonia all morning and though Javier had noticed her behavior he did not comment on it. Neither of them had seen Lars yet this morning and figured he was still asleep.

"No, I haven't, but the *alcalde* of Dos Passos recommended I go there. That's where the main events of the *Festival de Los Amantes Muertos* will be, right?" She sipped her coffee, enjoying its richness and Javier's company.

"Yes. There will be a big parade there to start the festival and flamenco dancing in the streets and more food than you can imagine. The locals will have booths set up to sell their homemade wares and many of the so-called gypsies will also come out to sell their goods which will probably be mostly items from the United States and Europe like jeans and Nikes and Barbies and such. There will be games and magic and costumes and the crowning of the king and queen of the festival. You will love it."

"It sounds amazing. I can't wait." Antonia was genuinely excited about this event and she hoped to make it the centerpiece of her article.

"Did I mention that during the festival the king and queen will make love and then be sacrificed?" Javier watched her face, expecting a reaction to that statement. He got one.

"What? What do you mean 'sacrificed?'" Antonia exclaimed, her face paling.

"Yes. They will make love on an altar of stone and at the moment they both, shall we say, experience their release, they will be sacrificed."

"No! I don't believe it. By whom? How? That's impossible...it's illegal!" Antonia's voice rose with each word she uttered.

Javier could see that she was getting agitated, believing his words to be the truth. He loved seeing this passionate side to her, finding it to be very sexy as well as sweet.

"I'm joking," he laughed and reached over to run his hand down the length of her bare arm. "Making love in public and human sacrifices are both illegal in Spain just as they are in most places in the world. The truth is the king and queen will kiss and then sink to the ground where festival-goers will shower them with rose petals. Then they will rise from the mountain of roses and lead the villagers to the sea where they will scatter more roses over the water and kiss once again. It's very safe and simple and no one dies."

"But what does it mean?" asked Antonia very interested in the tradition and wondering about the significance.

"The legend goes that once many years ago on this island, there was a man named Pablo who loved a woman he could not have because she belonged to someone else. She belonged to his brother, Ramon. Ramon had to go away on a hunting trip with the other men of the village but one man from each family had to remain behind to oversee the village and protect the women and children. So one day Pablo found himself alone with his brother's wife, Marta, the love of his life. Marta did not know that Pablo was in love with her and had always desired her from afar. Marta had asked him to meet her in private because she had something important to tell him. Pablo was very excited about the meeting, assuming she was going to confess her love to him. She had told him to meet her by the large rock at the western end of the island and he arrived there first, nervous and anxious. He imagined what it was going to be like holding her in his arms, smelling her skin, tasting her lips. He was beside himself with desire. When Marta arrived she came to him smiling but acting a little nervous. A couple of times she looked over her shoulder as if expecting someone else to show up. Pablo was so sure about what Marta was going to say to him that he did not let her speak first. Words of love and devotion tumbled from his mouth and then he grabbed her and they kissed with a passion that he had only ever dreamed of. Marta was shocked by his admission of love for her and startled by the passion in his kiss. But then a strange thing happened. Marta's sister Maria walked out from behind a rock where she had been watching this exchange. She screamed at them and accused them of adultery and accused Marta of luring her there under false pretenses. Marta was supposed to tell Pablo that Maria was in love with him but he was already in love with Marta. Marta was supposed to bring them together not drive them apart. In a rage, Maria threw a rock at Pablo who had broken her heart through no fault of his own, but Marta, for reasons no one truly knows, threw herself in front of Pablo and was struck in the head by the rock. She sank to the ground and died in Pablo's arms. Maria was so horrified that she walked straight into the sea and was never seen again. And poor Pablo died of a broken heart. Villagers found his body lying wrapped around Marta's hours later. And if that was not bad enough, when Ramon returned from his trip and learned that his wife, sister-in-law and brother were all dead, he threw himself off a mountain into the sea. This island is named after Marta and every year in October the dead lovers are honored and Isla Marta's birthday is celebrated."

Antonia was stunned.

"Wow. What a story. I should have been writing this down. That's amazing." She sat back in her chair thinking about the lovers and the misunderstanding that led to their deaths. She tried not to read anything into it that might suggest a parallel with her own romantic entanglements.

"It is sad but strangely beautiful," he said. "Would you like to go to Maladita today?"

"I would love to go but only on one condition…" she said teasingly.

"What is that?" he asked, amused.

"I get to drive," she laughed.

"*Dios mio*!" Javier exclaimed, crossing himself and shaking with laughter.

"Hey! That's exactly what Lars did the first time I drove," said Antonia, pretending to be hurt.

"What did I do?" asked Lars, coming in the door, once again wrapped in a towel and wet from an early morning swim.

"We thought you were still sleeping," said Javier. "But it seems you were the first one up." He glanced at Antonia, wondering if the sight of Lars in a towel would affect her, but she showed no notice of his attire.

"I like the feel of the sea in the early morning. So what did I do?" He looked back and forth between the two of them.

"You crossed yourself the first time you let me drive," smiled Antonia.

"Oh, yes, it's true," Lars grinned. "But she did fine."

"Not exactly, but thanks for saying so," said Antonia. "Would you like coffee?"

"No, thanks. I'm going to take a shower. I'll make some later." He started toward the hall but Javier stopped him.

"We're going to Maladita on the western side of the island this morning, Lars. Would you like to come with us?"

Lars looked at Antonia and searched her face for an answer. He hated the thought of the two of them going off alone together but he didn't want to be a fifth wheel either. He decided he would have to beg off for the sake of making Javier happy even though he would be miserable.

"You two go. I'm going to make some phone calls and practice some music. Have fun." He gave them a salute and headed down the hall to his room.

Antonia finished her coffee, her thoughts racing. She hated knowing that Lars would be alone and wished he had agreed to come with them. But for some inexplicable reason she was happy to be with Javier for the day. She made a vow to herself that she would explore her feelings for him today and try to figure out how she really felt about him. He was causing confusion now that he had not caused before—before she had met Lars.

"I have to get my camera. Be right back," she said pushing her chair away from the table.

Javier stood up and pulled her into his arms. He kissed her tenderly on the lips, a kiss that was meant to be chaste but that soon turned to one of passion—a kiss that was witnessed by Lars who stood just outside the kitchen door in the passageway. He cursed under his breath and returned to his room, quietly, so they would not know he had seen them.

What kind of game is she playing? he asked himself as he stripped off his wet trunks and hung them to dry on the towel rack in the bathroom. *And what am I going to do about it?* He turned on the water in the shower and when it was warm enough to suit him, he stepped in, pulled the curtain closed and began to sing "*Miserere*" at the top of his lungs.

* * * *

Antonia couldn't remember when she had had so much fun. She had driven them to Maladita without incident and Javier had been impressed with her driving abilities.

"It's as if you've been driving a stick your whole life," he had complimented her. "Lars must have been a very good teacher."

"Or maybe I'm just an excellent student," Antonia replied with a grin.

"I'm sure that's it," said Javier, brushing his hand through her hair, his fingers gently caressing the back of her neck. Antonia locked the car and put the keys in her purse, then Javier took her hand and they set off to explore the town.

They walked all around the village of Maladita, often encountering fans of Les Passionistes and friends of the Garza family. Javier was gracious to everyone who approached them, and signed autographs and posed for pictures for all those who asked. He had introduced her to the *alcalde* of the town who had given her more information about the festival including a book about the legend that Javier had told her about earlier. She interviewed shopkeepers and café owners, took photos and made notes about hotels and bed and breakfasts.

In the afternoon Javier treated her to lunch at Café Julio where she unwittingly ate bull meat. She had exclaimed over how delicious everything was and then Javier broke the news to her about what she was eating.

"Oh, no!" she exclaimed. "I thought it was a hamburger!"

"But you liked it, yes?" laughed Javier.

"Actually, it was pretty darned good," she smiled, finishing her french fries. They shared a dessert of fresh mascarpone torte with strawberries and *café con leche* then slowly walked back to the car.

"You can drive home, Javier. I'm too tired," she smiled, handing him the keys. Once inside the car, she slipped her feet out of her espadrilles and stretched her legs, rubbing the calves. "We did a lot of walking today. My legs are sore but in a good way."

Javier watched as she massaged her calves and rubbed her fingers over her feet. The action was getting under his skin. He turned to her and spoke softly.

"Antonia…?"

"Yes?" She put her feet back down on the floorboard and looked at him.

He leaned toward her and pulled her close to him, touching his lips to her cheek.

"You are irresistible, do you know that?" He whispered the words in her ear, his lips making a slow pilgrimage along her cheekbone to her lips. "I want to make love to you."

"Javier," she breathed his name, feeling her heart beating rapidly in her chest, threatening to burst through. She felt dizzy just as she had with Lars. *Lars.* She saw his face in her mind and felt a stab of guilt. But Javier's hand sliding under her blouse, making contact with her breast, was forcing the guilt away. She groaned when his thumb touched her erect nipple and she felt herself involuntarily lean closer to him. He kissed her with such intensity that she feared she might faint.

"You want me, too. I can feel it, Antonia," he whispered against her jaw, his tongue finding its way to hers. The kiss became almost rough and when they parted both were panting to catch their breath. Javier looked into her eyes. "It's only a matter of time, Antonia."

He leaned back in his seat and started the car. Naturally Antonia's eyes drifted to his hands, one on the wheel, the other manipulating the gearshift. The thought of his hands on her the way they were handling the car made her cry out softly. Her hand flew to her mouth and she looked away in embarrassment.

"What is it?" asked Javier.

"Is there any way you can drive this car without touching that damned gear shift?" she exclaimed. "I can't stand it!"

He looked at his hand on the gearshift and at her reddened face and laughed, a loud deep, sensuous laugh. He reached over and tousled her hair, his fingertips grazing her jaw.

"Am I—how do you say it—turning you on?" he laughed. "Because if I am, I will drive the car all over this island until we run out of gas."

She laughed and put her hand on top of his on the gearshift. He drove them home, her hand on top of his all the way there.

* * * *

Lars walked along the beach wondering about Javier and Antonia. The more he thought about the two of them together, the more he convinced himself he had to leave the island. Isla Marta was not big enough for the three of them and he could not shake the fact that Javier had met Antonia first. And, he was not sure exactly how he felt about Antonia. He didn't remember ever feeling such confusion where a woman was concerned as he felt with her. In the back of his mind, the fear that he was looking for a replacement for Katarina kept rearing its head. He picked up a handful of shells and stones and threw them one by one into the sea. Finally he decided he would go back to the house and wait for Javier and Antonia to return. He would watch them together, see how they acted with one another and when the moment presented itself he would get Antonia alone and have a talk with her. If she were playing with them, pitting them one against the other, he would put a stop to it tonight.

* * * *

Deanna stood looking at the calendar, a slow realization washing over her. She stared at the date and wondered if Antonia remembered what today was. She went to the phone and dialed Antonia's number figuring she would get her voicemail as usual. She was surprised when Antonia answered.

"Hey! What's happening on your little island?" asked Deanna glad to finally reach Antonia directly.

"Deanna! How are you? How's Sean?" Antonia was thrilled to hear her friend's voice.

"We're fine. I hadn't heard from you in a while and thought I'd better check in. What's happening there?"

Antonia walked into her room and closed the door behind her. She had left Javier and Lars talking in the garden with Manolo who was doing something to his fire pit.

"They're both here, Dee. Lars and Javier at the same time," Antonia said breathlessly.

"Damn! That must be surreal. Are they as hot in person as they are on TV?" she laughed.

"You have no idea," Antonia whispered. "Dee! I'm going crazy here. I wish you could come and help me save myself from these two."

Deanna laughed. *Oh, to have a problem like that*, she thought.

"Are they fighting over you?" she asked.

"It seems more the other way around," sighed Antonia.

"What do you mean?"

"I'm totally in love and it's making me crazy."

"With which one?" asked Deanna, holding her breath in anticipation of the answer.

"That's the problem. I have no idea."

"Damn, girl! That is a problem. What are you going to do?"

"Not a clue." They both laughed and then Deanna brought up the delicate subject that had been the reason for her call.

"Antonia…do you know what today is?"

"I've lost all sense of date and time since I've been here. Why?" Antonia was puzzled, fearing she had forgotten someone's birthday.

"It's Jeff's wedding day. I just wanted to make sure you were OK and not upset about it. But if you're in love with two hot foreign opera singers than you must be over Jeff anyway," Deanna laughed.

Antonia didn't speak for a moment. She *was* shocked. Shocked because she realized in that moment that she didn't care that it was Jeff's wedding day. She hadn't given him a single thought since she'd arrived on the island.

"I forgot." She said it almost proudly.

"Thank God. You're over him. That's a good sign." Antonia could hear the relief in her friend's voice.

They talked a few minutes more and then Antonia closed her cell phone and sat on her bed organizing her notes from Maladita. She finished up and was just about to go find Lars and Javier when there was a knock on her door.

"Come in," she called out.

Lars walked into the room, shut the door behind him and walked over to the bed.

"We have to talk," he said his voice low and serious.

"OK," she said, her heart beating faster. "What is it?"

"Are you playing some sort of game with me?" He sat down on the edge of the bed, pushing her notes away so he wouldn't sit on them.

"What do you mean?" she asked, her nerve endings on edge.

"You just spent most of the day with Javier. And don't tell me you didn't kiss him or touch him." Lars felt his temper on the rise and fought to keep it in check.

"Where is Javier? He could find us in here," she said anxiously, looking around Lars toward the door.

"So what if he does?" Lars said rather harshly. "He went somewhere with Manolo. Now tell me, Antonia, what game are you playing?"

"I'm not playing games, Lars. I'm confused."

"*You're* confused? That's funny because so am I. Is there something between us or not? I was under the impression there was." He tried to mask the frustration in his voice.

Antonia felt her own sense of frustration and confusion bubbling beneath the surface of her skin. She looked into Lars' eyes, trying to read his emotions.

"Correct me if I'm wrong, but aren't you the one who said that nothing could happen between us because of Javier? Well, it didn't stop you from kissing me…and more."

"It didn't stop you either, as I recall," Lars ran his hands through his hair and sighed audibly. "Tell me the truth. How do you feel about me? And Javier? I want to know where I stand."

"Oh, Lars. I don't know." Tears threatened behind her eyes and she fought to keep them from falling. She got up from the bed and walked toward the window, her back to Lars. "I truly don't know anything. I told you I'm confused. Please don't pressure me."

Lars closed the distance between them and folded her into his arms. Then he turned her around and kissed her hard on the mouth. After a few moments they pulled apart and Antonia gasped for breath.

"Think about that Antonia. About the way we kiss and the way we feel together. We'll talk more later." He kissed her again and left her there by the window feeling more confused than ever.

She collapsed on her bed and cried tears of frustration. She thought of Javier and felt her spirits lift. Then she thought of Lars and felt her heart sink. This was impossible. The house suddenly felt too small and the island too confined. She needed to clear her head and get some air. She changed into her bathing suit and grabbed a towel. A swim in the sea would calm her down.

* * * *

Peter Anderson was one lucky son of a bitch. Acting on a tip from his co-worker at Celebrity Photos International, he had finally found out where the other member of the hot group Les Passionistes was vacationing. And he had also found out from another photographer that Javier Garza was at the same place as Lars Kohler. Apparently Javier's father was better and so Javier had returned to Isla Marta to finish his vacation. It would be great if he could get a picture of them together. His company had already made a killing on the photos of Antoine de Cadenet and Andrew Jones, so this coup would be sweet, especially if he could catch one or both of them in a compromising position.

He settled into the cramped seat on the small plane to Isla Marta. He hoped he wouldn't have any trouble finding his way around the island once he got there. He had arranged to rent a little Mini Cooper at the airport and figured someone there would be able to give him directions to the Garza home. All he needed was one or two good pictures and he would be set. He had his eye on a new Range Rover, a black one, fully loaded. These pictures, if they were any good at all, were his ticket to that new vehicle. He looked out the window at the Mediterranean Sea below. They would be landing soon. He was anxious to get the job done and get back home to his girl in Paris. If he could get the pictures before sunset tonight, he could hightail it out of there and be back on the last flight back to Barcelona tonight. That would be sweet indeed.

* * * *

When Javier returned from the village with Manolo where they had picked up a very large pig from the butcher shop, he found Lars standing on the veranda staring off into space.

"Hey, Lars!" He waved to him as got out of the car. "Give us a hand with this beast, will you?" He opened the trunk and indicated the large wrapped package nestled inside. "This is tomorrow's dinner!"

Lars clambered down the steps and together they carried the pig into the kitchen where Marta was waiting to work her magic over it. Manolo stayed to help her and Lars and Javier went back outside.

"Where's Antonia?" asked Javier looking around.

"In her room, I think," said Lars. He looked at Javier and decided there was no time like the present to lay the proverbial cards on the table. "I need to talk to you about something."

Javier nodded. He didn't seem surprised that Lars wanted to talk. He had been expecting it.

"About Antonia, yes?" asked Javier.

"Yes. Can I be honest with you, Javier?"

"By all means," said Javier, assuming his matador stance again, back straight, hands in his pockets, one leg slightly forward of the other.

"I think I'm in love with her and I just wanted you to know," Lars looked into Javier's eyes, expecting—waiting for Javier to react physically. If he got hit, he would deserve it.

Javier inhaled deeply and let out his breath slowly and quietly as he returned Lars' gaze with a piercing one of his own.

"You see, Lars, that is the difference between us," he said mysteriously, removing his hands from his pockets and folding his arms across his chest. "You *think* you are in love with Antonia. But I *know* I am."

Lars was stunned at Javier's words. For a moment he stood there, speechless, not knowing how to respond. Javier had trumped him and it angered him. Before he could think of something to say in return, Javier continued.

"Listen to me, Lars. I understand what's happening to you. You and Katarina were together for a long time and you are probably missing the companionship that a woman provides. And then you come here to this island and what do you find? A beautiful, American woman who is hard to resist. But I can assure you, Lars, that Antonia is in love with me. I do not want to fight over her with you nor do I want to lose your friendship, but on this issue we must have an understanding."

"Did she tell you she's in love with you?" Lars didn't believe Antonia could turn so easily. She had been ready to make love with him the other night and they would have if they had had protection. She didn't seem the type to toy with one man, let alone two at the same time.

"Not in so many words, but I can feel it in her kiss and I see it in her eyes, even if she doesn't know it herself. But soon she will."

Lars wanted to tell Javier the whole truth about what had happened with him and Antonia while Javier had been in Madrid but something stopped him. He valued Javier as a friend and a colleague and it seemed pointless now to hurt him. But damn it, he had felt something in Antonia when he had kissed her and held her and that had to count for something.

"Maybe we should ask Antonia how she feels," Lars said, immediately wishing he could take back the words.

"Right, then. I will get her." Before Lars could protest, Javier strode purposefully into the house in search of Antonia. He walked from room to room but she was nowhere to be found. In the kitchen he asked Marta if she had seen Antonia.

"I saw her leave earlier in her swimsuit. She was going to the beach, I think," said Marta.

Javier walked back out to where Lars was standing under the huge palm tree.

"She has gone to the beach. Let's go." He said the words as a command.

"Fine," said Lars. He really didn't want to do this now but he felt like Javier had issued some sort of unspoken challenge and he hoped that they were all up to the task, particularly Antonia. He followed Javier down the path to the beach.

* * * *

Peter parked his green Mini Cooper behind some brush at the end of the drive, feeling confident that it was hidden from sight. He would probably have to hide out for awhile waiting for someone to come out of the house. He readied his camera equipment and decided he would head toward the beach and get some shots of the beautiful landscape. Just as he was about to barrel down the path, he heard footsteps and ducked behind a tree.

Bingo! His targets were together and walking quickly toward the water as if on a mission. They had angry looks on their faces and he sensed that something big was about to happen. When they had passed by the tree where he was crouching down, he slung his camera over his shoulder and slowly followed them, being careful to stay off to the side in the trees out of sight should they have reason to turn around.

Down at the beach, Peter saw a large rock, tiptoed over to it and slunk down behind it, watching intently at the unfolding scene. It was spellbinding and he had to remember why he was there—to get pictures. And what pictures they would prove to be.

* * * *

Antonia heard footsteps approaching behind her. She sat up on the blanket and was shocked to see both Lars and Javier walking purposefully toward her. She felt a shiver down her spine and stood, pulling her blanket around her.

"What's wrong?" she asked them anxiously. "Has something happened?" It was obvious something untoward had happened to put these looks on their faces.

"That's what we want to know, Antonia," said Javier softly, his voice comforting in spite of the fact that something bad was about to happen. She just knew it.

"What are you talking about?" she asked, willing her teeth not to chatter. She tightened her grip on the blanket.

"I want to know what happened between you and Lars when I was in Madrid." Again Javier spoke gently. Lars looked into her eyes and waited to hear her response.

She looked into Lars' brown eyes and willed him to answer the question so she wouldn't have to. But he remained silent.

"Nothing happened," she lied. She hated the look on Lars' face when she said those words. "Why?"

"You don't have to lie," said Lars. "Tell him how you feel."

Tears started behind her eyes and she fought them. Why were they confronting her like this? What had she done wrong?

Javier's heart went out to her. He wanted to take her in his arms and tell it was OK. But he had to let her speak. He had to know where he stood.

"I don't know what you both want me to say," she said, tears falling slowly down her cheeks."

"Tell Javier that you're in love with me," said Lars. He started to walk toward her but Javier put out his arm and stopped him.

"Let her be," he said, holding Lars' arm.

Lars looked down at Javier's hand on his arm and froze.

"What are you doing, Javier?" asked Lars, feeling anger and frustration threatening to overtake him. He towered over Javier by about four inches but Javier stood up to him defiantly.

"Don't touch her. Give her a chance to talk."

"I can't do this," she cried. "Please stop. The truth is I love you both."

"That is not possible," said Lars, shaking off Javier's arm. "Who do you want, Antonia? I'm tired of playing games."

"Please, Lars. Stop saying that. This is not a game." She sobbed and turned away from them.

"You've upset her now," said Javier. He wanted to go to her but again he resisted.

"What did you expect? I'm sorry, Javier. Your friendship means the world to me but I love her."

"No, you don't," responded Javier calmly.

"Yes, I do," said Lars, his voice raising.

"You couldn't possibly," said Javier.

"Why the hell not? You think you're the only one capable of love around here, Mr. Romantic?"

And then all hell broke loose. They went at each other like little boys on a playground fighting over a toy. Antonia wasn't sure who threw the first punch but suddenly fists were flying and she heard a mix of German and Spanish as they punched each other. Lars hit Javier in the jaw and Javier responded with a right hook into Lars' stomach. She screamed at them to stop but they didn't seem to hear her.

"Please! Stop!" she screamed louder. Javier glanced over at her. He wanted to stop this nonsense now for many reasons not the least of which was that his jaw felt like it was on fire. Lars popped him on the other jaw and they went down in the sand, rolling over and over, letting loose on each other.

"Stop!" Antonia screamed again. She couldn't bear to watch this any longer. She dropped her towel in the sand and ran toward the sea, her eyes blinded by tears. She ran into the cold water and headed for the large rock way off in the distance. She needed to get as far away from them as she could. She swam hard, getting further and further away from shore.

"Stop!" shouted Javier. "Enough!" They were back on their feet, panting hard, out of breath. Lars rubbed his nose while Javier massaged his jaw. They both looked at the same time out to sea and saw Antonia going further than it was safe to go.

"Damn it! I told her not go out there!" shouted Lars.

"*Dios mio*!" yelled Javier. He tore off his shirt, buttons flying and dashed out to sea with Lars close behind him.

Behind the rock up the shore, Peter Anderson got it all on film. He was thrilled that they had made so much noise that they couldn't hear his camera snapping away. He wanted to cry he was so ecstatic. This was so much more than he ever could have hoped for. He knew he should sneak away while he had a clear chance to get out unseen, but this was too compelling to walk away from. He reloaded his camera and continued his watch.

Antonia was out of breath. She was almost at the rock but it was so much further from shore than it appeared. She was so close but the pain in her side was threatening to do her in. She looked over her shoulder and saw that Lars and Javier were swimming toward her. She was nearly at the rock—so close. She slipped under the water, her side splitting, on fire. She sucked in seawater and bobbed to the surface, coughing up the salty water. She gagged and went under again. She wanted to call for help but she didn't have enough air in her lungs to hold her breath until she could resurface again. Panic set in and she knew in that moment that she was going to drown. She felt herself spiraling downward and she fought with all her strength to reach the surface. She could see it. She had to keep fighting. Her hand broke the surface and something grabbed it hard. She felt strong arms around her and a voice telling her not to panic…to be still…stop fighting. A few moments later she was being pulled up on the rock with Lars and Javier beside her. She felt someone's arms turn her on her side and she coughed hard, water pouring out of her mouth. She lay there shaking as Javier whispered to her in Spanish and Lars wiped the hair out of her face.

"Antonia…? Are you OK?" asked Lars. "You scared the shit out of us."

She coughed again and tried to sit up. Javier helped her into a sitting position. She sat with her head between her knees, struggling to get her breathing back to normal. Javier caressed her back gently and whispered in Spanish to comfort her.

"I'm…so…so…sorry," she cried, her shoulders shaking.

"It's OK, shh…," said Javier. He exchanged glances with Lars who looked distraught. "Everything is fine now. You're safe now."

Antonia's shoulders shook and Javier gently rubbed her back. Lars wanted to touch her, to comfort her, but he didn't dare. He saw something in Javier that stopped him. He saw the look in Javier's eyes, the fear and the love for Antonia. And he knew he had lost her. It was useless to let this go on. He stood up and looked toward the beach.

"How the hell are we going to get Antonia back to shore?" Lars asked. He looked down at Javier who was now holding the shaking Antonia in his arms.

"Manolo has a small boat. It's usually stored by the bathhouse. One of us will have to swim back for the boat." Javier was more than willing to go back to shore for the boat but he was not willing to leave Antonia alone with Lars to do it.

"I'll be back," Lars said and dove into the water. Javier watched him swim away, his heart heavy and his body hurting from the intense swim and the blows he had taken from Lars.

Javier turned to Antonia and put his hand on her chin, tilting her face to his. Her face was red, her breathing still rapid and he leaned down to kiss her softly.

"I'm so sorry, Javier. I couldn't stand to see you both fighting. I don't know what I was thinking." She sounded lost.

"It's OK. We never should have bombarded you like that. I'm sorry. Lars will be here soon and we'll get you home and dry and get you something hot to drink." He kept his arms around her, trying to quell her shivering. They sat in silence waiting for Lars. Javier saw him reach shore and run up the beach out of view.

Antonia laid her head in Javier's lap and tried to will herself to relax. She was afraid to go back to the house—afraid to see Lars. She prayed that they would be able to talk and work things out. She only wished she knew what she should say to them both.

"Here he comes," Javier whispered.

Antonia lifted her head and saw Lars heading their way. It was a small motor boat and he arrived quickly. When he came abreast of the rock, they noticed that he looked angry and sullen. Antonia worried that he might lose his temper and fight with Javier again. But his words shocked her.

"You're not going to believe this, Javier. I just spotted a member of the paparazzi hiding in the bushes. I don't know how long he had been there but he thanked me for the great footage. Fucking asshole!" Lars pounded the side of the boat with his fist then rubbed his hand in pain.

"Unbelievable!" Javier was livid. "This is ridiculous. They have no shame." He stood and helped Antonia to her feet. Lars held out his hand to her and helped her into the boat. Her arms tingled when he touched her and she felt goose bumps creep along her skin. Javier climbed in after her and Lars turned the boat around and in a few minutes they were back on the beach. Lars and Javier carried the boat while Antonia grabbed her blanket and sandals and followed them back to the house.

She hurried down the hall to her room, stripped off her bathing suit and stood in the shower letting the hot water rush over her. The spray hit her face and mingled with tears. If only she could stay in here all night in the safety of her room, but she would have to come out sooner or later. She couldn't hide away forever.

Lars and Javier both showered quickly and met in the kitchen. Lars wanted to talk to Javier before Antonia joined them—*if* she joined them.

"I'm going to leave tomorrow," said Lars. "And I'm sorry I hit you."

"I forgive you," Javier said, suppressing a grin. "I apologize, too." They were silent a moment and then Javier asked Lars about Antonia.

"Are you going to talk to her before you leave?" he asked, his voice low.

"And say what? 'I love you, but Javier got here first?'" Lars said bitterly. "I'll say good-bye. What else is there to say?"

"Fine then. We should probably call Samuel or Colin about the paparazzi incident."

"I'll call." He left the kitchen and walked toward his room. He met Antonia in the hall. She was warm and clean and dry and naturally he could smell her shampoo and her skin. They didn't speak but he touched her arm gently then went inside his room and shut the door. She stood a moment feeling confused and hurt, then went to the kitchen.

In his room Lars turned on his cell phone and saw that he had another message from Katarina. He listened to the message. "Lars, you must have your phone turned off. If you get this message, please call me. I have something to tell you. It's important. I love you."

"Damn it!" he cursed under his breath. He paced around the room and then placed a call to Colin. Colin was easier to deal with sometimes. He would let Colin tell Samuel about the paparazzi incident. When he finished his call he debated joining Javier and Antonia in the kitchen but his appetite overruled him.

Javier was preparing dinner for them and Antonia was sitting at the table drinking hot tea that Javier had made for her. Lars came into the room and stood in the doorway. An uncomfortable silence settled around them. Antonia felt a wave of exhaustion wash over her and she had to get out of the room. She finished her tea and stood up.

"I'm going to lie down for awhile," she said and left the room abruptly.

"Did you call Samuel?" asked Javier. He flipped the omelet over in the pan and adjusted the flame on the burner.

"I called Colin and left a message. I'm sure he'll be calling back when he hears it."

Javier put the food on a plate and set it on the table. He pointed to it with the spatula.

"Here, it's for you," he said gruffly.

"Did you poison it?" Lars asked facetiously.

"Why don't you taste it and find out?" snapped Javier.

Lars sat down and began to eat the omelet. It was surprisingly delicious. Javier made one for himself and joined Lars at the table and they ate in an uncomfortable silence. When they finished Lars offered to do the dishes. Javier bit back a snappy retort and let him clean up.

"I'm going to see if Antonia is hungry," said Javier and left Lars alone in the kitchen with the dishes.

He tapped on her door but there was no answer. He opened the door slowly and peered inside. Antonia was asleep on top of the bed. He went to the linen closet in the hall and found a blanket, and put it over her. She murmured in her sleep and he leaned down and kissed her cheek, then left her alone.

Lars and Javier avoided each other the rest of the night and eventually they went to bed. Javier lay on his bed thinking of what had happened today. He wondered what would happen after Lars left. He was going to prove to Antonia one way or another that she loved him. And he had an idea of just how to do it. He would seduce her through his music.

* * * *

In his room, Lars packed his clothes, mixing the clean with the dirty, the dry with the wet, not caring that the suitcase was a mess. He wanted to be ready to go first thing in the morning. This vacation had been a total bust and now he was going back to Switzerland. Normally home was the best place to be, or it was once upon a time. He wasn't sure what, if anything, he could do about Antonia but no matter what, he had to work with Javier and he had to preserve their friendship for the sake of Les Passionistes. He finally relaxed and fell into a fitful sleep.

As for Antonia, she fought with her dreams all night—troubling, exhausting dreams. She was glad when morning came and she could get up and start a new day—a strange day.

Chapter 11

Antonia was the first one up the next morning. Or so she thought as she walked through the quiet house to the kitchen. She saw a piece of folded paper on the table propped up in front of the ceramic napkin holder. She opened it up and read Lars' words:

"Javier and Antonia: I'm going back to Switzerland. Manolo is taking me to the airport. I'm sorry for the trouble I caused and I hope we can put it past us and move on. Javier, you are my best friend and partner. I honor that relationship. Antonia, you are sweet and beautiful and I'm so glad we met. I will never forget you. Be safe, you two. All the best, Lars."

Tears streamed down her face at the realization that Lars was gone and she had not had the chance to say good-bye to him face to face. She laid her head on the table and sobbed quietly. She did not hear Javier come into the room. He stood back watching her, seeing the note in her hand. He knew it must be from Lars. He waited until she had stopped crying and then walked over and took the note from her hand. He read Lars' words.

"Why are you crying, Antonia?" he asked softly, taking the seat next to her at the table.

"I wish I could have seen him before he left," she said, wiping her eyes with a napkin. "He probably hates me now."

"Lars has no reason to hate you." He said it matter-of-factly, as if he were finished with any talk about Lars. He scooted his chair over closer to hers and took her hand in his.

"I'm going to tell you something and I want you to listen to me. You don't have to say a word, just listen, OK?" His voice was tender and patient now and she looked into his dark brown eyes, noticing that errant lock of hair on his forehead.

"I'm listening," she whispered.

"I've fallen in love with you. You're beautiful and smart and a very good driver, too," he was teasing her now. "I just want you to know that no matter what happened with you and Lars while I was gone, it doesn't matter. I love you and I hope you feel the same. If I have anything to say about it, you will feel the same soon enough, if I have to sweep you off of your shoes."

"Feet," she corrected him smiling.

"Whatever," he smiled. "Now I know you must be starving. Shall I fix you my world famous omelet?"

"Please," she said. She tried not to think about Lars as Javier chopped peppers and onions and shredded cheese for her omelet. She poured herself a glass of pineapple juice and sat at the table as he fixed her food, concentrating on his deft movements as he worked.

He watched her eat breakfast and then told her was going to see if Marta and Manolo needed help with the pig.

"We're going to put it on a spit and roast it all day. Manolo and Marta's family will be here to eat with us. Then we will go to the opening of the festival in Maladita later this evening. How does that sound to you?"

"Wonderful," she smiled.

"Good."

Javier kissed her chastely on the cheek and left to find Manolo. Antonia sat at the table and thought of Lars. She missed him and wished he was still here and yet, perhaps it was for the best that he was gone. At least that was what she told herself.

* * * *

Colin listened to the message from Lars again. This was not good. Samuel had only just sorted out the problem in New York with Andrew and now this mess with Javier and Lars. He wondered just what the pictures would show that the photographer had taken. Lars had not been too forthcoming with information, only to say that photos had been taken of them 'sort of not getting along.' What did that mean? He wished he had more information and debated calling Javier. He had been unable to reach Lars. He should probably warn Samuel but maybe this would turn out to be no big deal and the pictures would end up being worthless. Better to wait until he had more information.

*　*　*　*

Marta and Manolo's three grown children and assorted grandchildren arrived in the afternoon for the pig roast. Manolo had been worrying over the pig for hours and finally declared that it was ready to eat. Antonia had offered to help Marta in the kitchen preparing side dishes but Marta had politely refused all offers of help. So Antonia had walked about the grounds watching the children play hide and seek and then a raucous game of stickball with Javier. They finally talked her into playing with them and she reluctantly joined in. It turned out to be fun and she had a good time. Manolo called them all together and performed a ceremonial slicing and dicing of the pig and they filled their plates and found spots to sit and eat about the grounds on chairs that Manolo's sons had brought up from the bathhouse.

When they had finished eating and cleaning up the dinner aftermath, it was time to go to the opening parade of the festival, which was to be in Maladita. Manolo's family piled into their cars and left for the parade with Manolo and Marta following in their old Fiat. Javier and Antonia were the last to leave. Javier offered to let Antonia drive but she declined which caused much teasing from Javier.

"You just want to watch my hand on the gear shift, is that it?" he teased.

"I wasn't even thinking that, I swear," she exclaimed, her face reddening.

They got into the car and before Javier turned on the engine, he leaned over and put his arms around Antonia and kissed her gently on the lips.

"Have you enjoyed yourself so far today?" he asked, nuzzling her jaw with his nose.

"Yes. I never knew I liked roasted pig," she laughed. His closeness was doing something to her—something maddening. She smelled his cologne, so different from Lars,' yet so sensual. She felt a stab of guilt at the thought of Lars, wondering where he was—*how* he was—and pushed the thought aside. Javier pulled her as close as the gear-shift would allow and kissed her mouth, his tongue melding with hers. Her head spun with desire and she felt confounded that two such different men could do this to her. Javier whispered Spanish words of passion in her ear and the sound of his voice was like honey dripping over her. She groaned against his mouth, knowing in that moment that if he made any moves of a sexual nature on her tonight she would be a willing recipient of his ardor.

They drove into Maladita, up and down the twisty, narrow, cobbled streets looking for a place to park. It seemed that everyone on the island had turned out for the festival. Javier eventually paid a handsome sum to a café owner in order to leave the Volvo behind his restaurant. They walked along the streets until they came to the town-square where the parade would begin, eventually wending its way to the sea. Javier saw a spot in front of the local pharmacy where they could watch the parade. He stood behind Antonia, his arms around her waist holding her close.

The parade began with the ceremonial kiss between the newly crowned king and queen who were then bathed in rose petals tossed by the crowd. They walked toward the sea followed by a group of musicians playing traditional flamenco music with women in their colorful flamenco dresses and men in tight black pants and white shirts, string ties and bolero jackets. They twirled in time to the music as they made their way down the street. Antonia took many photos of the people in their finery as well as of the young children who followed in colorful animal costumes. A military regiment marched by and a small contingent of horses pranced along, their manes tied with bright ribbons, their tails braided in elaborate designs. The parade lasted about half an hour and then Javier ushered Antonia into the streets where they held hands so as not to get separated in the throng making its way to the sea. Once they reached the water, the king and queen who Antonia figured were each about sixteen, kissed again and threw roses into the water. Then somewhere in the distance the sound of a cannon rang through the evening air, making Antonia jump in fright. She wished Javier had warned about that. He laughed and squeezed her hand tightly in his.

Later they made their way back to the town-square and Javier bought them cold beers from a street vendor. In the square, musicians were set up on a stage to play music for a street dance. Javier saw the *alcalde* and made his way toward him, holding tightly to Antonia's hand as they weaved their way through the crowd to the stage.

"Javier!" The *alcalde* greeted him, extending his hand. "You made it. *Muy excelente*! The band is prepared. They've been practicing all day!"

"Good," said Javier. "I have not rehearsed with them so this could be a complete disaster on my part. If so, I apologize in advance."

Antonia turned to Javier, a look of confusion on her face.

"What are you guys talking about? Are you going to sing?" She could hardly believe it.

"I have a surprise for you, Antonia, but I must warn you we have not rehearsed together—the local band and I—and also, I am used to singing this song with three other voices. So wish me luck. And don't move from this spot."

Javier kissed her lips tenderly and squeezed her hand. Then he walked up on the stage where the *alcalde* was ringing a bell to get the crowd's attention.

"Ladies and gentlemen, we have a special treat tonight. Spain's own Javier Garza of the world famous opera quartet Les Passionistes, has agreed to perform a song for all of us tonight. Please join me in welcoming this amazing voice to our stage. Javier Garza!"

The crowd erupted in wild applause as Javier took center stage. He signaled the band to begin the intro to "Surrender to Me" and then he began to sing in his rich, baritone voice.

Antonia was shocked. Javier was singing her favorite Les Passioniste song—the one that made her melt every time she heard it. She thought back to a few days ago when she had stood in the garden listening to Lars sing the same song and how it had made her feel. And now Javier was singing it and it sounded so amazing. His voice was truly a gift and Antonia felt hypnotized by each note. He sang to her, his eyes on her face and she never looked away. If this were some kind of spell he was casting upon her, it was surely working overtime. Javier held the last note for a long time, and the crowd, sensing the end was near, burst into wild applause. He smiled his appreciation to the crowd and bowed to them. They screamed for an encore but since the band knew only the one Les Passionistes song, Javier sang an a cappella version of a selection from *Beauty and the Beast.* When he finished the song, he came off the stage and embraced Antonia, then whispered in her ear.

"Let's go home."

Antonia didn't speak as Javier took her hand and they made their way to the café where they had parked the car. He opened the door for her and she settled in, her heart racing, her palms sweating, every fiber of her being on fire with expectation. She knew there was no way on earth she could resist Javier tonight. It was inevitable. She could still hear his voice singing "Surrender to Me" in her head and she concentrated on that and not on his hands as he drove them down the twisted streets toward the house.

He parked under the palm tree and they didn't speak as they entered the house. Antonia was nervous to such an extent that she could barely breathe. She forced herself to move slowly through the house, slipping off her sandals by the front door and setting them neatly aside, perfectly aligned with one another.

Javier walked to the kitchen door, his hands in his pockets, and stopped, turning to her.

"Would you like a drink? Some wine, perhaps?" he asked, a most sensual smile on his face, his voice sexy and low.

Antonia surprised herself completely with the words that tumbled unbridled from her mouth.

"No. I want to be completely sober," she said softly.

Javier needed no further invitation. He walked toward her and she met him halfway, their arms filling with each other. He kissed her tenderly and suckled softly on her lower lip. His tongue found hers and his body pressed against hers. She could feel him harden against her hip and she brazenly reached down and touched him, putting pressure against him. He groaned and kissed her neck, whispering words of passion in Spanish against her throat.

"Antonia, what are you doing to me?" he whispered, his breath ragged. "I want you."

"I want you, too," she whispered, knowing she was helpless to resist him, knowing she didn't want to.

He pulled back and looked into her amber eyes and smiled, bringing his hand up to caress her cheek.

"Are you sure this is what you want? Are you sure *I* am the one you want?"

"I am very sure," she breathed out the words in a slow sigh. She thought of Lars for a moment, Lars whom she had lusted after only days ago, but he had not made her feel like this. What was different now? It was a sweet mystery to be sure, but the way she felt in this moment made her realize that what she had felt for Lars was something animal, born out of sexual desire. But now with Javier, her feelings transcended lust and desire—they went much deeper than that. She felt a strange sense of security she had not felt with Lars, a feeling that this was heaven and she didn't want it to end. She couldn't be entirely sure what was different with Javier this time, but everything seemed heightened and as it should be.

Javier took her hand and led her down the hall to his room. He opened the door and let her enter first. She walked part way in and stopped, feeling nervous and anxious about what was happening between them. She saw the bed, neatly made, waiting for them. Antonia had never been so nervous in her life nor had her senses ever been so alert to every movement, every touch, every taste, every sight, every sound and every scent. She turned to Javier and he embraced her again, kissing her softly.

"Let's take it slowly, Antonia," he whispered in the semi-darkness of the room. "I want to savor every part of you."

"What if I can't hold out?" she said, again surprising herself with her bold words.

"Then perhaps we should not waste another moment." He led her to the bed and turned her to face him. He slowly unfastened the tiny hook on her navy sweater and pulled it over her head. He dropped it to the floor and brushed her brown hair out of her eyes. His hands moved over her stomach, sliding over her ribcage to her back and deftly unhooked her bra in one try. He slowly brought his hands around to the waistband of her khaki trousers and unbuttoned them, then worked the zipper down. She shivered when his hands touched her hips, easing the pants down, past her thighs, her knees and down to her feet. She stepped out of them and kicked them away. He leaned back and looked at her tanned, beautiful body and whispered in Spanish. He suddenly pulled her to him, a little roughly, causing her to gasp.

"I'm sorry, *querida.* But you are so beautiful that it hurts my eyes." He smiled against her cheek, weaving his fingers through her hair. He kissed her lips and felt her breasts rubbing against his shirt. He brought her hand up to his top button and she began to unfasten each one, finally arriving at the point where the shirt was tucked into the waistband of his black pants. She pulled the shirt free and undid the last few buttons, pushing the shirt back over his shoulders, letting it fall to the floor. He had the most beautiful chest, chiseled and muscular, with swirls of soft, dark hair in abundance. She teasingly ran her fingers over his nipples causing him to cry out and crush her against him. He kissed her roughly, then let his tongue make a path to her throat. He guided her hand to his belt and she unfastened it, undoing the button and the zipper. She pushed the pants over his lean hips and he pulled them off in one swift motion.

Javier stepped to the bed and pulled her down gently with him on top of the blanket. He leaned over her, trailing his lips down her neck, to her breasts where he suckled each hard, pink nipple, causing her to arch her back and moan with pleasure. As he passed his hand slowly down her stomach to the waistband of her underwear, he kept his eyes on her face, watching emotions pass over her. He felt the goose bumps on her skin as his fingers slipped beneath her silk panties, down into the soft hair there. She moaned, arching her back and he leaned down and kissed her, his tongue searching and tangling with hers.

Antonia was nearly out of her mind. She was on fire and thought she would explode before he ever touched her. She felt him slide her underwear down and she lifted her hips to make it easier to get them off. Finally she was naked under his hands and he ran his fingers along the length of her thigh, down to the knee and back up again. She reached for his underwear and he helped her pull them off. She saw him for the first time and took him in her hands. He was hard and ready for her and she was more than ready for him.

"Javier," she whispered. She had to let him know how close she was to release. She knew if he touched her wetness, she would explode. "Please...," she gasped.

"Do you want me inside you when you come, *querida*?" he asked against her jaw.

"Yes. You're making me crazy—*loca*," she smiled against his jaw.

"I need one thing. Give me a moment." He leaned down to the floor and found his pants. He pulled the package from the back pocket and pulling out a condom, he fitted it over himself. Then he positioned himself over her and brought their bodies together. She spread her legs, wrapping them around his back and he slid into her as far as he could go. She came instantly as she knew she would, and shivered and moaned against his neck. He kissed her, then raised up to look into her eyes. She watched his face as he moved over her in a poetic rhythm with much more control than she had had over herself. He pushed himself into her as far as he could, filling her up till she thought she would burst and then he cried out in Spanish, shuddered hard and lay on top of her, breathing into her neck. He lay still for a moment and then fearing he might be crushing her, he raised up and looked into her eyes. He leaned down and kissed her slowly and softly. Already Antonia was ready for him again as she thrust her tongue into his mouth, acting the aggressor this time. They kissed passionately for some time and then Javier lay next to her, her body tucked into his, his hands caressing her breasts, her face and her hair.

"You are amazing, Antonia. I knew you would be."

"So are you," she smiled into his neck. "Javier…?

"Yes, *mi amor*?"

"Have you ever wished you could stop time?" she whispered, turning to him, her breasts brushing against his chest.

"Yes. I've wished it when we have been on stage performing before thousands of people and we are sounding better than ever and the audience is eating out of the palms of our hands. Then I wish I could stop time." He looked down at her, grinning.

"Is there any other time?" she prodded, smiling.

"You mean like right now?" he teased.

"Yes, you know that's what I mean."

"I wish for this moment to last forever," he said and kissed her tenderly. His words washed over her like warm honey. They lay together for a while, breathing each other in, reveling in the passion they had just shared. Antonia had never felt such perfect bliss—she had not even known it existed.

After a while Javier stood up and beckoned to her to follow him. He took her hand and led her to the bathroom, then turned on the shower.

"Come in with me, *querida*."

They stepped into the tub and the cool temperature of the water made Antonia shiver. Javier stood under the spray and pulled her into his arms, caressing her back and bottom gently. She handed him a bar of soap and he began to wash her back and her stomach, then her breasts. She took the soap from him and returned the favor, lingering on his private parts, washing him gently. He hardened instantly and she massaged him, feeling his breathing becoming labored. She knelt down before him, the water rushing over them both, and took him in her mouth. She moved up and down, licking and sucking him until he couldn't stand it another minute, and finally, his body on fire, he exploded into her, emitting a guttural moan as he came. He pulled her to her feet and kissed her neck and her jaw, and then both breasts. He reached behind her and turned off the water and grabbed towels for them from the towel rack. He wrapped her first and then himself and led her back to the bedroom where he laid her down on the bed and opened the towel.

Antonia trembled with anticipation as Javier slowly kissed her on her mouth, then began a pilgrimage toward her private parts, stopping first to suckle each breast, to tease her bellybutton where the little diamond stud sparkled in the dim light of the room. She raised her hips involuntarily as his mouth got closer and closer, and finally, using his fingers to gently open her, he leaned down and tasted her sweetness, groaning as he licked and manipulated her with his tongue, her back arching, her breaths coming in gasps. It only took a few moments for her to reach a climax, one so powerful that it shook her to her core. Javier whispered words in Spanish as he kissed his way up her body back to her mouth where they kissed with such intensity it defied even the forces of nature.

It was now dark in the room and there was a bit of chill in the air. Javier pulled the covers back so they could get under them. He curled himself around her and they lay together for a while until they both needed turns in the bathroom. Antonia slipped into his black shirt and padded down the hall to her own bathroom to brush her teeth. When she returned he was in bed waiting for her. She saw a package of condoms on the nightstand and commented on them.

"They are for just in case," laughed Javier. "Just in case you attack me in the middle of the night."

"It could happen," she smiled. She settled into his arms and they talked softly about nothing in particular, then eventually fell into a deep sleep. Antonia had never felt such rapture in all her life. And Javier felt exactly the same way.

Chapter 12

"That was a short vacation," said Urs, helping Lars put his luggage in the trunk of the car.

"It was getting a little crowded on that island," Lars said gruffly.

Urs looked at his brother, noting the grim line of his mouth and the darkness in his eyes.

"You want to talk about it?" he asked. He started the car and they pulled away from the airport.

"No, I'd rather not. Have I missed anything around here?" he asked, his gaze on the passing landscape.

"Not really, but I need to tell you something."

Lars didn't like the sound of this. He really wasn't in the mood to hear news of any kind—good *or* bad. He didn't respond, knowing Urs would tell him anyway.

"It's about Katarina, Lars. She isn't doing well. Her mother called Father and said that she has not been taking care of herself. She hasn't been to work in days and she isn't eating properly. Her parents are very angry with you. If they know you're home, they will seek you out. I thought I should warn you." Urs glanced at his brother's expressionless profile.

Lars sighed, passing his hand through his hair. *Why did I come back here*? he thought. *I should have just gone to London.*

"What do they expect me to do about it?" he asked in a toneless voice.

"I don't know. Other than giving Katarina what she wants, there isn't much you *can* do, I guess."

"Me, you mean?"

"You *are* what she wants," said Urs, taking the exit that led to their neighborhood in the western suburbs of Lucerne.

"Well, that isn't going to happen. And seeing me again is only going to make it harder for her. It's best for me to stay away from her," Lars said adamantly.

"You have to see her. She wants to tell you something. It's something she needs to get off her mind. You have to call her when we get home," Urs said firmly.

"What is it? Do you know what this is about?" Lars was getting irritated with his brother. He wished he would just say whatever the hell it was and get it over with if he knew anything.

"No, but it wouldn't be for me to say even if I did. It's important—that's all I know. It's something she needs to tell you herself anyway, or so she said." Urs suddenly turned the car into the parking lot of a gas station, put the car in park and let it idle. He turned to Lars, his face serious. "And there is something else I will tell you. Katarina's parents aren't the only ones mad at you."

Lars stared at Urs, waiting for him to continue. He figured Urs was talking about Mother and Father although Mother had been supportive when he had told her about breaking it off with Katarina. After a long moment in which neither brother spoke, Urs broke the silence.

'I'm talking about Frederick."

"Damn it!" cursed Lars. "I knew you were going to say that." News that his older brother was angry with him wasn't such a shock, really. Once upon a time, Katarina had dated Frederick, before she set her sights on Lars. He should have seen this coming.

"What did he say?"

"He hates that you've hurt her like this. You have to know that he still loves her. But because he loves her and because he loves you he has stayed quiet, minding his own business all the time you've been with her and when you've been gone."

"Well, she is a free agent now," said Lars harshly. "Anyway, I thought he was over her."

"You *would* think that since you're never here anymore to see what's happening in this family. You weren't here when Grandmother passed away, Lars. And our parents' marriage is falling apart, but did you even notice? And you've destroyed Katarina. As for Frederick…I just don't know."

"Why are you doing this to me, Urs? Is any of this my fault? Are you blaming me for everyone's problems because I have a successful career and I'm famous now? And I was home for Grandmother's funeral, remember? I loved her! Maybe you should just turn this fucking car around and take me back to the airport!" Lars cursed harshly.

"I'm sorry, Lars. I don't mean to hurt you. It's just that things aren't as rosy around here as maybe you think they are. The least you can do is talk to Katarina and see what she has to say. And maybe talk to Frederick. He's coming over to the house tonight. He knows you're coming home."

"Fine. I will talk to them both. And I will see Mother and Father and then in a couple of days I'm going back to London. Maybe I can get some peace there."

"Did something happen on that island?" asked Urs. He put the car in drive and headed toward home.

"I told you I don't want to talk about that." Lars folded his arms across his chest and stared out the window for the rest of the drive home.

* * * *

"Right when I think everything is going to be fine, another damned complication," barked Samuel to Colin. "And you do not seem very surprised about this. Did you already know?" Samuel paced around his office, his face red, his blood pressure on the rise. He had just returned from New York to find an advance copy of the *London Inquisition* in a manila envelope on his desk. It had been delivered while Colin had been at lunch with some of the producers. Now it lay front page up on his desk with Lars, Javier and some woman on full display on a Spanish beach, the two of them apparently beating the shit out of each other in each frame of the photos—and there were a hell of a lot of them.

"I'm sorry, Samuel. I was going to tell you but you were in it up to your neck with Andrew—good work getting those charges dropped, by the way. I knew Andrew wasn't the violent type—and I really didn't have any facts other than what Lars had told me. He wasn't exactly a fountain of information. Frankly, I'm surprised at how fast this has hit the news."

"Have you spoken to Javier about this?" asked Samuel, staring at the photographs in disgust.

"No, I haven't but..."

Samuel cut him off.

"Why the hell not? Get him on the phone in a conference call with Lars immediately! This kind of activity could spell the end for Les Passionistes. If those two are really fighting over a damned woman—and who *is* this woman, by the way?—then we need to find out if the situation has been resolved between them or not. Because if it hasn't, then we need to get those two back here and get this taken care of before any more damage is done to the reputation of this group. Is that clear?"

Colin nodded, speechless, and backed out of Samuel's office, shutting the door behind him. He made a mad dash for the phone. He prayed fervently that he would be able to get them both on the phone at the same time or Samuel might get mad enough to fire him.

In his office, Samuel reread the article. The headline was glaring: *"More Trouble for Hot Opera Gods: Lars and Javier Caught in Fist Fight Over Mystery Woman on Spanish Island."* He noted that there wasn't much to the actual story, just speculation about Lars and Javier caught up in an apparent lovers' triangle and fighting over a woman on the beach. He studied the pictures intently. Yes, it was definitely Lars punching Javier in the face. And in the next frame he could plainly see Javier giving Lars a good one in the stomach. He looked at the girl, wrapped in a blanket apparently crying. The pictures continued with shots of the girl running into the sea, followed by Lars and Javier swimming after her. The story concluded with the statement that this latest scandal, after the Antoine de Cadenet affair and the Andrew Jones arrest, could spell the end for Les Passionistes.

"When hell freezes over," muttered Samuel. He closed the paper and sat back in his seat to wait for Colin to get Lars and Javier on the phone. Obviously it was time to cut their vacations short and get Les Passionistes back home to London where they belonged.

* * * *

Deanna saw the pictures on the Internet and nearly had a stroke. She saw them when she read her Daily Dish from Celebrity Central, the online news source that specialized in hot celebrity gossip. She stared at Antonia, wrapped in a blanket, a distraught look on her face, the two, hunky Les Passionistes guys beating the hell out of each other.

"Oh, my god!" she screeched. "What the hell is happening over there?" She looked at every picture in disbelief. She glanced up at the timeline noting that the photos were apparently hot off the proverbial press taken sometime in the past forty-eight hours. *People* and *US* magazines both had the story on their web-sites with teasers about more information coming in their next issues.

"Oh, Antonia," she muttered. "Your dad is going to have a stroke when he sees this." She wished Sean were home so she could tell him about these latest developments. "What have you gotten yourself into?"

She paced about her apartment, suddenly dreading the massage appointment she had later with the Olsen twins' personal fashion stylist. She tried to call Antonia but got her voicemail—it was pretty late over there anyway—already after ten o'clock. She left her a message urging her to call immediately.

"I bet Antonia hasn't even seen these pictures," Deanna said aloud. She read all she could find on the Internet about the mysterious fight and decided she would check out the television news. The E! channel might have more. She hated getting news like this secondhand but until she heard from Antonia that would have to suffice.

* * * *

When they arrived at the house, Lars went to his old room and sat on his bed. He thought about the irony of being such a mega-success in his professional life and yet his personal life was a royal mess. Why couldn't they both be perfect at the same time? He let his mind drift to Antonia. He wondered what was happening there with her and Javier and another irony came to mind, which made him laugh bitterly aloud. Now he knew how Javier must have felt when he went back to Madrid to see his father, leaving Antonia alone with him. He felt the negative feeling now—the feeling that something of his was being taken away from him. He hated this feeling. Maybe he should not have left Isla Marta. Maybe he should go back and put up a bigger fight. Or maybe he should just go to London and work on the music in preparation for going back into the studio in November to begin work on the new album. Maybe work was where his mind should be.

There was a knock on his door.

"Come in," he said expecting it to be Urs or his father who was due home from the office soon.

"Hello, Lars," said Katarina.

He looked up, shocked to see her.

"Katarina…," he said, standing up from the bed. He subconsciously slipped his hands into his pockets and kept the distance between them. "Why are you here?" he asked softly.

"I had to come, Lars. We need to talk. When you left before things were bad between us. And I didn't get to say everything I needed to say to you. Will you give me that chance now?" Her voice was thick with tears which she fought hard to keep from falling.

"I don't see how anything you say can make a difference, Katarina. I'm not trying to be cruel. I don't want to hurt you anymore." Lars kept his voice low and his eyes averted from her sad ones.

"Remember last year when you were in Italy shooting those videos for the album?" she asked him.

"Yes. What about it?" He failed to see how this could be important.

"Well, while you were gone, I found out that I was pregnant."

Katarina's words stunned him. He looked at her, standing there with her arms folded across her chest, looking small and frightened.

"What the hell are you talking about? Why are you telling me this now?" He said the words with anger in his voice, anger at her betrayal—that she would keep something so important from him.

"I tried to call you several times but you never returned my calls because you were always working—recording or shooting the videos or whatever. I tried for a damned week to call you to tell you my amazing secret. I was so excited. I couldn't wait to tell you. And then finally you called—ten fucking days later. *Ten!* But by then it was too damned late, Lars, because I had lost the baby. I lost our baby that fast, in the third month before I'd hardly had time to believe it was even real."

"I'm sorry…" Lars said softly, stunned at her words. "But when I did finally call, you never said a word about it. Why?" A part of him wanted to go to her, to offer her comfort, but he knew that would be poor judgment. So he stood across from her waiting for an explanation.

"When we finally talked I was so upset because you hadn't called sooner. Do you remember that fight we had?" She tried to keep her voice calm and under control.

"We've had so many, Katarina, I can't remember one from another any more." Lars sighed, not really wanting to take a trip down memory lane but he could see she had more to say.

"Do you remember my asking you about our relationship? About our future? About having a family one day?"

"I remember asking you to move to London to be with me but you wouldn't leave your family and the restaurant. *That* I remember."

"You knew I couldn't move that far away from my family. My life is here in Switzerland," she cried, wanting him to understand how close she was to her family.

"You made that perfectly clear," he said impatiently.

"I asked you that day on the phone how you felt about having a family and you made something clear to me, though I didn't really believe it. You said children weren't a priority and that your career was the most important thing in your life. You said you didn't really know one way or another if you would ever even have children."

"That's not true. You must have misunderstood me," Lars was sure she must be wrong.

"You made yourself perfectly clear but because I love you I let it be. And I decided not to tell you about the baby because I was afraid you might be happy that I had lost it."

"I might have been relieved, Katarina, but not happy. Anyway, that was a long time ago. It doesn't matter now," Lars wanted her to go. He didn't need this right now.

"Why can't we work this out, Lars? Why? Were you telling me the truth when you said there's no one else?" Katarina stepped closer to him. He felt cornered and didn't like the feeling. He needed for her to go. And now he had a new truth for her to hear.

"It was true at the time," he said quietly.

Katarina gasped, the tears flowing freely now.

"I knew it," she sobbed, backing toward the door.

"It's someone I just met. *After* you and I broke up." Lars knew she would never believe the truth—it was too farfetched.

"I don't believe you. You're a liar! Who is she? One of your groupies?" She stopped in the doorway her hand on the doorframe. "Who is she?"

"I'm not talking about this with you. I'm sorry, Katarina. It would be better if you just left now and tried to forget me."

"How do you expect her to do that?" asked Frederick. Lars' older brother stepped into the room, putting his arm around Katarina. She turned her head into the crook of his arm and sobbed.

"Frederick." It was all he could think to say. He looked at his brother's face so like his own they could pass for twins. His quiet brother who always wore his heart on his sleeve and who never dated another girl seriously after Katarina. His brother, with the amazing tenor voice, who was too nervous to sing in public and share his talent with the world. Lars decided in that moment as he watched Katarina and Frederick standing there together that maybe they should find a way to be together. He needed to remove himself from this situation and hope that nature would take its proper course and bring these two together as it seemed they should be. Finally he spoke.

"I have to go. I'm going back to London. I should never have come home."

"You're always running away, aren't you, Lars?" Katarina spat out the words.

Lars didn't answer. He picked up his suitcase and walked past them out to the sitting room. His father was just coming through the door.

"Lars! How are you, son? Home so soon?" He was thrilled to see Lars.

Frederick and Katarina walked into the sitting room and went for the front door. Katarina tried to force a smile for Mr. Kohler's sake but it was impossible to do.

"I'm taking her home," said Frederick. He nodded to his father and to Urs who had been waiting it out in the kitchen, wondering what was happening with Katarina and Lars in the bedroom. Frederick closed the door behind him and a pall hung in the air with his departure.

"What the hell is going on here?" asked Mr. Kohler.

"I have to go to London, Father. I will see Mother first and then I have to get back. Urs will explain."

At that moment his cell phone vibrated in his pocket. He looked at the dial and saw that it was Samuel's office.

"Excuse me," he said and walked down the hall to take the call. When he finished the conversation, he *knew* he was going back to London.

* * * *

"I finally have Lars on the line, Samuel. But I haven't been able to reach Javier. I'm sorry." Colin hoped this would be good enough for Samuel whose mood had not improved all evening. He patched the call through and waited for Samuel to finish with Lars. A few minutes later, Samuel came out of his office.

"Lars is on his way to London tonight. I told him about the story in the papers. It will be all over the news tomorrow. It's already all over the Internet. Lars assured me that there is no bad blood between him and Javier and the integrity of Les Passionistes has not been compromised or harmed in any way. For the group to be a success these four men must respect and admire one another. They are irreplaceable. Each of them knows this. Lars will explain everything tomorrow when he gets here. Please try to reach Javier again and if you have no luck, try first thing in the morning. Andrew and Antoine will be here tomorrow as well. I need them back here together. *All* of them."

"Of course," said Colin. Samuel went back into his office and shut the door. Colin again tried to locate Javier but came up empty.

*　*　*　*

Javier awoke before Antonia. He watched her sleep, willing himself not to touch her, to let her rest, but she made it so difficult. She finally stirred and opened her eyes, catching him staring.

"Good morning," she said, smiling.

"*Buenos dias, mi querida*," he whispered, kissing her jaw. She snuggled into him, breathing in his scent. Instantly she remembered the amazing night they had just spent, the lovemaking, the kissing, the touching, the tasting, and she held him tightly, her face buried in his neck.

"Antonia, we should get ready to go to the festival. There are many activities for you to see which you can use in your story. Do you want to go?"

"Do we have to?" she laughed, preferring to stay in bed with him for the rest of the day.

"It is up to you. We don't have to go right now if you have enough material for your article. We can always go later for the evening's festivities. You decide." He stroked her hair, twirling its silkiness in his fingers.

The only thing Antonia wanted to do was make love again with Javier but she thought of the reason she had come here to Isla Marta in the first place and realized that if she didn't get enough good copy for her story her father would be very unhappy. So she reluctantly forced herself into a sitting position.

"I guess we should go. Work comes first, right?" she laughed.

"Unfortunately that is sometimes the case. Speaking of work, I should call London and see if there is news on my band-mates and that photographer who spied on us. I feel so out of touch with my other life."

Antonia felt a stab of jealousy at his words and it must have shown on her face because Javier immediately pulled her down beside him and kissed her tenderly.

"But I would trade it all to be here with you forever," he smiled sexily at her.

"Liar!" she laughed and tried to tickle him but he caught her hands and held them tightly above her head.

"Let me prove it to you then," he said, leaning down and kissing her lips, then blazing a trail with his tongue down to her breasts. She moaned as he loosened his grip on her hands and she pulled him on top of her. He reached for the last condom in the package, then pulled it on and quickly entered her, filling her until she cried out.

"Am I hurting you?" he whispered.

"No. Please don't stop," she begged.

He moved over her, their rhythms matching as she rocked her hips and he moved inside of her, their passion once again overwhelming them both as they reached their climaxes at almost the same time. He lay beside her, kissing her face and she burrowed into his chest. Finally she spoke.

"Let's get this festival business over with, shall we?" she smiled at him.

"*Muy excelente*. You shower first and I will call my manager and see how things are with everyone. I also need to call home and check on my father. I'll meet you in the kitchen." He kissed her tenderly on the lips and she left to go to her room to shower and change.

Javier found his cell phone and turned it on. He hated cell phones and computers—they could be so confounding. He would rather memorize an entire opera in Italian than use either one of them. He saw his messages and was surprised at how many had come from Samuel's office. That didn't bode well. He decided he would call home first and then see what Samuel wanted. It was probably about the photos on the beach. He thought of Lars and hoped there were no bad feelings between them. Time would certainly tell.

* * * *

The taxi dropped Lars off in front of his flat and he let himself into the dark foyer. He flipped on lights as he walked through, already feeling himself relax now that he was back in his own home in London. It felt so good to be back where he belonged. He walked about the apartment, looking at his things—his computer, his stereo, his big screen TV that he never had time to watch, his espresso maker, his waffle iron. He played the messages on his answering machine, most of them sales calls or calls from the studio. There were some from Katarina but he erased them without listening to them—there didn't seem to be a point.

He dragged his suitcase to the laundry room and dumped the contents on the floor then sorted the mess out, some of it still wet from his last swim in the sea. He put a load in the washing machine, then went to the fridge and was dismayed to find it empty. He was starving but it was too late to go to the store, they would all be closed anyway. It was even too late to order take out from a restaurant.

The phone rang, its shrill sound shattering the silence of the apartment.

Who would be calling me at this hour? he wondered.

He picked up on the third ring, surprised to hear Andrew's voice on the other end.

"Andrew! It is so good to hear from you. What the hell happened to you in New York?"

"What the hell happened to you in Spain?" asked Andrew, laughing.

"How the hell do you know about that?" Lars smiled to himself as he stretched out on his chocolate leather sofa.

"Everybody knows. It's all over the Internet and on the news. What happened?"

"Tell me your story first. Where are you by the way?"

"I'm at the airport about to catch a flight back to London. I'll be there in the morning."

"Thank God for that," sighed Lars. "Now tell me your story about getting arrested."

Andrew proceeded to tell him about taking his girlfriend, Jenna, to the restaurant for a romantic dinner where she then broke the news to him that she wanted to end the relationship. The news had taken him by surprise, not because her words had hurt him so much, but because he wasn't as crushed by the news as he thought he should have been. The surprise was more in how badly he *didn't* feel than how badly he should have felt. For some reason Jenna became upset about his reaction and started an argument with him, which got loud and embarrassing.

"I mean here she is breaking up with me and I'm freaking making it easy for her by not getting upset and she goes ballistic on me," said Andrew.

"So how did chairs get broken and the place get wrecked?" asked Lars, secretly glad he wasn't the only of them with romantic troubles.

"I went to take her hand to get her to quiet down and accidentally knocked over her wine right into her lap. And she seemed to think I did it on purpose and the next thing I know, she pours water on me and then some guy at the next table gets up and accuses me of harassing her and he throws a punch at me and I try to defend myself. And then a table tipped over when the guy got up and after that it got really weird and nasty. Someone called the police and there goes Andrew taken away in handcuffs. My mother was so proud when she saw *that* on the news." Andrew was being sarcastic but it was still funny and Lars laughed.

"I know it isn't funny and I never believed you were at fault. I know you too well."

"Thanks, man. Samuel came and got the charges dropped and now I can't wait to get back to a more civilized country—and I never thought I would say that about England," he sighed. "Now tell me what happened to you."

But before Lars had a chance to answer, he could hear Andrew's flight being announced in the background.

"Hey, that's my flight. I've got to go. I'll be over to see you in the morning." They said their good-byes and Lars hung up the phone, glad that he didn't have to get into the story of what had happened with Antonia and Javier. It could wait until tomorrow. He thought of Antoine and hoped he was on his way home from Paris. It would be so good for the four of them to be back together—at least he hoped it would be.

* * * *

Javier had purposely ignored the messages from Samuel's office. He had listened to them but he did not return any of the calls. The way he figured it he was on vacation and his private time was his to do with as he pleased. And he was not ready to leave Antonia. Hell, he would never be ready for that. But he knew that his job was important and he would have to return to London whether he liked it or not. But he would make them wait a day before he called.

He and Antonia had gone to the festival and had a wonderful time, listening to music, shopping in the gypsy market and eating their way across the village of Dos Passos. At a jewelry store, Javier bought a silver ring with a turquoise stone for Antonia to wear as a symbol of their time together on the island. And she bought him a leather necklace with a silver double helix, which she tied around his neck. After walking all over the village most of the day, they were tired and slightly sunburned when they returned to the house after sunset.

They had showered together and after drying off, they snuggled together in Javier's bed. He curled himself around her, amazed at how perfectly her body fit into his.

"I hate to even bring this up, *mi querida*, but in the morning I must call my manager and I am fairly certain he is going to ask me to return to London. I had many messages from his office and there are things we need to take care of pertaining to the various messes we have all found ourselves in lately. I just wanted you to know." His voice was low and tinged with sadness.

She turned to him, kissing him tenderly on the mouth.

"I knew this couldn't last forever," she sighed. "You think you'll have to go back right away?"

"I am fairly certain. But I can't imagine leaving you." He leaned over her, kissing her along the line of her jaw. She put her arms around him, holding him tightly, wishing she could suspend time.

"I can't imagine staying here alone," she whispered.

"Come with me to London," he said against her neck, touching his tongue to her earlobe, causing her to shiver.

"I wish I could but I have to go back to New York. Besides it might be awkward being in London with...you know..." her voice trailed off. They had not spoken of Lars since he left and she knew it was a potentially touchy subject.

"You are thinking of Lars," he said, more as a statement than a question.

"Yes." She pushed the lock of hair off his forehead and kissed his mouth, letting him know that Lars was not a threat—not any more.

"I have an important question to ask you, Antonia," he said, pulling away so he could look into her eyes.

Her stomach knotted fearing he would ask about Lars—about what had happened between them and about how it had made her feel. But his question was not about Lars at all.

"Is it possible that you might be in love with me?" he asked quietly.

Antonia smiled, relieved. This was an easy one to answer.

"Yes," she said.

"Yes, you think it's possible or, yes, you *are* in love with me?" he grinned.

"Yes," she said again and laughed.

"Oh, you tease me now," he growled sexily and pushed her back into the pillows. He moved over her, kissing her passionately, teasing her with his tongue on her breasts and her stomach. He pulled an unwrapped condom from beneath the pillow and slipped it on, then entered her, causing her to squirm and squeeze him hard with her muscles. They moved rhythmically together for some time before Javier finally could not wait any longer and let himself feel release. He murmured Spanish words under his breath, then slid off of her, slipping his fingers into her wetness and manipulating her until she came as well. They lay together in the afterglow and soon slept.

In the morning, the aroma of sausage and pancakes awakened them. Marta, looking very happy at the turn of events that had brought Javier and Antonia back together, had whipped them up a veritable feast. They fixed their plates and took them out to the veranda where they ate and talked about their lives after Isla Marta.

Antonia would have to go back to New York and get caught up on her work. She had columns for upcoming issues to write and she had this big story to put together, plus there would be new assignments. And Javier and his band-mates would be starting work on their new album, a process that would take several months.

"I really cannot imagine being apart from you for too long," said Javier. "We will have to do something about that."

"What did you have in mind?" asked Antonia, feeling excitement grow in the pit of her stomach.

"Well, the simplest thing would be for you to marry me," he said matter-of-factly.

Antonia's eyebrows raised and she nearly choked. He handed her a napkin, grinning slyly at her.

"Did I shock you?"

"I'll say," she gasped. "Are you sure you know me well enough to marry me?"

"I know everything I need to know and already I treasure the years of learning more of your surprises." He took her hand in his and kissed her fingertips softly. "I love you, Antonia."

"I love you, too." It was the first time she had uttered the words to him and it felt so right to say them.

"So marriage would solve many problems then," he said.

"Is that an official proposal?" she asked coyly.

"It is a proposal but it's not official. Not until I get a diamond to replace that turquoise ring on your hand."

She laughed and kissed him. They finished breakfast and then Javier stood up.

"I have to call my manager. I don't want to do this, but I must get it over with. I will be back in a few minutes, *mi querida*." He disappeared into the house and Antonia took a walk around the grounds, thinking about all that had transpired between them in such a short time. And she realized that she had not given him a definitive answer to his unofficial proposal. But she knew what the answer would be. For a moment she allowed herself to bask in the knowledge that she would quite possibly become the wife of a member of Les Passionistes. It seemed surreal—impossible. It was amazing.

Javier returned some time later and found her in the garden behind the house. His face was dark and sullen. Her heart thudded as she realized he was about to tell her he had to leave.

"You have to go back to London, don't you?" she asked feeling her heart sinking.

"Yes. It seems that Antoine, Andrew and Lars have already returned. They are waiting for me to join them. Samuel is planning some appearances for us to show the world that Les Passionistes are still very much together, as if we wouldn't be," he said, the slightest hint of annoyance in his voice.

Antonia walked into his arms and they embraced, holding each other for a long time and not speaking. Finally, she asked him the dreaded question.

"When do you leave?" She held her breath as she waited for his answer.

"Tonight. Samuel has scheduled a television interview for tomorrow morning and rehearsals in the afternoon. He does not waste time."

Antonia's heart sank at his answer but she put on a brave face just the same.

"How are your friends—the other Les Passionistes members?" she asked quietly.

"They are fine—all of the troubles seemed to be sorted out. Apparently Antoine is sad that he has been all over the news for having an affair with a hot Hollywood actress and he has nothing to boast about because it isn't true. He feels he has let himself down, not to mention men worldwide."

They laughed and walked toward the house. Manolo was on the porch waiting for them. He was holding a folded paper in his hand.

"Javier, I thought you might want to see this. Marta just saw it at the newsstand in town and brought it for you." He handed Javier the latest issue of *Hello!* magazine with his and Lars' and Antonia's pictures splashed all over.

Javier took the magazine and looked through it at the pictures, which seemed to tell an accurate story of what had happened between them only a few days ago.

"Can I see it?" asked Antonia nervously.

Javier turned the pictures around for her to see and she covered her mouth in shock.

"This is terrible!" she cried in disgust.

"Don't let this worry you, Antonia. Everything will work out." He read quickly through the article and reassured her that her name was not even mentioned in it.

"They have no idea who you are so you should not have any problems with the press." He thanked Manolo for alerting him to the magazine and then they went inside so he could begin packing. He let Marta know that he would be leaving later that evening and made his flight arrangements while Antonia scanned in her latest pictures from the festival into her laptop. They ate a light dinner and then it was time for Javier to leave for the airport.

"Should I get Manolo to take me or do you think you can handle it on your own?" he asked, teasingly.

"I can handle it," she assured him.

They loaded the car and Antonia drove them to the airport. She parked the car and went inside with him all the while not believing that he was actually leaving.

When he was checked in for his flight to Barcelona, they sat in the coffee shop and had *café con leche.*

"When will you go back to America?" he asked her.

"I think I will make arrangements to leave tomorrow. When we will see each other again, Javier?" she asked anxiously.

"As soon as it can be arranged. We will work something out, I promise."

His flight was announced and they walked to the gate. He pulled her into his arms and she nestled into his neck, breathing in his scent, drinking him in. They kissed fiercely, with such intensity that other passengers and employees took notice but they didn't care.

He pulled away from her reluctantly and touched her cheek. She put her hand over his and felt tears burning at the backs of her eyes. She tried not to let them fall but it was pointless. He brushed them away with his thumbs and kissed her again.

"It's alright, *mi amor.* We will be together soon. I love you. Always know that." He hoisted his flight bag over his shoulder and walked to the plane. She stood in the window and watched until his plane was in the sky and then she drove herself home without incident.

Suddenly she felt as if she couldn't get off this island fast enough. She made arrangements for a flight out tomorrow morning to take her to Barcelona where she would catch an afternoon flight to New York. She called her father and let him know she was coming home a little early with plenty of copy for the article. She also called Deanna who was very relieved to finally hear from her. She promised to tell her over dinner everything that had happened on Isla Marta as soon as she arrived home.

CHAPTER 13

"I only wish I were having as much as fun as the press seems to think I'm having," said Antoine. He and Andrew were sitting in Lars' apartment waiting for the limo that would take them to the television studio where they would tape an interview for later broadcast on a popular, local entertainment show called *Afternoon Tea with Chauncey and Cherry.* Javier would be meeting them there and they were both a little apprehensive about Lars and Javier seeing each other for the first time since they were on the island. Andrew had expressed dismay that their first meeting since that time would be in front of tabloid TV presenters but Samuel had assured them that it would be fine. He had no intention of letting any of Les Passionistes say or do anything that would backfire against them in full view of the public.

"What about me?" laughed Andrew, teasing Antoine. "Now I have a reputation as mister tough guy on the block. I'll take your problems any day."

Lars was quiet as he listened to his band-mates laugh about their troubles. He had told them very little about what had happened between him and Javier, saying just enough to satisfy their curiosities. He simply told them that they had had a misunderstanding about the American girl staying at the house and that it had led them to lose their tempers and act like immature boys. He had said it was his fault and he was looking forward to seeing Javier so he could apologize to him in person and they could get on with making their music.

The limo driver knocked on the door, announcing his arrival, and they left the apartment together. Samuel was inside the limo waiting to give them a 'talk' on the way to the studio. He told them exactly what to say and what not to say and reminded them that the talk show hosts would be listening for their chance to pounce on anything they said that remotely resembled scandal.

Samuel turned to Lars.

"I know that you have not told me exactly what happened between you and Javier and I respect that. But can I have your word that you will not provoke Javier in any way, if this business between you is still unresolved?"

"You have absolutely nothing to worry about, Samuel. The interview will be perfect and when we are finished the hosts will be frustrated because they still know nothing. Antoine's story is the most fascinating anyway. Let him do all the talking." Lars stretched his long legs out in front of him and leaned back against the seat.

Samuel seemed satisfied with Lars' answer and spent the rest of the ride to the studio telling them about some of the other appearances he had tentatively scheduled for them.

When they arrived at the studio, Javier was already there signing autographs for staff members and fans who waited outside the studio every day to catch a glimpse of upcoming guests.

They waved good-bye to the fans on the street and entered the studio where Antoine and Andrew each embraced Javier in turn. Javier shook Samuel's hand and then turned to Lars. The others stood silently holding their collective breath as they waited to see how Lars and Javier would be in each other's presence.

"Lars…" Javier spoke first. He held out his hand to shake Lars' but Lars by-passed his hand and pulled him into his arms and hugged him hard. They stood like that for a moment, patting each other's backs and then pulled apart. Lars was silent, his face red.

"Good to see you, man," said Javier.

"You, too. Can we speak a moment in private?" Lars asked. He looked around the lobby and motioned for Javier to join him in the far corner near a potted plant.

Javier followed him over and made a joke about there being a hidden microphone in the plant.

"It's OK. They won't get much. Just my apology to you if you will accept it for my childish behavior…?" His question hung in the air.

"Of course," Javier clapped Lars on the back. "I'm sorry, too. We'll talk later when this is over. It'll be alright." He smiled and they walked into the studio where they met the hosts and then had their make-up done for the cameras.

A little over an hour later the interview was over and Lars had been right. The hosts got very little information and were both a little flustered at Les Passionistes' refusal to answer personal questions. Antoine kept them laughing with his cutting remarks about his love life or lack thereof, causing Samuel to roll his eyes on occasion. He was watching the interview from the side of the stage ready to call a halt to it should any topics get too personal. When they finished, the men posed for some still shots that the show would use in its advertising and then they left in the limo for the studio. Colin was there with lunch for them from the Italian restaurant that operated across the street.

They ate spaghetti and salad and then relaxed while the studio musicians finished warming up for the run-through of their repertoire. Since they had a few minutes to spare, Javier asked Lars to join him in the back of the building where they kept supplies and instruments. Andrew and Antoine decided to go out back to shoot baskets in the basketball hoop that management had erected for them while they waited to start rehearsing.

Lars and Javier walked back to the storage area and sat on folding chairs. Lars waited for Javier to speak first.

"Is everything OK with you?" he asked, trying to gauge how to talk to Lars, not sure what mood Lars was in.

"Everything is great. How about with you?" he asked, his voice quiet.

"Good, thanks. I've missed you guys." Javier genuinely had missed them, their camaraderie and the music they made together.

"Yes. It is very good to be back." He looked at Javier and asked the question uppermost on his mind. "How is Antonia? Is she still on the island?"

"She's fine. No, she went back to New York yesterday." Javier waited, expecting Lars to ask more questions about her. He debated telling him that he wanted to marry her but decided that that was more information than Lars needed to know right now. They didn't get a chance to talk further—the musicians were ready to begin rehearsing.

Andrew and Antoine came through the studio and they all went to the main room where they were to practice. Samuel listened in the control room as they sang through their entire album. They sounded great for the most part except for each of them having their moment of forgetfulness on some of the songs that were in languages other than their own, which for Lars and Antoine was every song. They laughed at this and the levity relaxed them all greatly. They took a few moments to study the music and a couple of hours later they sounded perfect, just as Samuel knew they would.

When they broke for the day, Samuel asked them to be back in the studio tomorrow to go over the schedule for the remainder of the year.

"Anybody want to go to the pub for a pint?" asked Andrew.

"You're sounding more like a native every day," laughed Javier.

"What can I say? Technically, England is my mother country," Andrew joked.

All four agreed to go for drinks and Andrew was happy that Lars and Javier seemed to be OK with each other. He and Antoine were both dying to get more details about what had happened and hoped that if they loosened their tongues with some ale, they could get more out of them. But that tactic didn't work. Lars had exactly one beer and then said he had to get home. He said good-bye and left the pub abruptly.

"For fuck's sake," said Antoine to Javier after Lars left. "What the hell is going on?"

"We had a misunderstanding. That is all. It's fine now." He sipped his beer and helped himself to some peanuts from the wooden bowl on their table.

"Give us a break, man," said Andrew. "We're all in this together. When something happens to one of us, it affects us all. Now give us more information or I might throw a fit and tear this place up with my bare hands," he teased.

"And I might pinch that cute, blonde waitress's tight ass when she brings us more beer. I'm famous for that you know," said Antoine proudly, nodding at the girl taking orders at a nearby table. "Now tell us who this American girl is."

"Right…" said Javier a little reluctantly. He told them about meeting Antonia at the house unaware that his father had promised her the place at the same time that he had promised it to Lars. He told them that by the time Lars arrived on the island, he and Antonia had become close but then he was called away to Madrid and Lars stayed with Antonia on the island. When he returned a few days later he could sense that something had developed between them and it had bothered him. So he and Lars had a talk and it unfortunately got out of hand and a tabloid photographer had caught it all on celluloid. Lars left the island and he and Antonia resumed their relationship, which was now quite serious.

"So this girl just goes back and forth between you two like a yo-yo?" asked Andrew, fascinated by the story.

"Are you demeaning the character of a woman you do not know?" asked Javier with irritation.

"God, no! I didn't mean anything by that. I'm sorry," said Andrew contritely.

"So, how serious is it with you and this Antonia?" asked Antoine, also captivated by the story.

"Very. We have even discussed marriage," Javier responded.

"Holy shit," breathed Andrew. "Is this going to be a problem for Lars? Does he know about this?"

"He has no idea and I want it to remain that way until I am ready to tell him. Is that understood?" Javier was not playing around and he wanted to make sure they got the message.

"Our lips are sealed," they agreed looking at each other warily.

They finished their drinks and went their separate ways. When Javier returned to his flat, he called Antonia. He could tell by the sound of her voice that he had awakened her.

"I'm sorry, *mi amor*. I have disturbed your sleep."

"It's OK. I have to get up anyway. I'm having dinner with my friend Deanna later and I need to get ready. I'm so glad you called."

"How was your flight?" he asked, imagining her lying in her bed and wishing he were there with her now.

"Long and boring," she laughed.

They chatted a while and just before they hung up, Antonia asked about Lars.

"How is Lars? Is everything OK with you two?"

"Everything is fine, *mi querida*. Have a good dinner with your friend. I love you and miss you. We'll be getting our schedule tomorrow and I am fairly sure we're coming to New York soon for some appearances and interviews before we go back into the studio. I cannot wait to be with you again and see you in your natural habitat." His voice was sensual and sexy and she hugged her pillow to her breast as he spoke.

"You make me sound like an animal," she laughed.

"Oh, but you are and I cannot wait to tame you again," he said teasingly.

They said their good-byes and then Javier went to take a shower. It would be difficult to sleep tonight after hearing her voice but he was exhausted and needed the rest no matter how hard it was to come by. He tossed and turned and finally after midnight he settled into a restless sleep.

* * * *

Deanna could barely contain herself. She had arrived at Antonia's apartment with a bag full of Chinese take-out, a vanilla cheesecake and a bottle of wine and was ready to hear everything that had happened during the past couple of weeks. But Antonia was having an inordinately long conversation on the phone with her father who was concerned about the stories and pictures he'd seen in the papers and on the Internet. Deanna heard Antonia tell her father that everything was fine and she would have a full explanation tomorrow at the office. Finally Antonia hung up and came into the living room where Deanna had set up their dinner on the coffee table.

"Tell me everything!" Deanna fairly screeched, she was so excited.

"Oh, my god, Dee. I don't even know where to begin. You have no idea. It has been the most surreal time of my life." Antonia sighed as she settled herself on the floor and reached for an egg roll.

"Start at the beginning and don't leave anything out," Deanna, said, pouring them each a glass of wine.

So Antonia started from the moment she arrived on the island and told Deanna how she had met Javier on the beach. She told her how she had been attracted to Javier but reluctant to trust him considering the reputation Spanish men have about conquering women and loving and leaving them.

"Hell, Antonia, all men are like that, not just Spanish men," interrupted Deanna.

"Still…" Antonia laughed. "I was afraid, though I'm not sure of what." She continued with the story and told Deanna about Lars' arrival and then Javier's sudden departure and being alone with Lars and how sexy he was.

"So, let me get this straight. You somehow managed to resist the Spanish god only to fall under the spell of the Swiss hottie? Explain that one to me."

"I was so attracted to Lars. Deanna, you have no idea how hot he is—his hair and his eyes and his hands and oh, my god…" Antonia leaned back against the sofa and closed her eyes. "There was this instant attraction and I don't know if Javier had loosened me up or what to make me more susceptible to Lars but I really wanted…" she stopped suddenly, feeling embarrassed and a little sad.

"What?" Deanna asked breathlessly.

"We would have crossed the line if we had had protection. I know we would have." She took a sip of her wine and thought back to that night with Lars. She remembered how tender he had been and how masterful he had been with his hands. Goose bumps rose on her arms and she rubbed the chill away with her hands.

"So you didn't…with Lars?" asked Deanna.

"Not that, no. And then Javier came back and there was this weird tension in the air and they fought on the beach and, well, you saw the pictures…" her voice trailed off.

"Hell, the whole fucking world saw the pictures," Deanna laughed.

"I know. That was so bizarre. Anyway, then Lars left and I was alone with Javier again and he just plowed his way right in. Into my mind, into my heart, into my…" She covered her face with her hands and shook her head in disbelief.

"*Wow,*" Deanna sighed. "I mean, *wow*. So you guys…?"

Antonia looked up and nodded.

"Oh, my god. How was it? *I. Have. To. Know.*" She spat out the words staccato-style.

Antonia's face reddened and her breathing changed dramatically. Deanna's mouth fell open in astonishment.

"Oh, my god. It was that good?" This was too much. Deanna thought she was going to have a stroke.

"You have no idea, Dee," was all Antonia managed to get out. She grabbed a pillow from the sofa and hugged it to her chest. "And then he mentioned marriage."

Deanna fell over in a heap on the floor.

"I. Cannot. Believe. This."

Antonia couldn't help but laugh at Deanna's reaction. Deanna pushed herself back up into a sitting position and drained her glass of wine in one gulp.

"It's all true," whispered Antonia.

"Are you going to marry him?" asked Deanna still in shock. She glanced down at Antonia's left hand and saw the turquoise ring. She grabbed Antonia's hand for a closer inspection.

"I have no idea," said Antonia, showing her the ring. "He got me this and said he wanted to replace it with a diamond."

"Wow."

"But now I wonder if we weren't just caught up in the moment. Now that he's back home in London he'll probably forget all about me. People say all kinds of crazy things in the heat of passion." Antonia hoped she was wrong but she was starting to think that the whole Isla Marta trip had been some sort of weird dream—that it couldn't have been real. Things like that just didn't happen to her.

"Can you forget about him?" asked Deanna quietly.

"No way," Antonia didn't have to think about her answer.

"What about Lars? Can you forget about him?"

Antonia hesitated, thinking of Lars' beautiful face, his hands and his silky black hair.

"No," she said.

"Are you in love with both of them?" asked Deanna.

"I thought so at first. But I don't think it's possible to be in love with two people at the same time. Somehow that defies the laws of nature." Antonia had considered this before—loving two men at once—but it was just too mind-boggling.

"Ask yourself this question," said Deanna, her voice taking on a therapist's rationale. "Can you live without them and have a normal life like the one you had before you met them? Think about them individually and tell me what you think."

Antonia thought about Lars. She had wanted him to make love with her, there was no doubt about that. And he had wanted her, too, she was also sure about that. But he had backed down so easily out of loyalty to Javier, and while that was admirable, what had that said about his feelings for her? And then he had left without even saying good-bye to her. Then she thought about Javier. He had been so gentle and patient with her and also with Lars in spite of the nasty fight on the beach. Thinking about Javier now made her realize that in every way that mattered, he was perfect. She had her answer to Deanna's question.

"No."

Deanna waited for her to elaborate but Antonia remained silent, her face pensive. Antonia felt tears churning and she didn't try to stop them. Deanna scooted over to her and put her arm around her friend and held her.

"Which one can't you live without?" She was almost afraid to hear the answer.

"It's Javier. And if I don't see him again soon, I'll go mad."

She sobbed into Deanna's shoulder and after awhile, when the Kleenex box was empty, they had some cheesecake and then Deanna had to go.

"Sean will be home soon. He had a late shift at the airport." She helped Antonia clear up their dinner dishes and fixed a doggie bag for Sean.

"When do you think you'll see him again?" Deanna asked at the door as she was preparing to leave.

"I'm not sure. He's going to call me with his schedule. He thinks they're coming to New York soon."

"Good then. In the mean time you'll just have to keep busy and try not to think too much—about *anything*." Deanna laughed and hugged Antonia.

But alone with her thoughts in her apartment, it was impossible not to see Javier's face in her mind, hear his voice in her ear, or wish that they were together. She tried to concentrate on some work, knowing that she would be swamped at the office tomorrow, but it was impossible. Between listening to her Les Passionistes CD over and over and studying their web-site, she was making herself crazy. She looked at the time in the lower right-hand corner of her computer, noting that it was the middle of the night in London. Javier was probably asleep. *Is he dreaming about me*? she wondered as she shut her computer down and went to get ready for bed. She tossed and turned all night, holding her pillow tightly to her chest, thinking of Javier, imagining a life with him—a home and children. It seemed too much to hope for. Just too perfect.

* * * *

Indeed, Javier was dreaming about Antonia. And in the morning he was anxious to get to the studio to see the new schedule so he could make plans to be with her again. He jumped in his Jaguar and raced to the studio, his mind wandering as he drove. He forgot where he was, making a left turn into the wrong lane and was startled into alertness by a swerving Mercedes, its driver honking his horn and gesticulating profanely at Javier.

"Damn it!" he cursed himself. He moved back into his own lane, his heart racing, adrenaline coursing through his veins. He had to concentrate and remember that he was in England now where they drove on the other side of the road—the *wrong* side as far as he was concerned. By the time he arrived at the studio his heart rate was steady again, his blood pressure returning to normal.

He was the first of the group to get there and waited for them in the lounge. Colin was already there, making coffee, and they chatted while they waited for everyone to arrive.

Andrew and Antoine arrived together, both in boisterous moods, ready to rehearse. The three of them talked about the material for the new album, which they had been looking over while they waited for Lars who was now quite late. Samuel had also arrived and was anxious to go over their schedule so that he could let them get to their music.

"Colin, would you please call Lars and see if he has overslept?" said Samuel, torn between annoyance and concern.

Colin went into the office to make the call but before he had a chance to dial the first number, Lars walked in, looking like he had not slept all night. His long hair was tousled, his clothes wrinkled and his voice low and gravelly when he said good morning to them.

"Whoa. You look rough, man," said Andrew. "Hard night?"

"My night was just fine, thank you for asking," grumbled Lars. "Sorry I'm late."

"That's fine," said Samuel. "We're just glad you're here." He noted Lars' disheveled appearance, exchanging glances with Colin who looked concerned. He handed them each a copy of the new itinerary and got down to business.

"I realize that you all expected to have the entire month of October to yourselves, but in light of certain events, I felt it better that you return to work early.

Your rehearsal yesterday was brilliant and I know today will be the same. The four of you always give one hundred and ten percent of yourselves every time you perform, and we appreciate that. Now, I have scheduled these appearances and interviews for the next couple of weeks so that we can get Les Passionistes back into the public eye and let the world see that you are four strong, that you are a tight-knit group and that all of the scandals of late have not harmed your reputation in any way. Also please note that you will prepare for the next album here in London during November and when we have narrowed the song selection to a manageable twenty or so we will be heading to the Stockholm studio for some of the recording. If there are any conflicts please tell me now so that we can make the necessary adjustments."

Javier looked at the printout of upcoming appearances and let out a slow sigh of relief when he saw the two New York events: *Good Morning America* next Thursday and *The View* on Friday. They were also scheduled to appear on *The Ellen DeGeneres Show* in Los Angeles the Monday after the New York appearances. Then they were to be back in Europe for an appearance in Germany for a benefit concert and then home to London by the second week of November. Plus Samuel had set up another interview for this Saturday afternoon with *Now!* magazine and a performance at Sunday's Party in the Park at Hyde Park.

"When do we leave for New York?" Javier asked Samuel.

"Wednesday morning. Colin has been making the travel arrangements. Is that OK for you?" he asked Javier.

"Can't we go sooner?" he asked. He looked at Lars' stony expression and wished he had kept his mouth shut.

"If you would like to go ahead of the others, Javier, by all means, you can do that. But you're scheduled for rehearsals here all day Monday."

"Fine. Then I will make my own arrangements to leave after rehearsal and I will meet the others there."

"Colin will take care of that for you. Just let him know where you'll be in New York so he can send a car for you to get you to the ABC television studio in time to practice before your performance."

Antoine and Andrew had been watching Samuel and Javier as they talked, their heads moving back and forth as if watching a tennis match. And they did not fail to notice that Lars was looking anywhere but at Samuel and Javier. On the contrary he appeared to be studying the schedule as if it held the key to a hidden treasure.

"Can we sing now?" Lars suddenly came to life, summing up energy from somewhere inside his tired body.

"By all means," said Samuel. "I'm anxious to hear you."

They went into the room where they performed and began to warm up with the musicians. They also used taped instrumentals but Samuel preferred live musicians whenever possible. For the next couple of hours they worked on their more difficult pieces until finally Samuel asked them to sing "Surrender to Me."

"It's Melina's favorite." He smiled as Antoine rolled his eyes.

"It seems to be everyone's favorite," muttered Lars, glancing at Javier as he spoke.

Andrew and Antoine looked at each, their eyebrows raised but they didn't speak. Javier ignored him and they began to sing. When they finished Samuel clapped his hands loudly, shaking his head in amazement.

"That is an excellent song. Why have we not released that as a single yet?" he asked no one in particular. He turned to Colin. "We need to get that released pronto. I can see many men proposing to their girlfriends to that song and just in time for the Christmas holidays."

Lars had had enough—enough practicing, enough togetherness, enough of everything.

"I have to go, guys. I have a headache," he said, looking at Andrew and Antoine who just shrugged, not sure what to say. They doubted the headache story but clearly Lars didn't want to be here a moment longer.

"Fine. Go home and relax, Lars. I'll see you all back here tomorrow—take the rest of the day off. Good work, guys." Samuel bid them a good afternoon and Lars disappeared instantly out the door.

"What the hell is wrong with him?" asked Andrew.

"I don't know, but I would suggest that Javier find out as soon as possible," said Samuel, standing by the door, his hands in his pockets.

"I intend to do that," said Javier. "*Hasta mañana.*" He dashed out the door after Lars and ran after him, catching up to him as he stood on the corner waiting for the light to change.

"Lars!" Javier grabbed his arm to prevent him from crossing the street. "Wait. We need to talk."

"We have nothing to talk about, Javier," said Lars, shaking off Javier's hand from his arm.

"Please, Lars. I thought everything was fine between us but I can see that something is bothering you and I want to work it out. I know it's because of me that you are feeling this way. Please, come to my apartment for lunch. We can get some food on the way and then talk things over. I *want* to talk to you."

Lars looked at Javier and saw the earnestness in his eyes. It wouldn't kill him to talk. Maybe it would even help, though that seemed highly doubtful. Reluctantly, he agreed.

"Fine. You're buying, I assume?" he managed a grin.

"*Por supuesto.* Oh, I forgot. You don't speak Spanish. Of course," he smiled and clapped Lars on the back. They walked back to Javier's car and drove to his place in Notting Hill. He stopped at the Indian restaurant up the street from his apartment and ordered their lunch and then they went on to his flat. Once inside, Javier got them both beers and set out plates, napkins and silverware. When they had the edge off of their appetites and had made small talk about their families, Javier broached the subject of Antonia.

"Lars, we need to talk about Antonia. Can you do that without getting angry and punching me out?" Javier tried to make a joke of it.

"Why do you think I would punch you? We can talk about anything you like. Andrew's the violent one, remember?" he forced a laugh.

Javier grinned and felt himself relax. Maybe this wouldn't be so bad after all. Lars' mood seemed to be lightening. He sensed everything would be fine.

"I want you to know what is happening with Antonia and me before you hear it some other way." He said the words quietly hoping to soften the blow.

Lars' face showed no change. He simply looked at Javier and waited for him to continue.

"I am in love with her but then, I think you already know that, yes?" he asked.

"I figured as much. That's great, Javier. I'm happy for you." Lars' voice continued to remain even, showing little emotion.

"Thank you." Javier sipped from his beer mug, feeling the need to do something with his hands.

"She feels the same way, I assume?" Lars pushed his plate away and leaned back in the chair.

"Yes. We have even talked of marriage though I have not officially proposed." He held his breath, fearing the worst.

"Marriage already. Wow. That is big news," said Lars. He let the words sink in, trying to assess how he felt about this revelation.

"Yes. When we are in New York I plan to ask her to be my wife. When something is so perfect, there is no need to wait for the passage of time for appearance's sake. I love her. And I want to know if I have your blessing. It would mean the world to me." Javier's voice dropped. His muscles tensed as he waited to hear Lars' answer.

Lars got up from the table and walked to the kitchen window. He looked out on the back patio, staring at everything but seeing nothing. He felt a knot in his stomach and it angered him at how Javier's words were affecting him. He shouldn't care about this. It shouldn't matter that Javier loved Antonia. It shouldn't matter that he wanted to marry her. None of this should matter. He didn't know how to respond.

Javier sat at the table waiting. He had the sense that this moment could spell the end of their friendship and he prayed fervently that that would not be the case.

Finally Lars turned from the window and looked down at Javier. He stood with his hands in his pockets and formulated words in his mind. But before he could say anything, the moment was interrupted by the ringing of the phone. It made them both jump.

"Excuse me," said Javier. "I'll take care of this quickly." He picked up the extension by the refrigerator and said hello.

Lars turned his attention back to the patio and listened to Javier's conversation.

A few minutes later, Javier hung up and cleared his throat. Lars turned back to him and waited.

"That was my mother. My father is to have a test at the hospital on Tuesday and she wants me to come for it. It is mostly routine and they are expecting no surprises but she really wants me there. I will still make it to New York on time for our performance Thursday morning and I will let Samuel know about my change in travel plans. It shouldn't be a problem."

"Of course it won't. Your family should come first. I hope the test is a success." Lars' words were heartfelt and sincere and Javier knew that he meant them.

Javier wanted to steer the conversation back to Antonia but now it felt awkward. The phone call had interrupted his train of thought but Lars took care of it for him.

"Listen, Javier. I'm going to get out of here. I need to get home and pay some bills. I wish you nothing but happiness." Suddenly Lars could not wait to get out of Javier's apartment and back to his own. "Thanks for lunch. I'll see you later."

Lars' departure was so abrupt that it left Javier stunned and frustrated. He wanted to stop him but couldn't think of what to say. He had not even had a chance to say good-bye. And he wanted to offer him a ride home but Lars was already hailing a taxi when Javier got to the door.

Alone in his apartment, Javier thought about what had just happened. Lars may have wished him well but he did not feel that he had his true blessing. He felt unsettled as he cleaned up the kitchen. He glanced at the clock and decided he would call Antonia. She would probably be at work now. He would feel better once he heard her voice.

CHAPTER 14

"Call for you," Carly said to Antonia. She was at her desk looking at the photos from her trip, selecting the ones that might work for the article.

She picked up her extension and was thrilled to hear Javier's voice on the line.

"Hi," she said breathlessly, turning her back to Carly who was suddenly hovering in the doorway, shuffling a sheaf of papers in her hands.

"*Mi amor.* How are you?" Javier asked, his voice low and sexy.

"I'm fine—very busy. How are you?" She felt a giddiness wash over her, her cheeks turning crimson just from the sound of his voice.

"Busy as well. And I have good news." He told her about the upcoming trip to New York for the television appearances. "But first I must go to Madrid to be with my father for a test he will have Tuesday. It is a routine test and everything is expected to go well. My mother wants me to be there more because I think she misses me than that she really needs me there. You know how mothers are," he laughed.

"Of course. So you'll be here Wednesday?" Antonia asked excitedly.

"If all goes well I plan to get the last flight out of Madrid Tuesday and I will arrive sometime Wednesday morning. How does that sound to you?"

"That sounds too good to be true," she said, smiling to herself. She glanced over her shoulder and saw that Carly had given up trying to eavesdrop and had gone back to her office. "Should I meet you at the airport?"

"No. I will take a taxi to your apartment. It will still be dark when I arrive because of the time difference. I cannot wait to see you again, *mi querida.*"

"Me, too." The thought of seeing Javier again was enough to make Antonia burst through her skin. She made sure he had her address and cell phone number and told him she would wait up for him.

"It will be quite late when I land, maybe after midnight," he reminded her.

"I don't care. I can't wait to see you," she sighed.

They finished their conversation and both reluctantly hung up, hating to sever the connection between them. Antonia floated around on a cloud the rest of the day, barely able to get anything done including gathering notes for her pop culture column which she had put off way too long and now the deadline was fast approaching. Her father stopped down to see her before she went home for the day and commented on her glow.

"You've been glowing all day, sweetheart. And I'm not talking about your tan. We didn't get a chance to talk earlier because I was in meetings with advertising off and on all day but I really want to hear everything. Why don't you come for dinner with your mother and me tonight and fill us in? We want an explanation for the pictures anyway."

Antonia wasn't in the mood for a family dinner but she knew she should go and answer their questions about the photos of her and Javier and Lars. She hesitantly agreed on the condition that they make it an early dinner.

"I still have jetlag," she grinned at her father.

"Alright. Let's go to Michaelangelo's at six. How does that sound?"

"Good." Antonia waved to her dad and went back to staring at the photos. It was all she could do to make herself work but eventually she had a good selection of pictures and a start on her column. At five thirty she joined her dad and together they walked the six blocks to the restaurant where her mother would join them and she would be subjected to their questioning. *This will give a whole new meaning to the term Spanish Inquisition,* she thought, laughing to herself as they entered the restaurant.

* * * *

Lars hung up the phone, thanking Colin for making the change to his itinerary. He paced around his apartment, suddenly feeling energetic and in need of a physical diversion. He changed into sweats and an old T-shirt, thinking that a run would do him a world of good. He was just about to head out the door when the phone rang. It was Katarina.

"Lars…hi," she said softly in his ear.

Lars closed his eyes, feeling the pent-up energy ebbing out of his pores. He sighed and said hello.

"How are you?" he asked, hoping this would be over quickly.

"I'm fine, thanks. I saw those pictures of you and Javier and that American girl. She's the one, isn't she?" Katarina's voice was matter-of-fact and sure.

"Why do you keep doing this, Katarina?" Lars sighed, trying to mask his exasperation and knowing he wasn't doing a good job of it.

"I'm not doing anything, damn it. Don't I have a right to know, Lars? You think you can be with me for as long as we were together and just suddenly throw it all away in one moment because you met someone else?" He could hear the tears in her voice.

"I told you before that I met her *after* we broke up. That is the truth. Why can't you let this go and get on with your life? I care about you and want the best for you but the best for you is not me. Now, please, Kat, let this go." He paced around the living room feeling desperate to get off the phone and get outside where he could breathe.

"You'll never be rid of me, Lars. Ever. I'm going to marry Frederick."

Her words sent him reeling. He leaned up against the front door and shook his head in disbelief.

"No, you're not. You don't love him. You're doing this to get at me. For the love of God, I don't know why, but you are. Why would you want to hurt Frederick by marrying him when you know you don't love him?" Lars had to make her see the foolishness of her words—his brother's happiness depended on it.

He heard the tears in her voice, more pronounced now as she struggled to catch her breath.

"Because he's as close as I can get to you," she whispered, her voice choking on a sob.

His heart went out to her. Who was he to judge her behavior when he knew what it was like to want someone he couldn't have? But still, his brother was a decent and kind man who deserved to be loved for himself and not as a substitute for someone else. He had to make her see that hurting Frederick wasn't the answer.

"Kat, listen to me," he said, his voice as patient and kind as he could make it. "Please don't hurt Frederick. The only thing he has ever done is to love you. Please don't marry him to get back at me. If you do, eventually he'll find out the truth and it will crush him. Do you care about him at all?"

"Of course, I do. And I love him, too, though in a different way than I love you. But anyway, it's too late now, Lars." She sounded calmer now, more in control of her emotions. Her change in tone scared Lars. He was afraid of what she would say next.

"What do you mean, it's too late now?" he asked, holding his breath, his muscles tensing.

"He asked me last night to marry him and I said yes. We're flying to Gibraltar next weekend to get married."

Lars was stunned. This couldn't be. Had Frederick lost his mind? He wanted to punch the wall, kick the door, anything to release the rage building inside of him.

"Don't do this, Katarina. You don't love him. This is wrong."

"I have to. He's as close as I'll ever get to you." She sounded resigned and her words pierced him.

"Listen to me, Kat. If you do this—if you marry my brother—if you hurt Frederick, I will never forgive you. I will loathe you for the rest of my life. Is that what you want?"

"At least it's something besides this indifference you suddenly have for me," she spat out the words. "You've changed so much. What has made you so cold, Lars?" She would have continued speaking her criticisms but Lars stopped her.

"Then why would you love me if I'm so bad? Now I'm done with this conversation. I have some place I need to be. And Katarina, one more thing…if you really care about me so much, then please don't marry Frederick out of spite for me. You're a good and kind person and I know you don't want to hurt him. Please don't do this.

"Wait, Lars. Please, I love you. Don't hang up," she begged, crying loudly now.

"I have to go. Good-bye." Lars clicked off the phone in disgust and slid against the front door down to the floor. He sat with his head resting on his knees for a few moments, then he called Urs in Lucerne.

* * * *

Her words stunned him to the core. He stood in the foyer his heart beating fast, adrenaline racing through his veins. He had come over to surprise her with flowers, letting himself in the front door with the key he had had for years and never thought to return. And now he stood here with the purple tulips and the red roses in his hand, hearing the words that he should have already known. He shouldn't be so surprised. But still the truth hurt and he realized it had been a long time coming.

Katarina walked around the corner and saw Frederick standing by the door with the flowers in his hand. His face was ashen, his lips pressed together in anger. She gasped at the sight of him.

"Frederick," she whispered, coming toward him, her face red, her stomach on fire with fear. "How long have you been here?"

"Long enough to finally see through you. I brought you flowers." He dropped them on the floor at her feet and moved toward the door.

"Frederick, wait. I don't know what you heard but I can explain," she reached for his arm but he shook off her hand.

"I don't need any explanation, Katarina. This is not meant to be. Obviously it never was. Not with Lars and not with me. And don't get any ideas about getting Urs. He's smarter than that. Smarter than I am—or was—until now. Lars is right. You need to find a way to let go and move on." He opened the door and left without a backward glance.

Katarina slammed the door shut and crumpled to the floor in a ball. She sobbed until she made herself sick. And in the midst of her breakdown she realized that Frederick was right—she needed to let them go and move on. Sensing she needed help, she called her mother. She pulled the flowers to her face and breathed in their scent. She was still there on the floor ten minutes later when her mother walked through the door.

* * * *

Colin stared at the phone trying to decide if he should alert Samuel to the news that Lars had changed his flight plans to leave ahead of the other members of Les Passionistes, except for Javier who would now be leaving from Madrid after seeing his family Tuesday. Twice he started to dial Samuel's cell phone number, both times stopping himself for fear of provoking Samuel's ire at being interrupted at his massage appointment. Samuel's massages and various aesthetics appointments were sacred and he did not appreciate having them disturbed. He finally convinced himself that Lars was probably telling the truth when he said he wanted to go early to have more time to get over the jetlag that always seemed to affect him more than the other members of the group. He couldn't possibly be going early for any reasons connected to that American girl. He had assured everyone that that situation had been dealt with and there was no reason not to believe him. So Colin turned off the lights, locked the office door and headed home, feeling confident that all would be well in the end.

* * * *

The members of Les Passionistes were swamped the entire weekend. They were interviewed by a journalist for *Now!* magazine and had to endure one ridiculous question after another, not to mention a photo shoot that Antoine felt went on far too long. He was very anxious to get it over with because, as he put it, he had hot action lined up for the night.

"Who's the lucky girl?" asked Javier as the four of them climbed inside the limo that would take them back to the studio where they were to have a meeting with Samuel.

"A lovely French girl I met at the Spirit Club a couple of days ago. She is *fine*," he smiled proudly as he leaned back against the cool leather seat of the limo.

"Going back to your own kind, are you, Antoine?" teased Andrew.

"I have decided that I cannot dismiss an entire country full of beautiful women just because one among them had the stupidity to give up the best thing she ever had." He closed his eyes and sighed contentedly.

The others laughed at his complete acceptance of his own appeal—however he perceived it to be on any given day. They chatted easily among themselves for most of the ride back to the studio though Lars was quiet as usual and he and Javier did not talk much to each other along the way. Andrew watched them both, feeling the tension in the air that lately seemed to be present when the two of them were together in a confined area. For the first time since they had returned from their vacation, he had a sense that Les Passionistes were losing their innocence, that they were in danger of harming the best thing that ever had happened to them professionally. He looked at Javier who now sat quietly by the window lost in his thoughts and at Lars staring at the passing scenery. He became reflective about his band-mates. Javier, the romantic singer, was the oldest of the group and their unofficial leader, and always seemed to feel things more deeply than the others. He had said on more than one occasion that he was ready to meet the woman of his dreams and settle down and have a family. And Antoine, the modern singer and happy-go-lucky one, who masked his insecurities behind his sense of humor. And Lars, the traditional singer, who was quiet and reflective, often seeming to be millions of miles away. Andrew stifled a chuckle, thinking that his own life seemed relatively simple compared to theirs in spite of the fact that Jenna had dumped him so unceremoniously recently, but it hadn't hurt too badly. As the classical singer of the group, he was more in love with his career than a woman anyway. *These deep European types*, he thought, suppressing a smile. *They need to lighten up*.

At the studio they had a practice session with Samuel observing them. He felt they sounded a little off this afternoon but resisted criticizing them too much, knowing that even when Les Passionistes were 'off' they were still better than any other singers in the world. He told them he would see them the next day for warm-ups before their performance at the Party in the Park and then they went their separate ways. Colin usually locked up the offices after a practice session but he was at a family wedding and Samuel had let the other producers and secretary go home when the session ended. He sat in the studio and played back the last song that Les Passionistes had just rehearsed. It was a song that they didn't sing much at events—a very beautiful and eerie song about lost love. At least that's what Samuel thought it was about considering it was in Italian and he didn't know much Italian. The song was called "*Mia Tristezza*" which he knew meant "my sadness." He hoped his guys were all right and just experiencing growing pains associated with sudden fame and talents nearly too big to contain. He was glad he didn't have that burden. And he was even happier that they would be back in London and also Sweden soon recording. When they started work on the new album they would come back into their own—get the excitement back. He wouldn't let them peak too soon.

* * * *

Javier finished packing and waited for the taxi to take him to the airport. He was anxious to get to Madrid to see his family but more than that he couldn't wait to get to New York. He thought back to the phone conversation he'd had with Antonia very early this morning. It had been the middle of the night in New York when he had called her. He'd apologized for waking her but he had needed to hear her voice. They'd had a very sexy chat that had sent him straight for a cold shower when they'd hung up and now he was ready to get going and take care of his business so he could get to her. He heard a car horn honk and grabbed his bags and ran to catch his cab. He had only one more day to get through and finally he would see her again.

* * * *

The flight attendant handed Lars a small bottle of whisky and a Coke. He fixed the drink to his liking and ate a couple of the pretzels from the small bag.

He was relieved to finally be on the plane so he could relax. He hoped he would be able to sleep some on this flight but it was doubtful. They had performed beautifully at the Party in the Park on Sunday and had spent all of Monday in rehearsal and now he finally felt like he could concentrate on the matter at hand. He knew he had no guarantees or expectations about what would happen in New York but he needed to see Antonia. She had been on his mind continually since he returned from Isla Marta, though he'd tried to act as if he didn't have a care in the world, especially around Javier. The one thought that he had to force out of his head constantly was that he was experiencing what Katarina was going through but in a different way. He had a history with Katarina and he recognized that that had made the break-up more painful for her, but he also believed that his short time with Antonia on the island had impacted his future to the extent that it was now in limbo. He tried not to think about Javier when he thought of Antonia and it irritated him to no end that that was becoming nearly impossible. He was going to New York to get one of two things: Antonia or closure. And when it was all said and done, Antonia would know exactly how he felt about her and he would know how she felt about him. Only then could he get on with his life.

* * * *

"You look great, Father," said Javier, sliding his arm around his father's shoulders as they walked among the fragrant orange trees. "Good as new, I would say."

"I feel great, too, son. I can't believe your mother called you to come all the way down here from London just for my little test, which was perfect as I knew it would be." Juan tapped on the trunk of a tree and looked up into the leafy branches.

"It's fine. I'm glad to be here. But you know I'm heading to New York later tonight. I hope that's OK…?" His voice trailed off as guilt seeped into his conscience.

"Of course. Your mother told me about Antonia. She said you two talked while I was having my heart checked. I'm thrilled that you and Ted's daughter have hit it off like this. I've never met her but he is a good man and his daughter must be very special as well."

"She is. So special that I plan to ask her to marry me." Javier hoped this news wouldn't cause his father to have another heart attack considering he hadn't even known Antonia a whole month yet.

"Well, son, you know that I knew your mother exactly five weeks, three days and four hours before we were married, so I am a big supporter of short engagements," Juan laughed. "If you're sure and she's sure, then I wish you both a long and happy life together. And give me some more grandchildren, will you?"

Javier laughed and squeezed his father close to him as they walked along the orchard, eventually returning to the house where Juan wanted to sit on the veranda and have a glass of juice.

"I would rather have sherry but your mother would never go for that," he grinned at Javier.

"That's right, I wouldn't," said Maria joining them with a tray of grape juice. She sat down and passed around the glasses. Then she turned to Javier, pulling out a small, velvet box from her pocket and handing it to him.

"What is this, Mother?" he asked, taking the box from her.

"When you told me today at the hospital how you felt about Antonia—how serious you are about her—I thought you might like to have this to give to her when you propose. It was your grandmother's. Go ahead, open it."

Javier held his breath as he slowly opened the box. His reaction told Maria that she had done the right thing in giving him the ring.

Javier stared at the ring, a large diamond in platinum setting, with a smaller diamond on either side of the larger one. It was shiny and looked brand new. He was amazed and felt the burning sensation of tears at the backs of his eyes and throat.

"Mother, this is beautiful. It looks brand new." Javier cleared his throat, holding his tears at bay.

"It's such a coincidence that I just had it cleaned with my own rings last week. That must be a sign, don't you think?" she said, smiling.

"It must be," Javier said quietly. "Are you sure, Mother, that you want to give me this?"

"Absolutely. Even though we have not yet met Antonia, I trust your judgment. If you love her, then that's all that matters. Your grandmother—my mother—would love to know that her ring is being taken care of. I only hope it fits."

Javier tried to slip the ring over his own ring finger but it wouldn't budge past the knuckle. He smiled and hugged his mother tightly.

"It'll be perfect," he said, kissing her cheek.

"This calls for a champagne toast," bellowed Juan. "Someone bring on the *Dom Perignon*."

"Hush and drink your grape juice, Juan Garza, and be happy that you can," Maria admonished him lovingly.

They raised their juice glasses in a toast and drank to their collective happiness. And then Juan offered Javier a piece of advice.

"If I were you, son, I'd go to that airport right now and get to New York and put that ring on her finger before some gypsy gets her first." He laughed at his joke and Javier smiled as well, but his father's words unnerved him. An urgency he had not previously felt suddenly washed over him and he realized that his father was right.

"That's a great idea, Father. I really need to get to New York. Do you mind, Mother?" He stood up and looked at his parents.

"Go, my darling. Just promise me that the next time you come home, you will bring Antonia with you."

"I promise, Mama. Thank you for everything. I love you both." Javier hugged and kissed his parents and went inside to call the airline.

Juan took Maria's hand in his and held it tightly, both lost in their own thoughts. A few minutes later, Javier returned and informed them that he had a flight in two hours. He packed excitedly, knowing he would be with her sooner than she expected. She would be so surprised.

* * * *

Lars debated where to see Antonia. He did not know her exact address but he knew that she worked for *Passion* magazine and so that seemed like his best option. But he didn't want to walk into the building and ambush her in her office so he decided he would go inside the building to the information desk and see if he could get her office number and call her from the lobby. He wasn't even sure if she was at work today but he assumed she would be. He paid the cabdriver and stepped out of the taxi, his flight bag over his arm and stood in front of the Taylor Group building where the cabby had told him *Passion* magazine was headquartered. He went through the revolving doors and approached the young redheaded receptionist who had been looking very bored with her job and life in general until Lars suddenly appeared in front of her. He got her attention in a big way.

"May…I…help…you?" She was so flustered at his presence she could barely get the words out. He was fairly certain she did not know who he was—she looked more like the hip-hop type than the opera type—and figured she was reacting to him on a physical level. He decided he would use his charm to his advantage.

"Good afternoon," he said, turning on his German accent full blast. "I'm looking for an old friend who works here and I wondered if you could give me her office number so I could call her from the payphones over there," he said, pointing to the bank of phones near the elevators.

"You can use my phone," she breathed, standing up apparently to get a better look at him.

"Oh, no, I don't want to trouble you. If you could tell me her phone number that would be perfect." He dazzled her with his white smile. She sighed longingly and reached for the company directory, knocking over a metal cup holding pens and pencils. Flustered, she grabbed them before they could roll onto the floor and quickly put them back into the cup. Her face turned bright pink and she sank back into her seat opening the directory.

"What's her name?" she asked, staring at his chest.

"Antonia Taylor," said Lars, trying not to laugh.

"Oh, the boss's daughter. Wow. Hang on a sec." She located the number and offered to connect him there at her extension.

"If you could just write the number down for me, that would be perfect," he said, tiring of this game but finding it good for his ego just the same.

"Sure, OK." She jotted the number down on a little yellow sticky pad and pulled off the top sheet, handing it to him. "Here you go."

Lars made a point of rubbing his fingers against hers as he took the paper from her hand. He gave her a sexy smile and a wink and walked over to the payphones. He quickly dialed Antonia's number, his stomach churning nervously as he listened to it ring several times before going into voicemail. The message said she had left for the day and would return tomorrow.

"Damn it!" he cursed under his breath. He hung up the phone and weighed his options, which were non-existent at this point. He thought a moment and then an idea came to him. He walked back to the receptionist and smiled a dazzling smile that caused her face to redden again.

"It seems that my friend has left for the day. And she gave me her home address but I guess I must have lost it. Would you be able to get the address for me? I would really appreciate it."

The redhead hesitated and looked uncomfortable.

"We're not supposed to give out that kind of private information about the employees. I'm sorry." She shrugged her shoulders and gave him a sad smile.

"I understand, of course. It's just that I have come all this way from Europe and it would be such a waste if I could not see her and say hello. And she will be so mad at me when she finds out that I was here and I did not stop in to see her. I can assure you she won't mind and I cannot tell you how much I would appreciate your help." As he spoke he leaned over the counter to get a little closer to her. He only wished he had put on some more after-shave or cologne after the flight. That probably would have helped his case.

"I don't know..." she said hesitantly, her voice trailing off. "I could get into a lot of trouble..."

"No one will ever know, I promise you. And perhaps the next time I'm in New York you could have coffee with me...or not...?" He hated even saying the words but he had no choice. He needed that address any way he could get it.

"Well, OK. Hang on." She tapped some keys on her keyboard and found the company addresses. She wasn't even supposed to be able to access the addresses but figured out how one day when boredom threatened to put her in an irreversible coma. She scrolled down to the end of the alphabet and located Antonia's address. She grabbed the yellow sticky pad and wrote down the information as well as her own address and phone number, then tore it off and handed it to him, smiling widely at him and batting her obviously fake lashes.

"Here you go. And I wrote my phone number at the bottom...you know...for next time...?" she said coyly.

Lars took the paper and glanced down at where she had written her name and number. He smiled at her again and, because he just could not help himself, he reached over and took her hand and shook it gently. He glanced one more time at the paper and bowed his head to her.

"Thank you, Pamela. You are so kind." He backed away, waving, even forcing himself to look back at her bright and hopeful face as he left the building.

Once outside, he checked the address against the street sign, finding the location on his street map of Manhattan and determined that he didn't have that far to walk and so he set off in the direction of Antonia's apartment building.

* * * *

Antonia had left the office early. There was no point in being there when she couldn't concentrate anyway. She'd called her father and told him that Javier was coming in later that night and she had some errands to run before his arrival. And now she was finished with her errands and anxious to get home so that should could soak in a hot tub and try to calm her nerves and attempt to get rid of the butterflies in her stomach. Just the thought of Javier being here in a few more hours was enough to make her insides quake. She let herself into her apartment, going straight to the phone to check her messages hoping there would be one from Javier. They were all either sales calls or wrong numbers. She turned on the kettle for a cup of tea and while she waited for the water to boil, she ran a hot bath, pouring in a liberal amount of lavender scented bath salts.

The kettle whistled and she ran to the kitchen. As she poured the water into a big mug she caught sight of her Les Passionistes CD on the dining table where she'd left it this morning. She smiled as she added sugar to her mug, then scooped up the CD, taking it to the stereo in the spare bedroom, which she used as an office. She popped the CD into the stereo and turned it up as loudly as she dared without inviting the wrath of the neighbors, then went to the bathroom and undressed. She sank down into the water up to her neck, sighing as the heat washed over her. She sipped her tea slowly savoring the flavor of the chamomile. She felt the tension ebbing from her muscles as the warm bath worked its magic over her. She closed her eyes and sighed. *This is heaven*, she thought, as she let her mind drift away.

The sound of the doorbell, barely audible over the CD snapped her out of her reverie. She jumped, knocking her cup of tea off of the edge of the tub and onto the mat below.

"Damn!" she muttered, pulling herself up out of the water, spilling a ton of it over the side. "Damn!" She cursed again. She stepped out and grabbed the towel from the back of the bathroom door, wrapping it around herself. Quickly she rolled up the soaking mat and shoved it against the wall.

"Who could this be?" she muttered to herself as she sloshed down the hall to the front door. She wasn't expecting anyone unless.... Could it be that Javier had taken an earlier flight to surprise her? *Oh, no! I'm not ready*! she thought, panicking. She had a whole ritual planned involving candles and wine and new lingerie. She stopped at the door and peered through the peephole. She didn't see anyone and thought perhaps whoever had rung the bell had changed his or her mind or had gone to the wrong apartment. Or maybe she had not heard the bell at all and it had just been something she'd heard in the music. Without thinking she opened the door and looked around the hall.

"Hello, Antonia," said Lars. He was leaning against the wall beside her front door. "Do you always answer the door dressed like that?" He turned to her and smiled, his gaze traveling her length, taking in the towel and the water dripping on the floor in a puddle at her feet.

"Lars…," she gasped, pulling the towel tighter around her body. "What are you doing here?" She was stunned. She glanced up and down the empty hall then took a step backward.

"I had to see you," Lars said, his voice low and as sexy as she remembered it. "Can I come in?"

"Of course." Antonia stepped aside and let him in. Her nerves were on edge as she pushed the door shut with her foot and pulled the towel tighter around her damp body. "Please, come into the living room. I need to get dressed. Just make yourself at home. I'll be right back."

Lars walked to the living room and stood by the window looking down at the city. He heard his own voice singing in the apartment and felt a certain irony in the sound. He tried to block out the music as he waited for Antonia to dress.

In her room, Antonia hurriedly slipped on a pair of jeans and a sweatshirt, then quickly ran a brush through her tangled mass of wet hair. Her heart raced as she hurried to get back to the living room, stopping first in the spare room to turn off the CD player.

"Lars?" she said his name quietly. He turned from the window and looked at her, wanting to cross the room and take her in his arms and hold her. He had not even realized until this moment how very much he had missed her. He wanted to touch her hair and her face and kiss her lips and her breasts and every part of her. But he stood by the window with his hands in his pockets, his flight bag on the floor at his feet, and looked into her eyes.

"I'm sorry for just showing up like this, Antonia, but I needed to see you. I've missed you." He said the words softly and it caused a stabbing sensation in her heart.

"I've missed you, too, Lars. How are you?" She wrapped her arms around herself to stave off the shaking sensation she felt inside.

"I'm fine but I'm not either." He ran his hands through his long, black hair and Antonia noticed the dark shadow of his beard along his jaw-line. His eyes locked on hers and he held her gaze as he continued. "I need to talk to you."

Sensing that he was deeply troubled about something, she walked toward him and took his hands and led him to the sofa. They sat down together and she asked him to explain.

"What is it, Lars?" she asked softly, fearing his words, yet needing to hear what he had to say as much as he needed to say it.

He held her hands tightly in his and leaned toward her. They were so close that she could smell his breath against her lips. It smelled of spearmint. He looked into her eyes and spoke quietly.

"Were you ever in love with me at all?"

She took a deep breath and let it out slowly, trying to buy time to find the right words.

"I think I might have been half in love with you, yes…" She looked down at his hands on hers. "I was very attracted to you. You dazzled me."

He chuckled nervously and rubbed his thumbs along the tops of her hands.

"You dazzled me. You still do. And maybe if I had told you that on the island it would have made a difference."

"I don't know what to say, Lars. When we were together on the island it was amazing. I don't know what happened. You and Javier were both so overwhelming. It's so hard to explain what I was feeling."

"What are you feeling now? Are you in love with Javier? I need to know." He let go of her hand and reached up and smoothed a wet lock of hair away from her cheek. His touch was electrifying and she felt every nerve spring to life. She closed her eyes for a moment and tried to think.

"Lars…I…." Her voice faltered. Being here with him like this was doing something to her body, to her heart and making it hard to think. She searched for words but couldn't speak.

"What do you feel when I do this, Antonia…?" He pulled her into his arms and kissed her tenderly, his tongue slipping between her lips. Her tongue responded, tangling with his, their kiss deepening, causing her to groan against his mouth. He slid his hand underneath the back of her sweatshirt and caressed her soft back. He felt the goose bumps rise instantly on her skin. "You feel something for me, don't you, Antonia?"

She shivered under his hands. He was making her crazy and she had to make him stop so she could think. She pulled away from him, and took his hand from under her sweatshirt, bringing it back to his lap.

"I can't do this, Lars," she said, her voice low. She looked down at their hands. "I just can't."

"Do you love Javier?" he asked, taking her chin in his hand and tilting it so he could see into her amber eyes.

"I do," she said, feeling an unexpected confidence as she said the words aloud. "I do. Can you understand that?"

He didn't answer right away. He leaned back against the sofa and sighed.

"Actually, I can. If it were anybody else, I wouldn't get it." He laughed resignedly. "Javier is an amazing man. I'm closer to him than I am to the others and I respect his friendship and his amazing talent so much. I think that might be why I'm here."

"What do you mean?" she asked.

"All along I've been torn between my friendship with him and my love for you. I needed to know how you felt about Javier as much as I need to know how you feel about me. Tell me that now, please?"

Antonia thought a moment. She looked into his brown eyes and considered what an amazing man he was—honorable, in spite of the sweet kisses, kind and sensitive. It would be so easy to love him and she knew that if she had not met Javier she would have fallen in love with him completely and for always. But she *had* met Javier and that made all the difference.

"Lars, I'll be honest with you. I was—*am*—attracted to you. What girl wouldn't be? And I admit that you and I connected on a deep, physical level…but…" Her voice wavered a bit.

"Yes?" he said quietly urging her to finish.

"But with Javier, something else happened. We connected on…I don't know…maybe a spiritual level. I think that's the best way to describe it. When I'm with Javier I have a sense of being home and of being safe. And that's not to say that I might never have felt that with you. It's just that with Javier it was more obvious somehow, even though I didn't see it at first. In answer to your question before, yes, I am in love with him. But can I tell you that I love you, too, and I always will and have you understand that the love is somehow different?"

Lars didn't speak for a moment as he considered her words. Though it hurt to hear them, he thought he understood. And in that moment he knew that the next time he gave his heart to a woman it would be completely and there would be no doubts. It just wasn't his time *this time* with this woman.

"You're beautiful, Antonia. And Javier is a lucky man. I think I'm always going to love you. Are you OK with that?" He smiled at her and touched her cheek gently with his fingertips.

"I'm totally OK with that," she whispered, covering his fingers with her hand. "You've come a long way, Lars. You must be hungry. Can I fix you something to eat?"

"Actually, I'm starving," he laughed. He covered his stomach with his hand. "The food on the plane was pretty bad."

"Come with me to the kitchen and let me rustle up some grub for you." She led the way to the kitchen.

"Grub? I've never had that before. And how do you rustle?" he asked.

"It's an expression that means cook you something to eat," she laughed.

"That sounds better," he said, taking a seat at the table.

She fixed some pasta with a pesto sauce and made a salad and garlic bread. When the meal was prepared she sat with him and ate a salad. They each had a glass of wine. She enjoyed his company, the conversation flowing easily between them. While they ate he told her about Katarina and their break-up and about his fear that his brother Frederick would do something crazy though Urs had promised to make sure that didn't happen.

Lars caught Antonia stealing a glance at her watch and realized that he might be keeping her from something. Then he remembered Javier would be here soon.

"Javier comes tomorrow, doesn't he?" he asked, finishing his wine.

"Actually, he'll be here sometime later tonight," she said shyly, noting that it was already very late. She and Lars must have been talking for hours though she had not even noticed the passage of time. She glanced out the kitchen window and saw how dark it was.

Lars put his plate and glass in the sink and turned to her.

"Thank you for the...what was that word...grub?" he laughed. "But I guess I better let you get ready for Javier. I need to use your phone to call for a cab, if you don't mind?"

"Of course." She pointed to the kitchen extension. "The number to the taxi service I use is right on the front of the fridge." She pointed to the bright yellow magnet shaped like a car. "Where are you staying?"

"We are all booked at the Four Seasons—a very nice hotel. Andrew and Antoine will be here tomorrow. We're performing on *Good Morning America* Thursday."

"Yes, Javier told me. I can't wait to hear you." She put the dishes in the dishwasher as he made the call for the cab.

"The taxi will be here in a few minutes. I'd better wait downstairs." He went into the living room to retrieve his flight bag. Antonia joined him at the front door and slipped on her shoes.

"I'll walk down with you," she said, grabbing her apartment keys and slipping them into the pocket of her jeans. As they rode down in the elevator she commented on his baggage.

"You travel lightly," she teased. "You must be very low maintenance."

"Would you believe we have a wardrobe person who brings all of our performance clothing? Our official designer is Ermenegildo Zegna who makes all of our suits and tuxes. We are so spoiled." He laughed.

The elevator door opened and they walked through the lobby and out onto the sidewalk under the awning. It was dark outside, an autumn chill in the air.

Antonia shivered and Lars noticed that she was cold. He set his bag on the ground and pulled her into his arms.

"You don't have to wait out here. It's pretty cold," he whispered into her hair. It felt so good to hold her like this and he knew that this would be the last time he held her in his arms. He breathed in her scent and squeezed her tightly to him. Over the top of her head he saw the lights of the approaching taxi. "I think that's my cab," he whispered. They looked up and saw the cab pulling up to the building.

"I'll see you soon, Lars," she said, stepping out of his arms.

Impulsively, he grabbed her and kissed her once more, knowing it would be the last time. The kiss took her by surprise. It was tender and poignant and left her breathless. He let her go and turned toward the cab.

Inside the cab, Javier slapped the headrest of the passenger seat in front of him and snapped at the driver to wait. He opened the door and stepped out onto the sidewalk in front of them.

"Javier!" Antonia was shocked and thrilled to see him. "You're early!"

"It would seem that I am too late." He spat out the words in Lars' direction, then reached for the edge of the cab door, which was still standing open. Before he climbed back inside, he looked at Antonia, his eyes filled with pain. "You have hurt me, Antonia. I expected more. And you, Lars…You are pathetic. You can have each other." With that, he climbed back into the cab and told the driver to go. The cab sped off into the night, leaving Lars and Antonia in shock on the sidewalk.

Antonia covered her face with her hands and began to cry. This couldn't be happening. He had misunderstood and left before she could explain. She sobbed and Lars took her in his arms. But she pushed away from him.

"Oh, my god. What have I done? He has it all wrong and he'll never believe this was innocent. I've ruined everything." She sobbed into her hands in shock at what had just transpired.

"I'm so sorry, Antonia. I didn't mean for this to happen. I'll find Javier and make it right. Don't worry."

In the distance another yellow cab was approaching the building. Lars saw it and picked up his flight bag. He grabbed Antonia's elbow and pulled her hand away from her tear-stained face.

"It's going to be alright, I promise you. I'll find him and talk to him and I will convince him that you love him. Trust me." He touched her face and opened the back door of the taxi.

"Please," she begged. He smiled encouragingly at her as he shut the door. She stood on the sidewalk under the awning crying as the cab sped away. When it was out of sight she ran upstairs to her apartment and threw herself on her bed and cried until she felt sick. She hugged her pillow and looked at Javier's picture on the CD cover and felt as if her heart would surely break under the pressure of having hurt him. She prayed Lars would find him and make him understand how much she loved him. It was up to Lars now.

CHAPTER 15

"The Four Seasons," Javier barked at the cabdriver angrily. He knew he should not be rude to the driver and felt a stab of remorse at his nasty tone but he said nothing further just the same. His heart was pounding as they drove along, his breathing ragged from the emotions swirling violently through him.

He felt so betrayed—by his best friend and by Antonia. How could she choose Lars over him? He suppressed a derisive laugh at the thought. *No woman can resist Lars,* he thought. *But I was so sure Antonia was different. How could I have been so wrong?*

He put his hand in his jacket pocket and felt the box with the ring in it that he had planned to surprise Antonia with tonight. He was glad that this had happened before he had given her the ring. She was not worthy to wear such a gift. And how could he share a stage with Lars now? He would feel like a fraud singing beautiful romantic love songs knowing that his best friend had betrayed him with the woman he loved. It would be impossible.

The cab stopped in front of the Four Seasons hotel. Javier handed the driver two crisp one hundred-dollar bills and told him to keep the change. It was the least he could do to make up for his rudeness. He grabbed his bag, slamming the car door shut, and walked to the door where a bellhop offered to take the bag. He thanked him but declined the offer and strode quickly to the front desk. He wanted nothing more than to get checked in and get to his room so he could try to calm his nerves with a drink. The clerk handed him the key and he headed quickly for the elevator. In a few moments he was in his room. He wanted to hit something but thought better of it and settled for a drink from the mini bar. He tried not to think about how this evening was supposed to have played out and he tried to keep Antonia out of his head. But he kept seeing her face and it was making him crazy. He paced around the room like a caged animal all the while wondering how he would get through this—how he would face Lars without beating the hell out of him.

A knock on the door stopped his pacing. He walked over and yanked it open angrily and came face to face with Lars. They stared at each other—Javier's eyes flashing with anger and Lars' eyes showing something altogether different. Javier started to slam the door in Lars' face but he forced his way in, shutting the door behind him.

"What the hell are you doing here?" Javier spat out the words, his hands forming into fists at his side.

"Javier, please. Listen to me. You have it all wrong. I promise you." The words came out in a rush with a need to speak before Javier could hit him or throw him out before he had a chance to set things right.

"I got it wrong all right," he said, moving away from Lars and walking into the sitting area of his suite needing to keep some distance between them. "I have nothing to say to you. It's clear whom Antonia wants. I don't know why you're even here wasting my time.

Lars felt a surge of frustration and wanted to shake Javier to make him listen.

"She loves you. She told me so. She told me how when she's with you she's feels safe and like she's home. She couldn't wait to see you. You have to go to her. You're breaking her heart, Javier."

"I don't believe you." But how he wanted to believe Lars' words.

"Trust me. I wouldn't lie to you. I came to see her tonight to tell her I loved her but it's too late. She's crazy about you. And outside her building *I* kissed *her*. She didn't kiss me. It's all you, Javier. Believe me."

Javier heard something in Lars' tone of voice that gave him pause. If Antonia loved Lars then he would not be here handing her over on a silver platter like this. It must be true or else they were playing a cruel game.

Javier turned to Lars, his face stony.

"Tell me something, Lars. Have you ever made love to Antonia? Tonight or ever?"

Lars didn't hesitate.

"No, I haven't, but I wanted to. I'll be brutally honest with you, Javier. On the island I kissed her and I touched her and I wanted her but I did not make love to her that way. Now you need to go to her. She's yours. She always was." Lars felt no need to tell Javier just *how* close he had come to making love to Antonia and that lack of a condom had been the reason they had not consummated their union. That was immaterial now. All that mattered was making him listen to reason.

Javier paced about the room, stopping by the window. The lights of Manhattan glowed in the darkness. He thought about Lars' words and decided that he had to be telling the truth. And suddenly getting to Antonia was all he could think of.

"I believe you. I have to go. Thank you, Lars. This couldn't have been easy for you." He grabbed his jacket and walked past Lars to the door. Lars wanted to shake his hand, pat him on the back—anything in a show of support but he didn't move as Javier moved past him.

"Good luck," he said as Javier opened the door. Javier looked back and mustered a smile.

"*Gracias.*"

Lars followed him into the hallway and watched as he entered the elevator. Then he walked down the hall to his own room where he helped himself to a small bottle of scotch from the mini bar and sat by the window in the darkness looking down on the beautiful skyline of New York City.

* * * *

Antonia dragged herself off the bed and went into the bathroom. She tried to avoid looking in the mirror knowing that she must look like hell. Noticing the wet mess on the floor she bent down and cleaned up the spill from her cup of tea and the overflowing bath water. She threw the mat and towels in the washing machine and went back to the bathroom to take a shower. She showered quickly, scrubbing off the dried soap from her interrupted bath and slipped into her white terrycloth robe then went to sit in the darkened living room. She had never felt such an emptiness in her soul, not even when she and Jeff had broken up and this time she doubted her ability to recover, especially when it was all so pointless and so unnecessary. She got up and paced around the apartment trying to fight the tears that threatened to flow continually. Finally she decided to take action. She would not give up until Javier knew the truth. If he didn't believe her then at least she would always know that she had tried to fix them. In her room she dressed back into her jeans and a pink sweater and slipped on her Adidas sneakers. She rushed through combing out her wet hair and putting on some make-up, feeling a sense of urgency—that somehow time was of the essence. She sprayed on some perfume and declared herself as ready she could ever be to win back Javier. She slipped her apartment keys and some money into her pocket, figuring it would be just as easy to flag down a cab on the street as to call for one, and, taking a deep breath, she opened her front door.

"Antonia."

She gasped at the sight of him, so suddenly and unexpectedly present. Javier stood in the hall, his face tired but hopeful. He said nothing else as he opened his arms to her knowing there was no guarantee that she would come to him.

Antonia choked back tears as she stepped into his outstretched arms and sank into his chest, burying her face in his neck. She didn't know what miracle Lars had performed but she was eternally grateful. Javier tilted her face to meet his and kissed her with a fierceness that left her gasping for air. His tongue found hers and the kiss deepened. Javier groaned against her mouth, whispering words of love in Spanish to her. Finally she pulled away and looked into his deep brown eyes. They were heavy-lidded and filled with desire.

"I'm so sorry, Javier. I promise you nothing happened with Lars. I would never hurt you. We only just..."

He placed his fingers gently over her lips, stopping her explanation.

"I know, *mi querida*. Lars told me what happened. You don't have to explain or apologize. No one is at fault except maybe me for not trusting you more." He enveloped her in his arms and breathed deeply, the scent of her hair and the softness of her skin causing him to harden with a desire that needed release.

"Come inside," she said, pushing open the door and pulling him into the apartment. "You're early." She smiled as she led him to the living room.

"I caught an earlier flight. My father's appointment went well and he didn't mind my leaving sooner than planned. I couldn't wait to get here." He slipped off his jacket and draped it over the side of a wingback chair in the living room. He looked around her apartment lit only by the outside lights of neighboring buildings and the nearly full moon visible through the large window.

A sudden shyness washed over Antonia as she stood in the middle of the room, looking at Javier. His five o'clock shadow was pronounced even in the dim light of the room and his clothes were wrinkled from the long journey. He looked so gorgeous that she thought she would die if he didn't make love to her immediately. But she waited for him to make the first move.

"I'm glad you're here," she whispered.

"Come here, *mi amor*," he said, reaching out to her.

She crossed the room and melted into his arms. He kissed her, tenderly at first, then with a mounting passion they couldn't fight any longer.

"Let's go to your bed," he whispered. She took his hand and led him down the hall to her room. He kissed her again then slowly pulled the sweater over her head. She unfastened her jeans and slid them off and he followed suit, pulling off his own shirt and jeans. "You're not wearing anything underneath?" It came out as a question more than a statement.

"I was in a hurry to get to you. I was on my way to your hotel just now to find you," she said, shivering as he rubbed his hands over her backside. He leaned down and took each of her nipples in his mouth, suckling them and kissing them until she thought she would pass out from the pleasure.

He removed his socks and underwear and pulled her down with him on the bed. They nestled into the heavy, white down comforter and he leaned over her.

"Do you know how badly I've wanted this moment?" he said against her jaw. She felt his hardness against her thigh and reached down and took him in her hand. He shuddered and said something she didn't understand in Spanish, then began making a trail of kisses across her breasts and down past her stomach. He stopped and slid his fingers inside of her, reveling in the wetness he felt there. "And I think you want it as much, yes?"

"You have no idea." She reached her arms down to him and pulled him back up, kissing him again. "Don't make me wait any more. I want you inside of me."

"*Un momento, mi amor.*" He hated this interruption but he knew it was necessary. He found his pants and pulled out the package. He slipped the condom over himself and looked at her wistfully. "Soon *mi amor,* we will not use these. I want to feel you completely, skin to skin, but we must be safe for now."

"I know. Now come here," she begged, opening her legs to him. He positioned himself over her and slid into her wetness burying himself completely. She wrapped her legs around his back and they began a slow, rhythmic motion that brought them both to climax together. After a while, when their breathing began to return to normal, he slid off of her and pulled her into his arms, his body spooning around hers.

"*Dios mio* but I have missed you," he said, nuzzling her jaw with his nose, breathing in the sweet scent of her perfume.

"I've missed you, too. I can't believe you're here. Maybe we're dreaming," she laughed.

"If this is a dream I hope it lasts forever. I love you, you know."

She turned in his arms, offering her lips to his in a sweet and tender kiss.

"I love you, too. Or as you might say, '*te quiero muchisimo.*' She grinned against his jaw.

"Someone has been practicing her Spanish I see," he said, brushing the hair from her face.

"I'll learn it, I promise."

"There is plenty of time, *mi querida.* We have forever."

They kissed again and soon they were lost in their passion again. This time Antonia climbed on top of him, moving up and down, watching his face as he struggled to hold off, to make it last, but soon he couldn't wait and he shuddered hard, releasing himself inside of her. He cried out from the intensity of his climax and pulled her down to him. He kissed her lips, trailed his tongue over her jaw and moved her to lie beside him. His hand slowly moved down her breasts, across her stomach toward the hair below. When his fingers came into contact with the diamond stud in her navel he touched it, running his finger around it. Then he slid his fingers into her and began to manipulate and move them rhythmically as he watched her writhe under his hand. He kissed her jaw as she reached climax, reveling in her release.

Exhausted they let their bodies relax as they snuggled together under the comforter. It had become cold in the room and they held each other close for warmth and eventually they slept.

* * * *

Antonia had intended to show Javier some of her favorite places in New York City but he had other ideas. So she called in sick to work and they spent most of the day in bed. Eventually they took a shower together and by evening they both agreed they needed sustenance to make it through the night. They decided they would venture out of the apartment for dinner but Javier wanted to stop at his hotel first to change his clothes and to make sure his wardrobe had arrived and also to get instructions for the performance tomorrow morning on *Good Morning America.*

They took a cab to the Four Seasons and went straight up to his room. Antonia waited in his extravagantly beautiful suite while he changed clothes and made several phone calls. He came into where she sat looking at a spectacular view of Trump Tower. He had changed into a pair of black pants and a black shirt and he looked incredible.

"Wow. You look amazing—like Zorro," she smiled, her gaze moving over him. She walked toward him wishing she had dressed up more. She wore a pair of navy trousers and a white sweater. "I feel under-dressed."

"You look beautiful, *mi amor.* Now I have a question for you." He had a funny look on his face and she wondered what he was up to.

"Yes?"

"My band-mates are apparently dying to meet you. They are downstairs in the lobby arguing about where to go for dinner. Would you like to meet them? They may want us to join them for dinner though, so be prepared."

Antonia laughed and felt a surge of excitement at the thought of meeting the other members of Les Passionistes.

"I would love to meet them—definitely. As for dinner, that's fine, too, if they ask and if you want."

"Oh, they will ask. And Antoine will hit on you—is that how you say it in English?" He smiled as he took her hand and pulled her to him in a quick embrace.

"Yes, that's how you say it." She followed him to the door but caught his arm before he could open it. "Wait, Javier," she said.

"Yes, *mi querida*?"

"Will Lars be there?"

"More than likely. Is that a problem for you?" She heard a change in his tone when he asked the question.

"No, but what about for you?"

"It is not a problem for me. I am very secure, *mi querida*." He kissed her softly and ran his hands through her hair, pulling her close to his chest. "Whether you like it or not, you are mine now."

She smiled with relief and they went down to the lobby where Andrew, Antoine and Lars were standing in a huddle discussing something of apparent great importance.

Javier kept his arm protectively around Antonia as he made the introductions. Antoine took her hand in his and held it firmly.

"*Enchante′*," he said dazzling her with a sexy grin. "You are aware that we have the same name, no?"

"*Oui*," she laughed. "And that's the extent of my French. Enchanted to meet you, too."

Andrew shook her hand as well and resisted the urge to comment on the fact that he understood the appeal she had for Javier and Lars. It all made sense now.

Lars came forward and kissed her on both cheeks.

"Antonia. I see you and Javier have worked everything out. That's great." He looked at Javier who smiled and shook Lars' hand.

"All is well," Javier said. "Now what are you three planning for the night?"

Antoine spoke up.

"We're starving. Colin has made a reservation for us at a restaurant that seems too formal—something called The Ivy. We have The Ivy in London and it's not...how do you say...hip? We want something fun with music and good food and really hot girls."

Antonia laughed while the others rolled their eyes, used to Antoine's antics.

"Wait a minute," said Javier. "I thought you already had someone new—a French girl, wasn't it?"

"Javier, please. We are in America now. I have new lands to conquer. France will have to wait until I am back in England." He shook his head, amazed that he even had to explain.

"I know a place in Tribeca that has all of that," said Antonia, smiling at Antoine. "The food is great—it's Italian, the music is fun and the best part for you, Antoine, is the clientele. The place is a hotspot for celebrity watching. You might find a hot movie star or two to romance." Antonia realized she was going out on a limb with that remark considering Antoine's recent publicity but she decided to test his sense of humor. She saw Javier raise his eyebrows in what she hoped was mock dismay at her words.

"Javier, you've been talking about me, haven't you?" said Antoine, grinning. "She knows me already so well and we have only just met. I do have a reputation with the Hollywood babes, you know." He winked at Antonia.

"So I've read. Would you like to go to DiCaprio's?"

"Oh, I know that place," said Andrew. "It's Leo's place." He turned to Antoine.

"You will like this place. Supermodels hang out there."

"Then what are we waiting for?" bellowed Antoine. "*Allons*!"

They left together and Antonia was amazed to see a black stretch limo waiting in front of the hotel for them. The driver was standing by the back passenger door and he opened it, helping her inside. As soon as they were settled, Antoine went straight to the mini bar and found a bottle of champagne.

"Who will join me in a toast?" he asked, pulling glasses from their holders. He warned everyone to take cover as he worked the cork. It popped off and the liquid gold fizzed onto the floor. "Oops. What a waste," he said as he passed around the glasses and began to pour the champagne into the flutes.

"Let me make this toast, please," said Javier, holding up his glass. They raised their drinks and Javier turned to Antonia. "To my Antonia, the most beautiful girl in the world, and to my partners in crime and music, long may we reign."

"Here, here." They each seconded the toast in their own languages and clinked their glasses together.

Lars sipped his drink slowly and watched Javier and Antonia share a kiss. He had to admit that they did make a beautiful couple. And he also had to admit that he felt a strange sense of peace at seeing them together. Seeing the love they had for each other gave him hope that one day he would be as lucky. And in the meantime, he would concentrate on the music. That would be the focus of his life for the time being. He suddenly wondered what was happening with Frederick. He looked at his watch and knew that most of Switzerland would be winding down for the night. He would call tomorrow and check on his family.

They had a fabulous time at DiCaprio's. They ordered entirely too much food which they shared family style and Antonia guessed they must have gone through nearly five bottles of wine. She was feeling light-headed by the time she finished her third glass and knew she had to stop. At one point Javier reminded them they had to perform early in the morning and they needed clear heads to sing.

Antoine was in his element at the sight of a table full of supermodels with whom he flirted shamelessly though they were playing it coy with him. And then a group of four thirty-something women having a ladies night out walked into the restaurant, immediately recognized Les Passionistes and went completely insane. They gathered around the table, begging for pictures and autographs. This caused the supermodels to sit up and take a little more interest in the four handsome men and they asked to join in the party. Soon DiCaprio's was a madhouse as more and more people wandered in, wanting tables and a glimpse of the celebrities.

Antonia sat back and watched the spectacle Les Passionistes had unwittingly created. Andrew and Antoine were in their element and even Lars seemed to be enjoying himself. She noticed that he maintained a respectable distance between himself and the models who clearly wanted to get to know him better. Several models and fans attempted to flirt with Javier and he was polite to them but distant. She stole a glance at him, wondering what he thought of all this attention.

He caught her eye and leaned over to whisper in her ear.

"*Mi querida.* I think we need to get out of here. It's getting a little crowded, don't you think? Besides, I have a surprise for you but we need to be alone for it."

Antonia raised her eyebrows in wonder.

"What kind of surprise?" she asked, leaning closer to him.

"No, *mi amor.* Not here. Are you ready to go?"

She nodded and he turned to speak to Lars.

"Antonia and I are going to go now. You will make sure these two make it back to the hotel sober, yes?"

"Don't worry. We're about to leave, too. I just asked the maitre d' to call for the limo. Wait a minute and we can all leave together."

"Good. These women are crazy. So is Antoine. He is a bad influence on Andrew, I think."

Lars laughed and assured him that Antoine was harmless and just being himself. The maitre d' approached the table and informed them that their limo was waiting out front. Javier gave him Les Passionistes' official credit card to pay their exorbitant bill and when it was settled they made their way to the front door, a gaggle of women following behind them.

Out on the sidewalk the four of them posed for a few more photos under DiCaprio's huge green awning, trimmed in red, white and green twinkling lights while Antonia waited inside the limo. Finally Javier had had enough.

"Good night, ladies." He waved as the four of them got into the limo. Lars instructed the driver to take them to the Four Seasons.

"I think I made several good contacts there." Antoine reached over and took Antonia's hand, squeezing it gently. "Antonia, you were right. DiCaprio's was a brilliant idea."

She thanked him and smiled as Javier reached down and removed Antoine's hand from hers.

"Down boy," he laughed, putting his arm around Antonia and holding her close. He couldn't wait to be alone with her so he could give her his surprise. He kissed the top of her head and wished the driver would speed it up.

At the Four Seasons, Javier asked the limo driver to wait. They went inside, stopping in the lobby to go over the plan for tomorrow. The limo would arrive at six thirty to take them to the studio for a quick run-through of the two songs they were scheduled to sing. Javier told them he would be back in time to join them for the ride to the ABC studios, as he did not plan to stay at the hotel tonight. They said their good-byes and everyone went their separate ways. He and Antonia went up to his suite and he packed his overnight bag.

"So, what's this surprise you were talking about earlier?" she asked innocently.

"As soon as we get to your apartment, *mi amor*. You must wait a little while longer."

He took her hand and they went downstairs and into the waiting limo. Javier gave the address for Antonia's apartment. Then he put his arms around her and kissed her all the way there.

Once inside her apartment, Javier didn't keep her waiting long for his surprise. He took her into the kitchen and pulled out a chair from the table. He gently pushed her into the seat and knelt down on the floor at her feet. He felt a nervousness course through him and worried that he would not get the words out the way he meant to say them. The irony that singing operas and love songs in Italian and English was easier than proposing to Antonia was not lost on him.

She gasped as she realized what was about to happen. Her heart began to beat crazily in her chest and she was thankful she was sitting down. Her head spun, partly from too much wine and Javier's surprise. He reached into his back pocket and pulled out the small velvet box. Antonia put her hand over her mouth to try to still her quivering lips. Already tears were forming and she didn't want to become blinded by them. She fought them as best she could as he took her hand in his and spoke.

"*Mi amor*. My life changed for the best the day I met you. I cannot imagine a day not spent with you even though I fear we have some separations to get through. But what I mean to say is *te quiero ahora y para siempre* which is to say, I love you now and for always. Will you do me the honor of becoming my wife?" As he finished speaking he handed her the box.

Antonia tried to blink away the tears but they fell onto her cheeks anyway. She held her breath as she opened the box and saw the diamond and platinum ring nestling in the velvet lining.

"Oh, my god, Javier," she gasped. "This is the most…" her voice broke on a sob. She leaned down to him and he laid his forehead on hers.

"It was my grandmother's," he whispered. "My mother gave it to me to give to you."

"Your mother knows you're proposing to me?" Antonia couldn't believe it.

"Yes. And my father. And quite possibly half of Spain by now." He laughed and leaned back so he could see her face, wiping away her tears with his thumbs. "But you have not answered the question and that makes me very nervous."

"Yes. I would be honored to marry you," she put her arms around him and kissed him tenderly. "This is the most beautiful ring I've ever seen."

"Thank you, *querida*." He stood up and pulled her to her feet. She took the ring from the box and he put it on her left ring finger. It slid easily over her knuckle and fit perfectly, exactly as he had hoped it would.

"*Perfecto*," he smiled. He crushed her to him and kissed her lips, her cheeks, her jaw and trailed his lips around her neck and stopped at her earlobe. She moaned against him and held him, feeling his body blend into hers. Their tongues melded and Javier whispered to her.

"You're doing it to me again. I want you," he whispered, his voice deep and sensual.

She took his hand and led him to the bedroom. He lay down on the bed and reached for her but she hesitated.

"Javier. I have a favor to ask you." She felt nervous knowing she was about to ask him to do something he might find uncomfortable but she had to ask.

"What is it, *mi amor*?" he asked, waiting patiently.

"You might think it's a little strange...." Her voice trailed off and she felt her face redden.

"I will do anything you ask, Antonia. What is it?" He smiled and hoped she would not be afraid to ask him for whatever it was that seemed so important. He could not imagine denying her anything.

"I'll be right back." She left the room and he could hear her making noise in her spare bedroom. He thought he heard the sound of the computer and for a moment he feared she wanted to make an X-rated video for posting on the Internet. He shivered at the thought as he waited.

Antonia came back into the bedroom with her hand behind her back. Javier smiled nervously wondering what she wanted from him and hoping he would be able to deliver.

"You are scaring me, Antonia. What are you holding behind your back?"

She brought her hand around and showed him a CD. She turned it to face him and he saw that it was Les Passionistes' album. He raised his eyebrows in question.

"I know this sounds crazy but I've dreamed of your making love to me while this CD plays, especially one song in particular. Will you do it or would it be too weird?" She felt shy and silly now and hoped he wouldn't think she had completely lost her mind.

Javier threw his head back and laughed heartily. Antonia wasn't sure what to make of his reaction. When his laughter subsided he reached out to her. She sat down next to him and he took the CD from her hand.

"Please tell me it isn't 'Surrender to Me?'" he asked.

"How did you know?" She really felt silly now.

"*Everybody* loves that song," he sighed. "Do you have a CD player in here, *mi querida*?"

She took the CD back from him and removed it from the case and slid it into her CD player/alarm clock. Before pushing play she stood up and removed her clothes. Javier watched as each piece of clothing hit the floor. When she was naked she lay down beside him and began to undress him. When his clothes were on the floor with hers he pulled her toward him and kissed her then smiled against her cheek.

"You know, I don't even sing the lead on this song. It's Lars and Antoine. I might not be able to perform, if you know what I mean..."

"It's OK. We can always change the song."

"You know it's me singing the lead on 'Something About the Way You Look Tonight.' That might work better for me." He was killing her fantasy but he couldn't help it. Making love to her with Lars singing to them wasn't going to work. He could feel it already.

She laughed and pushed the button to play song number eleven. The music started and Javier was relieved to hear it was "Something About the Way You Look Tonight."

"It's still a little strange to make love to myself but we shall see," he grinned and playfully pushed her back on the bed and moved over her, kissing her lips, then sliding down to her breasts. She caressed his back, pulling him closer to her. She felt his hardness getting closer to her and then felt his hesitation.

"Do you want protection this time, *mi amor*?" he said in her ear, his tongue on her neck causing her to writhe beneath him.

"No," she whispered. "Not if you don't."

"I want to feel you completely this time—skin to skin." His voice sounded ragged now and she knew they would not last long.

"It's OK. It's my safe time." She pulled him to her and they kissed again.

"I love you," he said as he entered her. He moved in rhythm to the music, her arms and legs holding him tightly, urging him further in. He felt a sensation not unlike falling as he came inside of her. His movements slowed but he stayed in her as long as he could, knowing her release was imminent. When she came, they lay together, still connected until a new song began that killed Javier's mood.

"You better turn that one off," he moaned as Lars began to sing *'Miserere.'*"

She laughed and stopped the music and they lay together staring at her ring and talking about the future.

CHAPTER 16

Antonia knocked on the door of Deanna's apartment impatiently. She was giddy with excitement and couldn't wait to get inside to tell her about all that had happened last night. She heard shuffling on the other side of the door and the sound of Deanna unfastening her many locks. The door opened and she was surprised to see Sean standing there.

"Sean! Hi. I didn't expect to see you this morning." She smiled and held up the bag of breakfast she'd purchased at Pinelli's Bakery. "I brought breakfast—bagels and hash browns."

"Good morning," said Sean, stepping aside to let her in. "Deanna's still in bed."

"Well, she has to get up *now*!" Antonia spoke in a rush and ran to the living room to turn on the television. Then she dashed down to Deanna's bedroom.

"Deanna! Wake up! Come to the living room. Les Passionistes are going to be on *Good Morning America*. You have to see them. And you have to see this."

Deanna rolled over and popped her head up from under the blankets.

"Good Lord, woman. What are you doing here so early?" She smiled and sat up, pushing her blonde hair out of her face. "What is…oh, my god! *Oh. My. God*! What is *that*?" She let out a scream that brought Sean scurrying into the bedroom.

Antonia stood in the middle of the room, her hand out for them to see. The diamond sparkled in the early morning light streaming in from the window.

"Javier asked me to marry him last night!" she beamed. "Can you believe it?"

"Get over here!" Deanna beckoned for Antonia to come closer. She took her hand and inspected the ring. Her breath caught in her throat as she stared at the beautiful ring. "This is gorgeous," she whispered.

"It was his grandmother's. His mother gave it to him." Antonia looked down at the ring, still in shock that it was on her finger. "Now get up. They're going to sing. Come to the living room! Hurry!" She dashed out, brushing past Sean who stood in the doorway watching them. He grabbed her hand, stopping her in her tracks so he could get a look at the ring.

"Wow. That's gonna be hard to live up to," he said, winking at her. He glanced at Deanna and smiled. "Do they sell these things at Kmart?"

"*K what*? I can't believe you said that word in my presence!" She threw a pillow at him and he and Antonia laughed and retreated down the hall. Deanna put on her robe and joined them in front of the TV. Diane Sawyer was talking to Emeril Lagasse who was making something delicious with eggs, peppers, onions and lots of garlic.

Sean made them a pot of coffee and they spread their breakfast out on the coffee table while they waited for Les Passionistes. The show went to commercial with Diane promising a special treat from the newest singing sensation to hit the airwaves when they returned.

"Now, we have a minute. Tell me what happened last night!" Deanna set her coffee cup down and waited anxiously.

Antonia told them about their night out on the town, about meeting Andrew and Antoine and about the proposal later at her apartment.

"I can't believe this. This sounds like something out of a romance novel." Deanna shook her head in amazement.

"You haven't known this guy very long, Antonia. Aren't you rushing things a little bit?" Sean felt a sense of obligation to put things into perspective. He caught Deanna's frown and heard her sharp intake of breath.

"Time doesn't matter, Sean!" she snapped. "Just because you and I have been dating for five years! Is that your idea of not rushing it? I mean if you don't know me by now…." Deanna's face reddened as her voice faded.

Antonia had a sense that a can of worms had been opened and she felt guilty as hell but, thankfully, they were saved by the return of the show. Her stomach lurched as she saw Les Passionistes standing on the stage with Diane Sawyer who talked a little bit about the group, how they were created and what they were about to sing. The music started and the camera settled on the four of them as they began to sing "Something About the Way You Look Tonight." Antonia couldn't breathe as they sang. Deanna reached over and took her hand as they watched the flawless performance. The four of them were dressed in matching black Zegna suits, white shirts, black and white striped ties with red roses in their lapels. When they finished singing, the studio audience applauded and Diane positively swooned at their feet as they went to commercial break.

"They are pretty amazing," said Sean. "Not bad at all."

Deanna scowled at him and turned her attention to Antonia. She wanted more details. Antonia answered her questions and then the show returned and Les Passionistes performed "Surrender to Me." Antonia groaned and leaned back against the sofa.

"Oh, no…this song…" she sighed. They listened as Les Passionistes sang the beautiful love song, which naturally caused tears to burn behind Anontia's eyes. She watched as the camera moved from Antoine, who sang so expressively with his arms outstretched to his listeners, then to Andrew who smiled so brightly and sang with such pure, unadulterated joy. Then the camera went to Lars who looked so stoic as he sang, concentrating intently on the music and his individual contribution to it. And finally to Javier whose baritone resonated in the studio, his sparkling eyes always moving and his hands holding the microphone stand, one hand at the top of the mike, the other half-way down the stand as if he were holding a woman, pulling her close to his body. They finished singing and Diane could barely speak as she sent them to commercial.

"Wow," uttered Deanna. "They got to her—to Diane. Did you see that?" She looked at Antonia, saw the tears and then, unable to help herself, she cried, too.

Sean retreated slowly from the room, suddenly feeling as if he didn't belong. He disappeared into the bedroom, leaving the women to collect themselves.

"Antonia…why are you here and not at the studio? You should be with him," Deanna asked.

"He left really early this morning. And I have to go to work. I'm so behind on everything." She stood up and began to pick up their breakfast dishes. "I should get there now before my dad fires me," she grinned.

"He would never do that," said Deanna. "When do you see Javier next?"

"He'll call me this morning. I'll see him sometime today—soon I hope."

They walked to the door and Deanna embraced Antonia warmly.

"You're a very lucky girl. I'm jealous." She laughed but Antonia heard a somber tone in Deanna's voice.

"Is everything going to be OK with you and Sean?" Antonia asked, her voice low.

"We'll be fine—maybe. But he might have to change his name to Antoine and start speaking French if this relationship is going to continue." She hugged Antonia again and took one last look at the ring, sighing deeply.

"Kmart my ass," she grinned. She opened the door and Antonia stepped into the hall, waving good-bye as she dashed for the elevator.

* * * *

Just before noon Javier called Antonia who had been, once again, trying to work and not making any progress.

"Did you watch us this morning, *mi amor*?" he asked, his voice in her ear threatening to be her undoing.

"Of course. I watched from my friend's apartment. I made her get out of bed to see you." Antonia noticed Carly lurking nearby and turned her chair around to face the window.

"I will have to meet this friend soon. When are you free to leave work?"

"A soon as I have some copy for the editors but it's so hard to concentrate. I keep thinking about you." He heard laughter in her voice.

"That's as it should be," he said. "We have some interviews this afternoon but I will be finished by four. Where and when shall we meet?"

"I'll come to your hotel as soon I'm done here—no later than five o'clock."

She glanced at the clock on the wall by the window as she spoke, her heart sinking at the amount of hours between now and then.

They finished their conversation and hung up, Antonia's mind millions of miles away. She managed to conduct a couple of interviews with designers for her column and sent it to editing. She skipped lunch to finish up her listing of hot books, movies and music coming in the new year and finally, a little before five, she signed off the computer and sneaked quietly out of the office before Carly could start another chat with her as she had tried to do several times throughout the day.

She arrived at the Four Seasons just as Lars was walking out the door. They stood together on the sidewalk in front of the building, an unexpected awkwardness creeping into their conversation.

"It's pretty cold today," he said, noting the fierce wind whipping around them. He reached out and pulled her jacket closer around her body. "You should be buttoned up."

"It is cold—November weather, you know. But I would think you would be used to the cold being from Switzerland and all." She tried not to notice his long, dark hair, blowing around his face or his almond-shaped eyes sparkling in the sunlight.

"True, but we do get hot weather there, you know. We even have palm trees," he teased. He noticed the diamond sparkling in the light and took her hand in his. "What is this?" he asked, his voice taking on a low tone.

Antonia hesitated. Would her words hurt Lars? Had Javier not told him about their engagement? Would it hurt her to tell him? She wondered about these things as she looked up into his eyes, his hands holding hers as he looked at the ring.

"Javier and I are engaged," she said quietly, frustrated with herself that those beautiful words could cause such guilt to seep into her heart.

"And he never said a word this morning—that guy." He suddenly pulled her into his arms and held her tightly, her hair and her perfume filling his senses. "Congratulations, Antonia. Javier is the luckiest man alive."

They stood that way for a few moments, Lars not wanting to let her go and Antonia not wanting to feel the guilt that was bubbling up inside.

"Am I interrupting something?" Javier asked, irritation in his voice. He stood barely four feet away watching them intently.

Antonia jumped and moved out of Lars' arms. She knew she wore guilt on her face even as she mustered a smile for Javier and moved closer to him.

Lars came to her rescue.

"She was just showing me the ring, Javier, and I was congratulating her. I can't believe you didn't say anything this morning."

"Yes, well I had planned to tell you all later today when Antonia arrived." His eyes gave nothing away as he looked at them both but Antonia had a feeling that Javier was not happy. The thought left her slightly unnerved.

Lars, sensing her discomfort and Javier's annoyance, congratulated them again and said he had to go.

"I'm meeting Andrew and Antoine for a drink up the street. Should I keep your news secret or would you like to join us and tell them yourselves?" he offered.

"You can tell them. But, no, we have other plans. I'll see you later tonight."

Lars forced a smile and left them. Javier turned to Antonia and steered her back into the hotel. With his hand on the small of her back, he guided her to the elevator. They rode up in silence with several other people, finally arriving on Javier's floor. Once in his suite Antonia broke the jarring silence between them.

"Javier. Is everything OK?" she asked quietly, fearing his answer.

"Antonia…there is something you don't know about me but I'm going to tell you now. I am a very jealous man and though I try hard not to show it, sometimes it is impossible. And I'm afraid that where Lars is concerned, that jealousy might he hard to hide. I do not want to worry and wonder every time I see the two of you together that there is something between you. I know I should not worry this way but that's the way it is. Do you understand?" He stood with his hands in his pockets, looking into her eyes, holding her gaze.

Her heart went out to him. She understood jealousy.

"Of course I do. All I can do is promise you that you have nothing to worry about. Not now or ever. You have my word." She held up her hand, flashing the ring in his face. "I never would have accepted this ring otherwise. Do you understand *that*?" She knew she was getting agitated as she spoke but she couldn't help it.

"I'm sorry, *mi querida*. But the fact is that as long as Les Passionistes exists, Lars will be a part of our lives. I have to get used to that."

Antonia felt anger at his words. This was not the way Javier should speak of his friend.

"Lars is your best friend. He was in your life long before I was and his relationship with you is every bit as important as mine is with you. We are not mutually exclusive, Javier."

"What does that mean? I do not know that term in English unless you mean *mutuamente exclusiva* when acceptance of one means rejection of the other. Is that what you're talking about?" He walked to the window and looked down at the street below.

Antonia closed the distance between them. She took his arm and turned him to face her.

"That's exactly what I'm talking about, Javier. Lars and I are not mutually exclusive. That means you have to accept us both. He as your friend and band-mate and I as your soon to be wife. We can live in harmony. You know all about harmony, Javier. You perform it everyday." She pressed her body up against him, kissing his lips, her arms snaking around his neck, pulling him tightly toward her.

"You are more than a beautiful woman, *mi amor*. You are also *muy inteligente* and I could learn a lesson or two from you, I see." He returned her kisses with a fierceness that left them both breathless.

They debated going out for a walk around the streets of New York to soak up the crisp, autumn air or staying in to make love in Javier's bed. Lovemaking won hands down and they spent the next two hours exploring one another's bodies until they lay exhausted and hungry. They read the room service menu and Javier ordered chicken marsala and pasta for them with chocolate cake for dessert. Over a bottle of wine, Javier asked about wedding dates.

"I don't believe in long engagements, *mi amor*. I hope we are in agreement about this." He poured her another glass of wine as he spoke.

"I don't either. Shouldn't we meet each other's parents before we set a date? My father certainly wants to meet you." She sipped her wine and toyed with a piece of chicken.

"Let's have dinner with your parents this weekend. Would they want to do that? We have one appearance here tomorrow on *The View* and then we fly to Los Angeles Sunday to tape *The Ellen DeGeneres Show* Monday. This weekend is my only chance to meet your family before returning to London." He reached across the table and took her hand, already feeling the sadness their separation would bring.

"I'll call them. I'm sure they'd love to have dinner. I can't wait for them to meet you."

They talked about Javier's upcoming work schedule, which would be brutal with the start of rehearsal for the new album and the subsequent recording of it.

"Oh, I almost forgot to tell you. We will be performing here in New York City in early December with the Philharmonic. Samuel just told us about that this morning—a Christmas concert with other musical celebrities for charity. Then we will have to work on getting you to London."

The mention of the Philharmonic caused a chill to wash over Antonia. She had never mentioned Jeff to Javier—somehow the subject of old flames had never come up between them but now it seemed she would have to tell him about Jeff before he found out some other way. Her face must have changed significantly because Javier leaned toward her and stroked her hands with his thumbs.

"What is it, Antonia? I mention I'm coming to New York in December and you suddenly seem so sad. That does not make you happy?" His voice was full of worry and apprehension not understanding what had caused this change in her mood.

Antonia got up from the table and walked over to the window. Her nerves tingled as she wondered how to tell Javier about Jeff especially in light of his earlier confession about his jealous tendencies. This could put him over the edge. At least with Lars he knew with whom he was dealing but Jeff was an unknown factor. She swallowed hard and turned to him.

"Now there's something about me I need to tell you. But, please, Javier, know that you have nothing to worry about. I love you."

"*Dios mio*," Javier muttered. He put down his wineglass and came to join her by the window. "What is this about, Antonia?"

She didn't mince words.

"I was once engaged to marry the assistant conductor of the New York Philharmonic."

Javier didn't respond immediately. He looked at her, his eyes wary and Antonia feared she might have crossed a line. He remained silent considering her words. His rational side told him that it was perfectly natural for Antonia to have had lovers before him but up to this moment he had chosen to pretend they did not exist. But now the subject must be dealt with and put away once and for all.

"How long ago was this?" he asked, his voice even.

"We broke up earlier this year. As a matter of fact, he was just married a few weeks ago when we were in Isla Marta." She watched Javier's face wondering what he was truly thinking.

"So you came to Isla Marta to escape?" He felt agitation building and hated himself for feeling it and being unable to keep it out of his voice.

"No!" she cried. "I came to work. You know that." She wanted to go to him and hold him but she had done nothing wrong and so she stood her ground.

Javier paced around the room, fighting jealousy he had no right to feel. Finally he came to a stop before her at the window and took her hand in his. Her hand was cold and he rubbed it and kissed it tenderly.

"It's fine, *mi amor*. You see how quickly I felt the jealousy and let it go? No more talk of past loves or you will want to know about all of mine and we have not enough time in the day for that subject." He laughed at the stricken expression on her face. She pulled her hand away from his and tried to get around him.

"Are you trying to make me jealous now? Because if you are, it's working!" she retorted.

"No. I am just teasing. As far as I am concerned, you are the only woman in the world—past, present and future." He kissed her, his tongue tasting the red wine on hers, his hands rubbing her backside and pulling her hard against him.

She pulled away and looked into his eyes, suppressing a grin.

"Let's keep it that way. Now why don't we go for a walk and get some fresh air? You're going to need it for later."

He grinned sexily at her and kissed her, whispering unintelligible words in her ear. They grabbed their jackets and went out, spending the evening walking around the city lost in their own world.

*   *   *   *

The weekend flew by and suddenly Antonia found herself saying good-bye to Javier once again. They had spent the weekend together beginning with Les Passionistes' performance on *The View*. Antonia had been in the audience, deciding to ditch work again to be with Javier for as long as possible. When Meredith Vieira had boldly asked the men about their love lives, Javier proudly told the world that he had just become engaged to a beautiful American girl. Upon learning that Antonia was in the audience, the camera panned to her startled face and she smiled nervously. The sound of moans and groans from the audience could be heard all over the studio as the women realized that one of Les Passionistes would soon be officially off the market.

They had spent that night at Antonia's apartment and then had a raucous dinner with Antonia's parents, her brothers and Sean and Deanna at Il Fontanella's Italian restaurant Saturday night. That night she stayed with him at the Four Seasons. And now they were in the lobby, the limo waiting to take Les Passionistes to the airport to catch their flight to Los Angeles. Antonia had considered accompanying them to the airport but they both agreed that airport good-byes were too hard to get through.

Javier held her tightly as Andrew checked them all out. A bellhop gathered their bags, putting them on a trolley to take them to the car. Antoine and Lars watched from a distance as Javier reluctantly let go of Antonia.

"You OK with the two of them?" Antoine asked Lars quietly.

"I'm getting used to it," he responded, picking up his flight bag. He gave Antoine a wan smile and went out to the limo.

Javier kissed her again and took her hand, then followed Lars out the door.

"I'll call you when we land, *mi amor. Te quiero.*" He let go of her hand and climbed in. The limo sped away and Antonia walked against the wind the fifteen blocks to her apartment, fighting the stinging tears all the way home.

*   *   *   *

Once on the plane, Lars closed his eyes and thought about home in Switzerland. He had finally talked to Frederick who had told him that he was not going to marry Katarina. Lars was happy about the decision but also sad that now both he and his brother would not be spending their lives with the women they loved. Urs had gotten on the phone and told them both to snap out of it, which had lightened their burdens somewhat. Thank God for Urs. His parents had also decided to go ahead with their divorce and his father had made his peace with the decision. He was already looking forward to the future. Lars realized that now there were three of them not spending eternity with their soul mates. *How strange*, he had thought.

Frederick told him that Katarina had gone to a 'spa' to get herself together with her mother accompanying her. He understood the meaning of the word 'spa' in this sense and his heart hurt for Katarina, knowing he was the cause of her emotional pain, but there was nothing he could do that the passage of time wouldn't eventually fix.

They landed in Los Angeles and were whisked away to their hotel where they had a photo session with *Vanity Fair* magazine and then an interview. They kept up a frantic pace with the *Ellen* show and other interviews and appearances before heading to Germany and then finally home to London.

They settled into a routine that involved long days of rehearsals and recording, flying back and forth between London and Sweden. Lars was glad to be back to work—real work finally. He realized that music was where his head needed to be and he kept it there, his nose to the proverbial grindstone—most of the time. And it felt good to sing with his band-mates. Life was feeling good again. Even the news that Antonia was moving to London didn't get him down. He was happy for Javier and knew that Javier's concentration would improve once she came to stay.

They spent a whirlwind twenty-four hours in New York City in December for the Christmas concert with the Philharmonic at which they sang "Ave Maria" and "O, Holy Night." The concert was a success and several million dollars were raised for many charitable causes. Antonia had naturally been there and she had looked beautiful in a red sparkling gown. When he thought of her now he pictured her in that stunning gown, her long brown hair swirling down her back, her amber eyes bright and sparkling. He did occasionally allow himself to think about her as long as she did not interfere with the music. No one would ever know his thoughts anyway or so he figured.

Andrew and Antoine also experienced a renewal of sorts with the music. Antoine was excited that they were finally singing a song in French. For once he would have the upper hand in rehearsal. Andrew fell in deep lust with a new violin player—a Japanese girl the studio had hired—and spent a lot of time in extra, 'one-on-one rehearsals' with her.

Life was slowly getting back to normal for Les Passionistes and Lars felt peace—finally.

* * * *

"I still can't believe you're moving all the way to London," said Deanna. She helped Antonia seal the last box of books and CD's. "What am I going to do without you?"

"You're just going to have to move to London, too. They need massages over there, too, you know, and yoga, and all that good stuff," smiled Antonia. She marked the box with a felt pen so she would know what was inside later.

Deanna thought a minute, her face brightening considerably.

"You know—you're absolutely right. I can do my job anywhere." Deanna felt a sudden wave of buoyancy wash over her. "The more I think about it, the more I like the idea. Can you see me parading up and down the aisles of Harrods? All that Burberry! Oh, yeah. I might have to move to London, alright."

Antonia impulsively hugged her friend hard.

"I would love having my best friend nearby, but what about Sean?"

Deanna hesitated, her face clouding over. She looked away and shrugged.

"I'm not so sure about Sean anymore. I love him but things are different all of a sudden."

"Different how?" Antonia asked softly.

"I don't know exactly but you're having this great romance that seems larger than life and I feel myself wanting it, too. I want to be swept off my feet. Do you know what I mean?" Deanna sighed and looked away.

Antonia grabbed Deanna's hand and squeezed it hard—she understood completely. Then a funny thought occurred to her.

"You know, there are still two members of Les Passionistes available...if you get what I mean...." Her voice trailed off. She waited to see if Deanna would take the bait.

"Only two? Which two? Not that it matters. As I've said before, any of them could eat crackers in my bed anytime—yours included." She laughed, her mood lifting again.

"I'm talking about Andrew and Antoine. Javier says Andrew is all crazy about some new violin player who isn't all that interested in him and Antoine is still searching for 'the one.' So you see—they're ripe for the picking." She got up and pushed the box over to the front door. Deanna followed her, clearing her throat.

"So Lars has someone then?" she asked.

"Oh, Lars! Of course. I mean...no. He doesn't...I mean...not that I know of..." Antonia stammered. She blushed and turned away from Deanna.

"Did you forget about him?"

Antonia swallowed a non-existent lump and crossed her arms over her chest.

"No," she sighed. "I think I just..." She stopped, her mind suddenly befuddled.

"You just can't allow yourself to imagine him with anyone, can you?" Deanna knew this subject was sensitive but perhaps Antonia needed to get something off her mind.

Antonia sighed. She paced around the living room trying to sort her thoughts.

"He's not mine and he never will be, I know that. But I admit that it is a little hard to imagine him with anyone. But, Deanna, believe me when I tell you how much I love Javier. You do believe me, don't you?"

"Are you trying to convince me...or yourself?"

"I'm not trying to convince anyone," Antonia was quick to answer. "I love Javier and I always will. But there will always be a place in my heart for Lars. Does that make any sense or am I just plain crazy?"

"I understand. Hey, I've seen Lars. What's not to love? But you've got the best one. You know that, don't you?"

A grin broke out across Antonia's face as she realized just how right Deanna was.

"Absolutely—Javier *is* the best." She looked down at her engagement ring and touched the large diamond in the center. "I am so lucky."

"You are indeed. Now are you ready to go? Your party awaits, madam."

"Ready as I'll ever be."

They grabbed their coats and headed out to DiCaprio's where Antonia's *Passion* colleagues, along with her parents and brothers, were throwing her a going away party. She only had two more nights in New York—the movers were coming tomorrow for her household goods—and then she would be flying to London to live with Javier in his apartment until they found a bigger place. And she would be joining the staff of the London edition of *Passion* as their new pop culture editor. Her father had made all the arrangements for her job change and she was excited about learning the ins and outs of the London scene.

The next day the movers arrived early and carted away all of Antonia's belongings. When they had finished removing the last box and she was finally alone, she walked from room to room in her empty apartment, making sure she hadn't forgotten anything. She sang a line from a Les Passionistes song and laughed as her voice echoed off the empty walls. She knew she was going to miss New York but London was a great substitute for the Big Apple. She walked to the front door and flipped off the light in the foyer for the last time and let herself out, leaving her keys with the doorman as she left the building, suitcase in hand, and hailed a cab to take her to Deanna's.

She had already said her good-byes to her family and opted to spend her last night in Manhattan with her best friend. They had a take-out dinner from their favorite Chinese place—Ching Tao—and after stuffing themselves senseless, Antonia excused herself to call Javier. She knew it was after midnight there but she wanted to hear his voice—she *needed* to hear his voice. He picked up on the first ring.

"Antonia?" he said, sounding wide awake considering the hour in London.

"Hi. Did I wake you?" she asked, already feeling that breathless feeling the sound of his voice brought on so easily.

"No, *mi amor*. I knew you would call me. I've been waiting."

His voice sounded so sexy, Antonia felt her skin prickle.

"I'm leaving tomorrow afternoon. I can't wait to get there."

"I'm sorry I was not there to help you pack but Samuel would not let me get away. He is such a taskmaster—I think that is the word I heard Andrew use to describe him."

"It's OK. Everything's packed and on its way. I know it's late. I don't want to keep you from sleep. But I miss you and I love you and can't wait to see you tomorrow."

"I love you, too. Tomorrow begins the first day of our lives together—at least until the wedding. I cannot wait for that day."

"I can't either.

They spoke a few moments more and Antonia hung up the phone. She rejoined Deanna in the kitchen and they spent their last night together talking all night about wedding plans and babies and the possibility of Deanna's moving to London. They avoided the subject of Sean and Deanna was glad not to have to talk about him. She would let Antonia know in due time her decision regarding him and their future—or lack thereof, if that was to be the case.

At noon the next day, the airport shuttle arrived for Antonia. She kissed and hugged Deanna, waving good-bye with a promise to call as soon as she had recovered from the inevitable jetlag. She settled into her seat and sighed a deep cleansing sigh. She thought of her parents and her brothers, already excited about their upcoming visit for the wedding in March, to be held after Les Passionistes' new album was completed. And about Deanna and Sean. She secretly hoped they would go their separate ways. As great a guy as Sean was, Deanna was a beautiful, vivacious blonde who needed more excitement and passion in her life than Sean seemed able to deliver. She thought of Antoine and Andrew and how much she looked forward to spending time with them and getting to know them better. She couldn't help but think that Antoine would be perfect for Deanna—she could just feel it in her bones. She let her mind drift to Lars—beautiful, sexy Lars. It would be strange to be around him, she feared, but she looked forward to seeing him just the same. She wanted him to find love but still…there was a part of her that dreaded it. She hated herself for feeling this way but it was a reality she would live with. And then Javier—so sexy and sweet and kind and intelligent and generous. Goose bumps rose all over her body as she thought of his lips, his hands, his eyes and his voice. In a few hours she would have all of those parts of him and more, but especially the part that mattered most—his heart—filled with devotion and unbridled passion. And that was the best part of all.

EPILOGUE

Javier stood at the back of the church waiting for the priest to give him the signal to take his place at the altar. He adjusted his tie nervously, smoothing out his white tuxedo jacket. Andrew, Antoine and Lars dressed in the black version of Javier's tux, stood nearby talking quietly.

"I knew Javier would be the first one of us to bite the dust," joked Andrew, glancing at Javier who looked more nervous tonight then at any of Les Passionistes' performances in their history.

"Bite the dust? What is that?" asked Antoine, nervously adjusting his jacket and fiddling with the red rose in his lapel.

"It's an American expression for getting married—or dying," Andrew explained.

"Some might say that getting married and death are one and the same," joked Antoine.

Andrew grinned, nodding in agreement. He turned his body slightly so that he was facing away from Lars who had moved to stand near a stained glass window and now appeared lost in thought. "You think he's alright over there?" he said in a low voice, nodding his head in Lars' direction.

Antoine glanced over at Lars who now appeared to be talking to himself.

"He's a little crazy but, *oui,* I think he's fine. He's practicing his speech for the reception, I bet."

The priest entered the vestibule and smiled at Javier.

"It's time," he said.

Javier took a deep breath and held his hand out toward the doorway, letting Andrew, Antoine and Lars enter first. As Lars went to move past Javier into the sanctuary, Javier took his arm, stopping him. Lars looked at him and smiled.

"Everything OK?" Lars whispered to him.

"*Si.*" Javier looked at Lars trying to get a sense of how he felt. "I just wanted to thank you again for being my best man. I wasn't sure you would agree but you're my best friend and I couldn't imagine anyone else standing up with me, though some might think it strange." Javier squeezed Lars' arm and Lars patted his back affectionately.

"I'm happy to do it. Really I am. And not that many people know our true history. The world thinks it knows, but they really don't. Now, let's get you out there. You shouldn't keep your bride waiting."

"So this means that I have your blessing then?" Javier asked, his voice low.

"You have my blessing. Now get out there."

They walked into the sanctuary of London's St. Stephen's Cathedral and took their positions at the altar. Javier smiled nervously at his nephew and parents and gave a wink to his mother noticing that she was already crying and the ceremony hadn't even begun yet. He rolled his eyes and tried to suppress a grin. He was happy to see Marta and Manolo there, smiling proudly as if they were watching their own son getting married. He saw Antonia's mother and brothers sitting across from his parents and some of her colleagues and distant relatives who had flown over for the wedding. Most of the crew from the studio had turned out including Samuel and Melina and Colin and his wife. The wedding was small and intimate as he'd hoped it would be and he was more than ready for it to begin. His sisters and Deanna were Antonia's attendants and he was anxious to see them in their wedding finery. Just the thought of seeing Antonia, whom he had not seen in twenty-four hours, was enough to make him burst through his skin.

A quintet of musicians from Les Passionistes' personal orchestra began to play "Pachelbel's Canon in D," signaling the start of the processional. Javier's sisters walked slowly down the aisle in simple, pale pink strapless, floor-length gowns and took their places opposite Javier and his groomsmen before the altar. Deanna came down the aisle next in a slightly darker shade of the same dresses his sisters wore. Javier noticed that Deanna looked very beautiful and he wondered if his band-mates were noticing. He looked expectantly toward the rear of the church, knowing Antonia would be next. Her father appeared in the doorway in his black tuxedo and Javier saw him lift his elbow in offering. Javier held his breath as Antonia appeared in the doorway, sliding her arm through her father's. She wore a silk strapless body-hugging Carolina Herrera gown that accentuated her curves and her hair was up in a loose topknot. He felt as if he couldn't get his lungs to work properly as the music changed and Antonia and her father began the slow walk down the white carpet strewn with red rose petals.

He stole a glance at Lars who surreptitiously touched his elbow in support. Javier fixed his gaze on Antonia's veiled face and willed himself to hold it together. All he needed was to cry like a baby in front of his family and friends. His band-mates would never in a million years let him hear the end of it if he did. Lights flashed all around them as guests and their official photographer and videographer captured each moment. And before he knew it, Ted Taylor was lifting Antonia's veil, kissing her cheek and offering his daughter to Javier who moved next to her and took her cold hands in his. She was trembling and he wanted to hold her but he stood still, his dark gaze locked onto her amber one.

Later, neither of them would remember the vows they had taken, the exchanging of the rings or the words of the priest as he joined them in marriage. They knew they would be thankful for the pictures and videotape later so they could experience the wedding as their guests had done. Everything seemed to happen in slow motion as they pledged their lives to one another and Antonia had not been able to stop the tears when Javier sang "Something About the Way You Look Tonight." He sang the first verse alone and his band-mates joined him for the last verse—the Italian operatic version even more romantic than Elton John's original version. Then they received the sacrament and the priest's blessing before finally being pronounced man and wife.

The guests burst into applause when Javier kissed his bride, a long and tender kiss that melted every heart in the church. They made their way up the aisle and once in the outer vestibule, they kissed again and turned to greet their guests as they filed past offering their congratulations and best wishes.

Antonia felt as if she were having an out of body experience. Her wedding was more beautiful than she ever could have imagined it to be. When they gathered to pose for the official pictures she stole a look at Javier, amazed that she had found this perfect man. He was truly a once in a lifetime gift that she would cherish forever.

White stretch limos ferried guests to the reception at the Royal Court Hotel where they feasted on roasted chicken, boiled baby red potatoes, asparagus and sweet corn au gratin. The cake was a four-tiered vanilla confection with lemon butter-cream frosting covered in sugary roses of every color imaginable.

When they had finished dinner, everyone refilled their wineglasses for the toast. Lars stood at the table next to Javier and Antonia and cleared his throat. He had been practicing this moment in his head all day and finally he could say the words and then allow himself to relax. A hush fell over the room as he spoke, his gaze on Javier's face.

"As your best man, Javier, it is my duty and honor to offer this toast to your marriage to the beautiful Antonia. It has been my privilege to sing with you for the past almost two years now, and while all four of us bring something special and unique to the group, I do believe that you truly are the heart of Les Passionistes. I'm certain Andrew and Antoine would agree with me on that. And now you have found this beautiful woman to sing to for the rest of your life. How much luck can one man have?"

The guests oohed and aahed as he turned to Antonia.

"And you, Antonia, could not be more perfect for Javier. You complement one another in ways you are not even aware of yet—ways that will be revealed as your new marriage stands the test of time. I see the two of you old and gray with many children and grandchildren and I only hope that one day, before *I* am old and gray, I will have what you both have now. You are lucky to have Javier. He is the true best man here. Congratulations to you both—may your days together be many and your sorrows few and far between."

Lars raised his glass and the guests raised theirs, cheering loudly in appreciation of his poignant words. Javier and Antonia touched their glasses to Lars' and then Andrew and Antoine joined in the toasting with Deanna and Javier's sisters. Glasses could be heard clinking all over the reception hall as the crowd drank to the newlyweds.

Javier turned his head away a moment, choking back a tear or two that threatened to shatter his macho façade. Antonia was unabashedly crying, knowing what it meant to hear those words from Lars and what it must have cost him to say them. Javier collected himself and turned back to Antonia, kissing her tenderly on the lips and wiping away her tears with a napkin. Then he stood and embraced Lars who was choking back tears of his own now.

"Thank you," said Javier. He wanted to say more but words failed him.

Lars smiled and they both sat back down to finish their meals. The band began to play as guests rose from their tables and mingled with one another, stopping often to express their best wishes to Javier and Antonia. Eventually it was time to cut the cake and then the band started the music for the traditional first dance. Javier swept Antonia into his arms and they danced slowly, their bodies melded as if as one, while everyone watched in awe. Antoine asked Deanna to dance and soon many other couples joined them. They danced and partied until long after midnight and finally Javier whispered to Antonia that he wanted them to be alone. They were spending the night there in the Royal Court Hotel and he was anxious to get her to their suite and consummate their marriage. They said their good-byes, promising to send postcards from their honeymoon in Morocco, then slipped away to their room.

Andrew and Antoine joined Lars by the bar where he was debating having another drink.

"Well, he did it. One down, three to go," Andrew said jokingly. "I wonder who's going to be next?"

Lars smiled and looked at them both.

"I predict Antoine only because he is the one least likely and therefore he is the one most susceptible."

"*Non! Jamais*! Never! If I marry then I limit my options. What would that mean for the rest of the women in the world? It would be wrong." Antoine said it so seriously that Andrew raised his eyebrow questioningly.

"You're a strange guy, you know that, Antoine?" he grinned and slapped him on the back.

"That may be so but I know what I talk about. Shall we go to the pub now?" He shrugged his shoulders and looked at Lars in invitation.

"You two go. I'm going to head home. I'll see you next week at the CD launch when Javier gets back from his honeymoon." He bid them good night and grabbed his tuxedo jacket from the back of his dining chair and left the hotel. He started his BMW and pulled out into the street from the underground parking garage, his mind reflecting on the wedding and Javier and Antonia and how perfect they were together. He inadvertently glanced down at his hand on the gear-shift and laughed out loud remembering how that had driven her crazy. He reached between the seat and pulled out his new CD—the latest from Nightwish, his current favorite heavy metal band and popped the CD into the player. He turned the music up and sang along with them as he drove home, feeling the beat of the music in his chest. He had a sudden sense of weightlessness, knowing that with Antonia's marriage to Javier he was officially—regretfully—free to roam about the world and embrace all that it had to offer. If that included a soul mate or just a temporary fling—then so be it. Maybe he could learn a thing or two from Antoine about women. In the meantime, he had his music, his one constant companion since he had been a little boy growing up in Switzerland and the one thing that would never disappoint him. Maybe he could find a way to blend his two musical passions—metal and opera.

Wouldn't that be something else, he thought, smiling to himself as he drove home along the dark, quiet streets of London. An idea came to him as he parked his car outside of his apartment. He let himself in and went straight to his stereo, which was connected to his computer and the new digital composer. He would write a musical composition blending his two passions of metal and opera and he would do it tonight—and hope the neighbors were asleep and wouldn't hear. He would call it Passion Music and in the morning he would have a good laugh about it. And then he would put it away and get on with his life. Now that seemed like a good plan.

THE END

978-0-595-38237-8
0-595-38237-1

Printed in the United Kingdom
by Lightning Source UK Ltd.
121939UK00001B/251/A